THE WHIPPING BOY

The son of a distinguished surge[illegible]rrat was born in Liverpool in 19[illegible]n-chester and Trinity Co[illegible] attract attention [illegible] *The Schoolr*[illegible] war he joine[illegible] his wartime e[illegible] *Corvettes* and [illegible]946 he became a di[illegible]rvice in Johannesburg a[illegible]a. His most famous book, *The* [illegible] in 1954, is one of the most successful [illegible]me and was made into a film starring Jack H[illegible] Other famous novels include: *The Tribe That Lost [illegible]s Head* and its sequel, *Richer Than All His Tribe*, *The Story Of Esther Costello*, *The White Rajah* and *The Pillow Fight*. Monsarrat lives with his wife, Anne, in Malta.

By the same author in Pan Books

SMITH AND JONES
THE STORY OF ESTHER COSTELLO
THE SHIP THAT DIED OF SHAME
THE WHITE RAJAH
THE TRIBE THAT LOST ITS HEAD
THE PILLOW FIGHT
RICHER THAN ALL HIS TRIBE
SOMETHING TO HIDE

NICHOLAS MONSARRAT

The Whipping Boy

UNABRIDGED

PAN BOOKS LTD : LONDON

First published in 1936
This specially revised edition published 1969
by Pan Books Ltd, 33 Tothill Street, London, SW1.

ISBN 0 330 02295 4

2nd Printing 1972

Printed and Bound in England by
Hazell Watson & Viney Ltd
Aylesbury, Bucks

For my friends

HARRY and DORA ALEXANDER
this book, begun in their
house in Gloucestershire

CONTENTS

PROLOGUE

When Ian Carrington married Cynthia Wilder in the early spring of 1933 there were many who found it an astonishing union. Or, if not astonishing, at least in the unlikely class, and not the best of the season. 'I don't suppose they'll hit it off' was the common formula: or 'I never expected her (or him) to go through with it'. Pressed to explain, they would have confessed to an inability to put their respective fingers on it: but they might have said (if they were Carringtons) that the Wilders were a damned sight too stuck-up, and that Cynthia was probably just like the rest of them: or (if they were Wilders) that the Carringtons seemed an odd lot – in fact, who *were* they?

That vague dissatisfaction was as far as the thing went – there were no scenes, no grim words in the vestry, no more than the usual covert sneers at the opposing wedding presents; and clearly it was not the two principals who occasioned comment so much as the contrast between the two families. For they did not mix, either at the wedding or at any time thereafter: it was a case not of oil and water, but of axle-grease and some over-refined sewing-machine lubricant: the Carringtons had all the money, the Wilders all the breeding (a marketable asset, it was true); and gossip, with its tongue not so much in its cheek as protruding from its ear, said that old Carrington must have made a pretty handsome settlement on his son before the Wilders came up to scratch.

But come up to scratch they did: and Sir Henry Wilder led his daughter up the aisle at ten minutes past the appointed hour with all the assurance which a sixth baronetcy, and the best part of a bottle of Nuits St Georges at lunch-time, combined to give him.

It was remarked that Cynthia looked colourless and rather frail: the vultures, seeking what they might devour, pounced on this negative attribute. 'Not strong,' murmured the women, and wondered how she would take 'everything.' They classed her as that kind of bride, and not the other sort, whom one eyed closely and decided that she had taken 'everything' very well indeed a good while back. . . . Cynthia Wilder was Tennysonian to the backbone, or thereabouts.

However, the service went off without hitch or interruption, its smoothness due in no small measure to the fact that there were no child-bridesmaids to turn nasty and no little page-boys to play with themselves or break for the open in mid-service.

But even the most casual observer at the subsequent reception would have marked the contrast between the two families, and wondered at it. The respective fathers might have been taken as the prototypes of this contrast: on the one side Mr Carrington, tough and thrusting business-man – all square jaw and black wiry hair – too busy punishing the champagne and being the life and soul of the gathering to notice the acute embarrassment he was causing his neighbours: and on the other Sir Henry Wilder, talking gently and with exquisite gestures to a very old lady in a wheelchair, and betraying neither surprise nor resentment that the last of his cellar was being slaughtered to make a holiday for people whom he disliked and mistrusted on sight.

He made a speech later, as he was fully entitled to do, a speech full of wit and a sort of die-away elegance: it was enjoyed by his own circle, misunderstood and extensively misquoted by the opposition. Mr Carrington, 'not to be outdone' as they say in competitive circles, also made a speech, in a somewhat different tradition: a lot of it was laughter, some of it hiccoughs, and all of it shot through and through with what could only be described as sly digs of a procreative nature. But the 'tut-tuts' were lost in the loud laughter: everyone knew what a wedding meant – except the bride, of course, which was the cream of the joke.

One of the prettier bridesmaids was Helen Carrington, Ian's sister: during the course of the afternoon she found herself next to a fourteen-year-old boy who was wolfing wedding-cake as if he had waited ten years for the chance – which may have been something like the truth. Politely she expressed the hope that he would suffer no ill-effects: and was rewarded by a ferocious scowl and a small shower of crumbs. Later she worked out that the small boy, having been an usher in the church, was in fact Denys Wilder, the bride's only brother. She thought: if he's the next baronet, the line looks like dying out of over-eating. Then she forgot him. There were many far more interesting people, and she collected interesting people, though with no long-continued enthusiasm.

Cynthia Carrington – late Cynthia Wilder – was aware of the undercurrent of dissension in the party, and was rather depressed by it, as being something she couldn't possibly cope with. Ian Carrington too found himself hoping that things were going to be all right in the future, instead of knowing that they were going to be. But of course, as all brides and bridegrooms have to keep reminding themselves, they weren't marrying each other's family – they just wanted each other. The short view of life contains an infinite solace.

Finally they went off on their honeymoon, pursued halfway down Kensington Gore by Mr Carrington's voice shouting something questionable about not being bored during the daytime. His wife and daughter got him home, in fairly good shape, by five o'clock. The other guests filtered away, eyed by a depressed detective: Sir Henry retired to his study and his returning worries: Denys Wilder groaned in the upstairs bathroom and wondered if he were *really very ill*, and not just sick. Certainly marzipan and icing angels were no sort of things to be sick on – as that silly woman had pointed out.

The two families met occasionally, exchanged the barest civilities, and then forgot each other's existence. It could not be otherwise: the Carringtons' taste ran towards cinemas, and the more ephemeral type of night-club, and noisy week-ends in Paris, all of which was very far from being Sir Henry Wilder's cup of tea. The matter was complicated by the latter's increasing financial embarrassment: he juggled with his exiguous fortune in a manner for which he was quite unqualified, he would accept no advice from Mr Carrington (who knew the markets like the back of his own hairy hand): he went from bad to worse, and kept it to himself.

Finally he lost his grip entirely, and, after writing a number of scholarly notes to his nearest relations deploring his own incompetence, removed to Scotland and the most rigid parsimony; he would have been glad to have the use of the small amount of capital which he had settled on Denys, but that would have meant endless trouble with the income-tax people (inquisitive enough already), and he knew in his heart that the money would only go the way of all the rest. And after all, he thought as he bought the first third-class ticket of his career at King's Cross, after all it was better to have the boy settled and out of the way: he could stay on at Eton, even if he had to give the 'varsity a miss, and after that he could look around in London, and get himself a job.

So they went their several ways: Mr Carrington peered at the markets, thrust his jaw into them, and inevitably prospered: his wife ministered to him as best she could: Helen played ducks and drakes (especially drakes) with her allowance, her life being bounded by clothes, alcohol and that ecstasy which music-lovers know when they hear the throaty words 'I went down to St James's Infoimary': Sir Henry shivered in a decayed Scots shooting-lodge, and turned to Descartes and other outmoded philosophers, and Denys survived spots and 'art' postcards and his first glass of beer and fill of tobacco, and became a stylish oar, and rather pleasant in an unassuming way.

And Ian and Cynthia Carrington made a thorough-going mess of their marriage, and slowly frittered away whatever of tenderness, of understanding, of mutual loyalty had been theirs in the beginning. But Cynthia suffered most, because she was the slower to fall out of love, and tried to shut her eyes to the process, and thought that having a baby would make everything all right again.

Part One

STORY OF A HOLIDAY

CHAPTER I

I

Ian Carrington took leave of his wife, and made heavy weather of it.

'You'll be all right, dear, honestly you will,' he repeated, with that synthetic heartiness of tone which takes the place of genuine feeling. He didn't attempt to look at her (he hated the attributes of pregnancy, and he hated her also for so troubling his conscience); instead he wandered round the bedroom, lifting things up and setting them down again, fiddling with the ridiculous paraphernalia of the dressing-table, wishing that the taxi would arrive or that his conscience might somehow be set at rest. 'What *can* go wrong?' he went on, almost plaintively. 'Everything's been so splendid so far. And you do trust Dr Armstrong, don't you? – and you like the nurse. . . . And it's not as if I was going to the ends of the earth.'

He let fall one of the ivory-backed brushes with a clatter, and Cynthia closed her eyes to shut out the darting pain which the sound brought. The great burden within her stirred also, bringing to an end the interval of peace which had been allowed to her. Now she'd have *hell* for another hour or so. . . . Out of the twilight of agony her voice came to him, faint, too tired to support the assurance of her words:

'It's all right, Ian, really. I know I'm silly to be scared. It's just that I'd rather have you here when – when it comes. But I don't want you to miss your holiday. . . . Will there be snow, do you think?'

'I hope so.' Inwardly he raged at the idiocy of the question. He was going out for a fortnight's ski-ing with the family, and she said: 'Will there be snow?' Of course there'd be snow: snow had been paid for, in sterling. . . . And as if to echo his thoughts:

'Of course there will – how silly of me.' She roused herself. 'Just think, Ian – when you come back there'll be another in the family – a third.'

'Marvellous, darling. . . . I must go, I think.'

Her mouth drooped. 'Stay a little while.'

'I've got to call for your brother, don't forget. And father is sure to get to the station early, and you know how he fusses.'

'All the family together. . . .' She gave a little sigh, and checked it quickly. That *hurt*. . . . 'I wish I were coming, just to make up the six.'

That was the cue for 'So do I,' and the tenderest of smiles, but even at this moment he could summon neither: he only approached her bedside, staring down at her squarely for the first time since he had entered the room, and wondering, not for the first time, why on earth they had ever married each other. Of all the hopelessly unsuited couples. . . . There had been the usual eagerness on his part, of course: the usual glorified idea of passion and its fulfilment; and marriage must have come as a relief to her, after having no money at all and with that dry old devil of a father always demanding attention. . . . But that didn't square the present, that didn't alter the fact, the itemized debit, that she had never been more than moderately pretty: that they had been married four years: that motherhood was an essentially ugly thing – for so his thoughts ran, as he bent to kiss her.

'Take care of yourself.'

She put her arms round his neck, regardless of the great upsweeping of pain which the movement brought. 'Write to me, won't you?'

'Of course, darling.' A momentary compunction made him add what he knew to be untrue: 'Every day, too. . . . There's my taxi. Good-bye.'

He straightened up, patted her shoulder encouragingly, and crossed to the door. A glance back, and round their bedroom, brought no tender recollection to him, but simply the impatience and the damnable frustration of the last few months. Woman should be the mate only, the ready physical counterpart: motherhood was a natural imposition for which one never bargained. What was the good of a wife who ... He nodded to her, essayed a lying smile, and left the room.

Cynthia began to cry again, weakly, almost without emotional stress: she had tried so hard to make it a successful parting, and then she had been silly at the end and he had become restive and irritable. She knew exactly what he had been thinking when he kissed her: that was the adverse item of married life, that it gave you an awareness of *all* the other person's thoughts, not just the nice ones. ... Of course he was glad to go: he loved Switzerland (as she herself did), he loved his family, he liked her brother Denys. And it was true that she wasn't very attractive, just at the moment.

She clenched her fists, shaken by a fresh onset of weeping. Why was having babies such a filthy job, why couldn't she give him what he wanted? And how *could* he be anything else but glad to get away when she was no *use* to him at all. . . . Through her tears the brilliant showcase bedroom seemed only a hazy mockery of that uselessness, showing beyond doubt that he did not want the baby, that it had already come between them instead of uniting them, that now he did not want *her* either, on any terms.

Valiantly she persuaded herself that this was a new development, that he hadn't been bored with her before, that they never *really* quarrelled or got on each other's nerves, that they were truly suited to each other and not just another jumbled-up, shaken-together couple with nothing vital in common. But there kept recurring to her a line from a play she had seen somewhere: 'We are bound by the closest ties of mutual indifference.' It had been a funny play, but the reality missed the laughter and kept only the heart-break.

The nurse, starchy and eminently dependable, carried into the room a cup of something-or-other which must somehow be swallowed.

'There, there,' she said, soothingly. 'It'll soon be over now, and then you'll know it's worth while.'

Cynthia reacted dutifully to the professional gambit, taking the cup, disposing of its contents by degrees. She knew already that there were no new phrases in connection with child-bearing.

Down below Ian was exhorting the taxi-driver, with a kind of sadistic relish, to be careful with his skis. There was certainly no sense in being held up now, when he was so very nearly away.

2

Denys Wilder sat on a suitcase in the hall of his little flat, waiting for the taxi and his brother-in-law. His cigarette (no longer an adventure, but not yet a natural habit) sent a curl of unheeded smoke upwards, smoke which swirled and vanished in the biting draught from the doorway: he stared at the graining in the wood panelling opposite him, and felt rather sorry for himself and sorrier still for feeling so. For it should have been such a good moment: he had never been winter-sporting before, and it meant Christmas abroad and the chance of some sun. And it was nice of Ian to offer him a lift to the station. But in spite of everything it wasn't a good moment: he still felt as if he oughtn't to be going, or that it should all be somehow different.

He took a pull at his cigarette, and then threw it away half-finished. It was Ian, of course – Ian and Cynthia – who furnished the core of his depression: Cynthia was going to have a baby, very soon, and Ian had not changed his plans on that account, but was going out with his parents to Adelboden, as he did each Christmas. What was one to think of that? What was the right attitude? Had it, indeed, anything to do with himself at all?

He shrugged his shoulders, aware of this reluctance within him, uncertain how to deal with it. At eighteen, he was still universally tolerant by reason of his humility, still far from convinced that his opinions had even a shadowy weight or significance, and Ian's ten years' seniority was an effective bar to criticism of any kind. If the latter thought that was the right thing to do, then supposedly that settled it; if he thought Cynthia was well enough looked after to be left alone, that was his affair and his only. Denys, even as Cynthia's brother, had precious little say in the matter, whichever way one looked at it.

Then he heard the sound of a taxi at the end of the road,

and straightened up instinctively, trying to stifle his misgiving by brisk movement. Here was Ian, anyway, in very good time: and they *were* going to enjoy themselves, and Cynthia *would* be all right. As the taxi creaked to a standstill outside, and Ian's head appeared inquiringly at the window, he picked up his suitcase and passed out into the drab wintry street.

Their greeting was on its usual friendly level.

'Hallo, Denys! Feeling in good form?'

'Fine, thanks.' But he shivered involuntarily. 'It's damned cold outside, though.'

'You wait till you get to Adelboden – the wind goes right through you, however much you pile the clothes on.' Ian opened the taxi door and held out his hand. 'Give me your suitcase, and we'll get going.'

Climbing in, Denys asked as he did whenever they met: 'How's Cynthia? All right?'

'Pretty good.' Ian stared at the meter as the taxi gathered way again. 'I didn't want to go really,' he continued reasonably, 'but she got rather excited about my missing the holiday, and Armstrong thought perhaps it would be the best thing after all, if she was going to work herself up over it. And I know she'll be all right.'

Denys nodded to himself, secretly relieved by the words and the tone in which they were spoken. They put rather a different complexion on the affair; it seemed that Ian wasn't being just thoughtless or selfish, but had honestly tried to do the best for everybody, in the peculiar circumstances. His mood changing suddenly, Denys said:

'I suppose your family will be at the station already. Your father usually likes a good half-hour to marshal the luggage.'

Ian laughed, glad of the change of subject. 'We've never been able to break him of that kink. Mother's pretty hopeless, too: she missed a train once, on her honeymoon, and she's never quite got over it. By all the laws of eugenics I should be the same, but I'm not.' He looked out of the window, and up at the overcast sky. 'Rather a lot of wind. I hope Helen won't be sea-sick this time.'

Then they fell to discussing the snow reports, with a sense of anticipation which left everything else far behind. That was the best of a winter-sports' holiday: it seemed to start from the moment one saw the words: 'One-and-a-half metres fresh snow, crusted: sunny' tucked away somewhere in the morning paper on the day of your departure.

3

No one knew whether Helen Carrington was lazy, temperamental, or congenitally sulky, and very few people cared after the first few days of diverse infliction. All her life – twenty-nine years – it had been like that: she was pretty enough for trouble to be taken to get to know her, she seemed to welcome any escort, but the more progress one made the less help she gave to the making. She was hard work all the time, in the sense that she never seemed to gather any social or sensual momentum at all: one good remark didn't start her off in promising form, it merely made her expect one good remark a minute till midnight; and one bad one seemed to strike her dumb for the rest of the session.

Kissing her was rarely progressive and never climactic: she would become, by stages, capricious, mocking and downright inattentive, till at last the potential fountain-head dried up altogether. ... Clearly there was some basic discontent at the core of all her reserve: it might be entirely bound up with sex – a virgin ever on the defensive, a Messalina *manquée*; but whatever it was, it gave her a bad time which she did not hesitate to pass on to other people.

At the present moment she was standing by herself near the entrance to the Continental Departure platform and was thus more or less insulated from the despised encroaching universe. She had elected to remain there, while her father saw to the baggage registration and her mother lobbied for a cup of tea in the buffet: she could keep an eye open for Ian and Denys, she had said, with some determination – and had added, in answer to her mother's look of inquiry: 'It's very unlikely that anyone will try to pick me up at this stage – they've usually completed their arrangements by now.'

Though in truth, despite a rather sulky mouth, she was looking pretty enough that morning; most of the available males, however, were nearly off their heads with worry, so that her armour was never put to the test. She hated crowds, because they were impersonal and beyond the influence of her like or dislike; and the platform barrier, though sufficiently overwhelming, was far less of a shambles than either the registration hall or the refreshment room.

If she now had any worry other than a personal or introspective one, it was to do with her brother's inclusion in the party. The facts seemed patent and incontestable. By their whole family standard, Ian should have remained in London with Cynthia: that was how they had both been brought up, that was what their warm domestic childhood had taught them was correct. But throughout the argument on this point, ranging through two months or more and at times assuming an unbearable sentimentality, she had taken his side: less from conviction of righteousness than from her threefold dislike – of Cynthia, of the marriage tie and above all of the idea and the tradition of child-bearing.

It was revolting, that kind of sticky blackmail: it was beyond all bounds intolerable, that because Cynthia was going to have a baby – not a clever proceeding, but an essentially maladroit one – a basic gaucherie – they should all be expected to stand round and slobber sympathy and coo their chorus of lush platitudes. ... And Cynthia was so *bad* at pregnancy, too (Helen hunched her shoulders, shaking off some distasteful memory): it should be a secret thing, a rite hidden away until its culmination, and yet Cynthia, perpetually and obtusely unconcerned, had insisted on going about with them – to theatres and shops and concert-halls – till far too late in the day. ... It had been so obvious, so universally shameful, like coming on to the stage unbuttoned, like queueing-up at a lying-in hospital.

Ian was going with them, anyway, and that reunited the family: father and mother, brother and sister, with Cynthia – the true Wilder who did not fit into their family, the clumsy pathetic interloper – effectively left outside. She was glad of that, and yet worried for Denys' sake: it must seem odd to him that his sister's approaching confinement was not of sufficient moment to keep Ian in London. It might make him unhappy or preoccupied, and she didn't want him to be either:

she liked what she had seen of young Denys, not counting him as a Wilder at all – he was unassuming, he was rather sweet and immature and fresh, he did not have to shave more than twice a week at the most. ... And his body, like – what? Very white, probably – very smooth and untested. There was sufficient there for a day-dream, the sort of mental excursion into the unknown of which she was so fond. She embarked upon it.

A porter knocked against her roughly, apologized and was surprised to meet a most angelic smile. Momentarily he forgot to be class-conscious, and basked in it. You never could tell, he thought as he threaded his way towards the barrier: the toughest-looking were often the softest underneath. Come to hand nicely, that one would. But, of course, she was somebody's dish already, like every other scented she-dog on the boat-train.

4

Henry Carrington, doing nothing very much at tremendous tension, was in his element and likely to stay there. He harried his porter, he counted and recounted the luggage, he jostled his neighbours, he tried to jump places in the queue; priding himself on being a seasoned traveller, he had an immense contempt for the bunch of trippers round him and considered them fair game for any smart tactics whatsoever. And come to think of it, someone had to do the work: his wife was useless, Helen had no organizing ability at all, Ian hadn't even arrived yet. ... He took off his travelling-cap – that odd pepper-and-salt affair which, to his great annoyance, always seemed to look brand-new, and mopped his forehead: it was hot work getting all the baggage collected and registered at such a time, it took a man, a real business man, to see that nothing went wrong. There were six pieces, counting the little kit-bag: six pieces all duly labelled, and he was only a few yards from the scales now. Organization, that was the thing: Organization and Push.

His next-door neighbour, recognizing Push if not Organization, said: 'Pretty good crowd, what?' and he nodded fiercely without answering. Of course there was a crowd: this was the

CHRISTMAS RUSH, and the fellow ought to know about it. But then half these people never set foot out of England more than once in their lives.

5

A cup of tea, sugarless and half-slopped over into the saucer, had at last rewarded Mrs Carrington's efforts. Grasping her hand-bag under one arm, she began to pour the overflow back into the cup: but someone jogged her elbow half-way through, and quite a lot more was spilt, this time irretrievably, on the floor. She took a sip of what remained, and tried to imagine that it was pulling her nerves together. There was, proverbially, nothing like a nice cup of tea, and nothing at all like this one.

But certainly she needed something of the sort. It had been a terribly trying morning for her: she had packed the night before, of course – Henry always insisted that the suitcases should be locked and labelled before they went to bed – but even so there had been a dozen things to see to, finicking things like paying the servants' wages and telling the newsagent, and it had been an unending rush from half-past seven onwards, and it wasn't over yet by any means – why, they weren't even in the boat-train yet – anything might happen, although it had never done so yet. And really, with Cynthia's baby so near, she wasn't at all happy about going. It was almost as if they were leaving London *because* the baby was coming – though that, of course, was ridiculous. But it did seem that Ian at least might have stayed behind: he had been out to Switzerland so many times before, and this one occasion wouldn't make any difference.

White Horse – Beer is Best – Smith's Potato Crisps.

One couldn't say anything very definite to him, though. Not now. Children grew up so quickly. The younger generation not only caught one up, they passed by at a rush, without looking.

Her tea was finished almost before she had embarked on it, and with a sigh she put down the empty cup on the nearest table and prepared to leave. Her mind jumped ahead a few minutes, in its usual orderless fashion. Soon they would all have collected on the platform: Henry was so busy and distinguished-looking, Ian frowning at the fuss (and, she hoped, worrying just the tiniest bit about Cynthia), Helen probably in a bad temper. ... And Denys – she smiled suddenly, glad that she had persuaded Henry to invite him. He would have been lonely, all by himself in London: Henry and she really took the place of his parents nowadays; and he was so young, he would cheer them all up.

She pushed back a straying hair underneath her hat, gathered her coat about her, and set herself to negotiate the revolving doors. Wouldn't it be awful if one got caught in them, and just went round and round and round. ...

6

All five of them converged on the platform barrier, as they had arranged.

That side of the station was in turmoil. There lacked only three days to Christmas, and the cross-Channel traffic was at its height: midday saw the line of taxis for the Continental Departure side stretching far back along Grosvenor Place, and the column of traffic at the station entrance was four deep, with a like clamour of impatience.

There were several major issues – the last-minute reservations, the weighing and registering of luggage, the catching of the earliest of the boat-trains instead of the last packed one; and within these several offensives there were the minor, individual, struggles – the decorous attraction of one's travelling companions fifty yards down the platform (perhaps a whistle was permissible, so near Christmas?), the determination to snatch a last whisky-and-soda, the wail of despair which marked the loss ('stolen, obviously') of that little blue hat-box, the threatening onrush of the four young men, already in ski-ing clothes, who had boundless effrontery and no reserved seats. ... The strange equipment to be seen everywhere seemed a special guarantee of the enjoyment ahead: stacked piles of skis, dangling ski-boots, grey rucksacks with a whole network of harness – all these gave a bizarre excitement to the temper of the crowd. Look, they seemed to say – we're all going winter-sporting together – aren't we lucky?

The movement and the clamour increased from moment to moment. It was now a quarter to one, and people poured out from everywhere – inquiry office, booking hall, luggage depot, buffet – making for the long queue forming at the barrier. Porters swung skis up on to their shoulders and set off down the platform, glad of their favourable place in the handicap: officials argued and cajoled and reassured, Cooks' frowned at the Polytechnic, who passed it on to Dean and Dawson, policemen strove to give form and direction to the struggling mass: fierce military gentlemen in ski-ing caps and third-class curling badges prepared to stand no nonsense from their neighbours. ... Then the barrier gate went down, and a ripple of humanity surged forward.

Ian and Denys had found Helen, and the three of them awaited the parents with varying degrees of unconcern. They stood a little out of the crowd – Mr Carrington had all the tickets, so they could not get through to the train; Ian was talking to his porter, Helen was humming to herself with her arm lightly through Denys'. It was a surprising gesture from her, and he liked it: he was eighteen, he was new to everything, he really liked any woman's arm anywhere, and this double novelty cheered him immensely. He stood very still, full of a most unmanly gratitude. Seeing life could, apparently, begin at home.

Mrs Carrington was the next to arrive. She kissed Ian, shook hands with Denys, and cast a fleeting glance upwards to gauge her daughter's mood: Helen was only intermittently a dutiful offspring, and the twenty-four-hour journey ahead could be made or marred by her attitude. Sleeping compartments were so cramped, so inescapably matey. ... At the moment, however, the omens seemed good.

Ian said: 'Where's Father?'

'Seeing to the luggage, dear.' Mrs Carrington glanced round her rather fearfully, mistrusting the hubbub and the swirling crowds. It seemed odd that anything so expensive should still be competitive. 'He won't be a minute, I expect. But no one can take our seats, can they?'

'No.'

She turned to Denys. 'Aren't you excited? You've been

abroad before, haven't you? Isn't it wonderful, how everyone seems to be enjoying themselves?'

Denys answered 'Yes,' which seemed to cover all three questions. But for that single instant he wasn't enjoying himself: he was wondering if, having surrendered Helen's arm to shake hands with Mrs Carrington, he could possibly take hold of it again. It had been so very pleasant a contact, and it still surprised him: this was the very first time that such a thing had happened to him, because he was always so shy in that direction and expected nothing to come his way at all. ... But it had been her idea, not his, and he could do nothing to re-establish it. He shifted his weight uneasily, and their shoulders touched; then she smiled, and once more laid her fingers on the crook of his elbow. He thanked God for them, with conspicuous lack of perception.

A voice smote them all, the crowds parted as if threatened with some disaster, and Mr Carrington arrived in the wake of a piled trolley. His cap was askew, and his face rather red.

'All here? – that's good. How are you, Denys?' Once more, maddeningly, Denys found that he must shake hands: but this time her arm followed his and the contact remained unbroken. Mr Carrington blew his nose in generous fashion. 'Well, Ian. How's Cynthia this morning?'

But as he said this his eyes inevitably swung back to Denys again, and a momentary embarrassment settled on the group. The topic had, at this late stage, a kind of fugitive significance: their holiday had started, and Ian was with them, but Denys belonged to both camps and his presence was a tangible reminder of what they were abandoning.

Ian's face was admirably blank. 'She's pretty well, thanks. Armstrong seems satisfied, at all events.'

'That's good.'

'I wish she could have come with us,' said Mrs Carrington wistfully.

Helen's chin rose imperceptibly. 'Hadn't we better be making for the train?' Her voice was without expression. 'It must be nearly one o'clock.'

The group sprang into activity, finding relief in movement. Mr Carrington, reassuming the burden of organization, swept round and sent his porter ahead like a shot from a gun: Ian shouldered his skis with a self-conscious frown; and then the five of them formed into line and joined the end of the queue, slipping at last into the machinery of export. England began to recede, falling back under the glamour and the greedy uproar of the station crowds.

The little board by the entrance said: 'Sea moderate.'

CHAPTER II

The little board by the entrance had, it seemed, a somewhat land-locked sense of proportion. The sea was not moderate: or rather, it was only moderate by some titanic standard of distress, as one might say 'a moderate thunder-bolt' or 'a moderate murder'; Nature might do things on a grand scale, but the reckoning of Man was always less ambitious. ... The travellers marked the warning signs: even as the boat-train ran into the harbour station, it could be seen – by the inshore wavelets, by the flying smoke, by the reluctant hovering of the gulls – that a brisk wind awaited them; and people turned from their carriage windows in silence, and marshalled their luggage with a certain deliberation, as if to demonstrate that there could be no point in hurrying now that the low ebb of the journey was at hand. Only arrival at Calais could match the mood of departure from Victoria.

Thirty seconds of Dover, glimpsed fleetingly as he struggled heavily-laden up the gangway, made Denys wonder if anyone knew what the town was really like. Did people ever do anything except pass through it like a sophisticated wind? There was the germ of a sad idea there: the Forgotten City, the Town that Wants to be Stayed In – but all it ever saw were swift travellers who collected no dust, wasted no time, a frieze of figures always in a hurry, spurning it out of the corner of one eye. ... He tried to give it a long look out of sympathy, but the realists behind him murmured and he passed on. He resolved that one day he really would take a ticket just to Dover and no farther (if such tickets were purchaseable), and treat the place as a separate entity instead of a draughty doorway labelled 'Aux Bateaux'.

Installed on board, the Carrington party split once more into its constituent parts. Mr Carrington was busy ramming all the luggage into a heap as near as he decently could to the outgoing gangway: his wife, with surprising tenacity, had commandeered a steward and was showing him the precise spot – amidships, and just behind the funnel – which a long and bitter experience had taught her was the least vulnerable for her deckchair. (Though it was precious little use, she knew well, when one's fellow-travellers were so magnificently unconcerned as to when or where they were ill.) Ian sought the bar, visualizing the three winking stars with which Martell beckons the apprehensive; and Helen made for the upper deck with Denys, seeking through the chaos of baggage and the diverse crowd – harassed or quietly indifferent or queasy already – for some reasonable anchorage. Reason demanded a modicum of privacy, as it always should do.

With such a Helen by his side, Denys had no need to clear the harbour to be on the crest of a wave. He had never known her to be like this before. It could hardly be said that she had taken any notice of him during the three or four years they had known each other: always she had been simply Helen Carrington – aloof, much older than he, the sister of the man Cynthia had married – the sort of chance contact which neither circumstances nor personal curiosity would ever prosper.

He remembered meeting her at the wedding, when she was the top bridesmaid and he a fourteen-year-old usher in his first morning-coat; he had drunk a phenomenal amount of champagne and eaten all such stray bits of marzipan as the other guests had rejected, and she had expressed a concern for the morrow which was slightly galling. Damn it, he wasn't just a schoolboy jumping at a chance to stuff himself sick. . . . Though in point of fact he *had* been pretty ill, and not exactly on the morrow either. But clearly that had set the standard of their relationship for all time: she was that much older, and he had never caught up. By such unscaleable personal barriers are the generations separated.

But she had always been friendly, and now, as they leant in

companionable silence against the pile of big life-saving rafts, she was certainly in a novel mood. It was as if, suddenly, he had become worth monopolizing, as if he had reached a stage of reasonable maturity and that she had decided to make use of it. He could not help being flattered, since that relationship – the pedestal for the woman, the praying-mat for the man – was still the one which most commended itself to his romantic imaginings: that was the *proper* outlook, and all else was conceit or insolence or worse. ... If she chose to honour him thus, he could only accept the accolade with grace and humility. Nothing more. She was still twenty-nine, and he eighteen. Such handicaps were not made up in a day, or even in a night.

A lurch, and a succession of grindings, interrupted his day-dream, told him that they were casting-off. The syren gave a terrifying salute as the boat, defying Nature as well as all the principles of mechanics, edged out sideways from the quay; deep down below them a bell rang, and the pervading rhythm of the engines took on a stronger pulse. A wise sea-gull flapped away from the mast-head and dropped astern. They were off.

Helen buttoned up her coat-collar, facing the brisk wind. Her mouth moved, the firm red lips softening, curving, reforming into speech. 'It's going to be cold. ... Shall we get chairs, and snuggle down properly?'

'All right.' Denys jerked to attention, and moved along the deck towards the pile of chaises-longues. He carried with him the words 'snuggle down'. . . . The phrase had an intimacy which swamped all consecutive thought. She was jolly nice really, when you got to know her. It was a privilege to do her service.

Helen smiled to herself, a most unusual proceeding for her. He was a darling, and perhaps she wasn't going to be ill after all. At present she could not analyse the swift excitement which the first sight of him, on the platform at Victoria, had brought her: he had come up to her, in his grey suit and very new Old Etonian tie, and with his skin as clear and as soft as her own, and she had suddenly known that he had significance instead of anonymity, that he was going to change the holiday from a routine entertainment into something with the true flavour of animation. It had been a most unforeseen development, but one on which she had acted straight away. . . .

She looked up now, as he drew near her again.

'That's good. Let's have them here, out of the wind.'

Denys arranged the chairs carefully, side by side, facing astern; he had brought a rug as well, and this he tucked round her knees with a diffidence which she found charming. The boys usually made a good deal out of that. . . . The ship passed the pier-end, and began to lift decisively: the noise of the water's attack made itself heard above the engine beat, while a warning drift of spray, cold and clean as snow itself, pattered on the deck beside them. A grey sky overhead showed a few ragged hurrying clouds slipping away towards the coast they were leaving. The stern rose and dipped majestically, the deck-promenaders laughed and clutched one another as their steps grew erratic.

She said: 'You're never sea-sick, are you?'

'I haven't been, so far.' He lay back, staring at the mast-head as it slowly cleaved the upper air. 'But then I've only been across the Channel two or three times, and then it was like a lake.'

'I'm not so lucky.'

He turned quickly to look at her. 'Are you feeling all right now?'

'Oh, yes. I just need to keep warm, that's all.' She leant a little towards him, smiling. 'So if I become rather affectionate, it's only because I'm getting shivery.'

There was a cue there for the most dashing remark, he knew, but somehow he didn't feel able to make it. She was so far out of his reach, so independent, so grown up. He stared at the mast-head once more, hoping that she would never grow disappointed with him. She must usually go about with such different people. All this holiday he must do his very best to deserve her company.

Some way aft, Mrs Carrington, coming out of an apprehensive day-dream, found herself listening to a formidable woman in the next chair, who was making some pronouncement about Rescue Homes. She did not find it easy to concentrate, menaced as she was by storm without and stress within; but fortunately the woman, who had on her own confession 'A stomach like cast-iron, my dear', needed no prompting and no rejoinder of any sort.

Rescue was her line and nothing else: Alma Mater with a dash of Dolorosa. ... She dealt at full spate with affairs from the irregular cradle to the unhallowed grave. There appeared to be no kind of Rescue – just in time, just too late, submerged, sinking, sunk – in which she had not had a hand: and the slight groans which Mrs Carrington was forced to emit at intervals might well have been her reactions to this back-stage saga of vice. But just occasionally, as she shut her eyes to blot out a heaving sky, she found herself wondering why she was so very often selected by people in need of this kind of conversational baffle-plate. Had she a receptive face? – or only a meek-and-no-back-answers one? It was, perhaps, not a distinction of any practical importance. They got their claws into you any way.

Presently the woman paused, having reached the end of the current tale of woe. Then she glanced solicitously at Mrs Carrington, and leant towards her.

'Are you all right, my dear? Does the rolling bother you?'

'Just a little,' answered Mrs Carrington faintly. She would rather not have heard the word 'rolling' brought out with such effective clarity, and she wished Henry were here to take the weight of the conference off her shoulders. Not that he knew anything about rescues. In fact, rather the reverse. 'It's silly of me, I know. And I'm much the worst of the family.'

'Ah, you have a family?'

'Oh, yes – a boy and a girl.' Aware of her companion's scrutiny, she added: 'And my husband, of course.'

'And is your daughter with you?' There was a kind of professional curiosity in the question which Mrs Carrington wished she had the strength to resent. Though it would be interesting to see Helen reacting to a Rescue. ... She answered briefly:

'Yes, she's somewhere with the others,' and closed her eyes again. The sooner they were started on the next sunken delinquent, the better for all concerned.

'As long as she's not alone,' said the woman thoughtfully.

'Sometimes people on these ships – men—' she waved her hand, as though to dispel the shadows of evil. 'But, of course, I know you never have any trouble with her.'

The assumption was to Mrs Carrington's mind such a large one that she felt herself unable to deal with it effectively. Instead she smiled vaguely, and answered:

'I expect she'll be with Denys – that's the brother of the girl my son married.' It annoyed her to have to reply in such detail, but her companion clearly would get at the facts in the end, possibly incorporating them in some Little Book. 'They're really very good friends.'

'Good friends. . . .' The woman repeated the words: the two syllables seemed to multiply themselves into a whole scarlet-bound novelette, purchased behind locked doors, or in some upstairs room. 'You believe, then, in throwing young people together quite freely?'

Here Mrs Carrington visualized, as she always did, a number of adolescents of both sexes piled into a heap and tipped down a well; and she wished she had sufficient daring to reply (as Helen would have done) on the same lines – such as 'No, I believe in keeping them well apart, sticking feathers in their ears, and using them for Badminton.' . . . Surely the woman knew that one did not throw young people together; they just met, in the neatest possible way; they had brought coalescence to a fiery, if not a fine, art. Nor could one rescue people until they had become worth rescuing; and after that one was, of course, simply a spoil-sport, for whom the little hanging sign 'Do not disturb' had been specifically invented. Mrs Carrington drew her rug about her.

'I have always trusted my children,' she said, as decisively as she was able. 'And Denys, of course, is only a boy – he's only just eighteen.'

The other woman raised her eyebrows. 'Eighteen? But don't you think . . .' she turned the rest of the sentence into a cough, and paused. Was it indelicate to hint that at eighteen years of age the young man might have comfortably made four years' hay, and still have a major store of sunshine to spare? That was the trouble with this kind of social work: it gave one knowledge which other people might find intensely disturbing.

Why, at eighteen years old some of the girls . . . and as for the boys . . . she frowned, eager to spread the gospel, but (like all evangelists) impatiently aware that it might be unacceptable. People were often so queer, so ridiculously shy; they preferred to live in a flower-garden world of their own, in which Sex might rear its ugly head, but little else besides.

Mrs Carrington, however, was prepared to stick to her guns.

'I'm afraid that we don't see things in quite the same light,' she volunteered.

It was, for her, a bold statement, but sea-sickness, with its accompanying end-of-the-world feeling, made her indifferent to any mere social contretemps. 'Surely it's quite possible for there to be an ordinary friendship between two people, without any need to suspect anything in it. One should try to keep an open mind, always.'

She rose unsteadily, and grasped her hand-bag. 'And now I think I will go below for a little. . . . Thank you for a most interesting talk.'

But on her way down to the security of the Ladies' Saloon she passed the small alcove where Helen and Denys were sitting. Helen was looking rather white, as she usually did during the crossing, and Denys had his arm round her. In the friendliest way, of course – the poor child needed to be kept warm. But Mrs Carrington was somehow glad that the rescue-woman wasn't with her.

Lolling against the bar, clasping his fourth brandy and second soda in a jealous grip, Ian was feeling in better form than he had done for several months. This was what one wanted, if one was in truth a man – freedom – freedom to throw a chest and breathe real air; London and the flat and Cynthia were all very well, but there was another side of life which had an equal importance and an equal attraction.

To be sailing away, on a holiday, and magically bereft of all responsibility, was the sort of luck he had been looking forward to all the winter. He had waited for it: it had arrived at last. And it was not only the brandy which urged him to play that luck for all it was worth.

His thoughts dwelt on the possibilities which Adelboden might hold for him; his eyes strayed over his surroundings, seeking to confirm by some agreeable image or other his potential disloyalty. For that, unconsciously, was what was in his mind: the passage of time, and the special circumstances of the past few months, had induced in him a desire for change, backed up by a complete indifference as to the method to be adopted.

Many things contributed to this mood: there was no major factor, but simply a number of doubts and a number of irritations. Perhaps he had married too early: perhaps he and Cynthia were basically unsuited: perhaps he was simply not of the faithful breed at all; the fact remained that he was sick of the whole thing, and if the chance offered itself, he was not going to forgo entertainment just because he had happened to marry four years ago. Life was very short; and a stern morality did not exactly contribute to its sweetness.

His eyes lighted on a manifest confirmation of this view. There was a pretty girl, looking distinctly lost, a few yards away from him. She had a pleasant, friendly figure, rather wider in the hips than a purist (a purist in the aesthetic sense, that is) would have chosen. Ian put on his best smile and offered his assistance.

But she only wanted to know where to get her passport *visa*-ed, and the little office was only just round the corner from the bar: the road to ruin was too short to be effectively trodden. . . . She thanked him prettily, making attractive play with her underlip. She was going to Neuchâtel, and that was really no good at all. . . . She refused a drink, and disappeared: her hips were mobile as well as wide. Ian sighed deeply, and turned back to the bar: the sea might be stacked with fish, but there weren't really so many warm-blooded young women in the world that he could afford to lose one.

'Now then, Ian, old boy. . . .' His father's voice, sensationally coy, made him, together with everyone else at the bar, turn round immediately. Henry Carrington slapped his son on the back jovially. 'None of that now, you young devil – thought we were all out of harm's way, didn't you?' He winked in the direction whence the girl had departed. 'Pretty girl, too. How do you do these things – a staid old married man like you?'

Ian laughed, sufficiently content not to be embarrassed. That was just like his father, making a joke out of something which, set out in plain terms, would have shocked him immensely. The family humour was always of that brand, exhibiting the same full-blooded reticence that made music-hall jokes go down so well – one could always glorify adultery by calling it 'a bit of fun'. ... He smiled back cheerfully.

'She just wanted some advice,' he answered. 'How about a drink for you?'

'Some advice, hey?' Mr Carrington continued to include the bar in the conversation. 'We've heard that one before, I think. It's funny how they always go to the young ones for advice. ... Here's your passport, before I forget.' He took one out of the pile of five passports, all of which he had had *visa*-ed, and gave it to Ian. 'It's all in order. Where are the others?'

Ian handed him a quarter-tumbler of brandy, and began pouring in soda-water with due circumspection. 'On deck, I expect. Helen's being ill, I dare say; but Denys can look after her.'

Mr Carrington sniffed his drink, decided that he had not been served with liqueur brandy, and took a substantial gulp. 'I like that young fellow,' he said presently, as if the words set the final seal on Denys' career. 'It was a good idea to bring him along. I hope he won't worry too much about Cynthia, though.'

'I shan't,' said Ian pointedly. Perhaps it was the brandy speaking for him, but he failed to see why Denys, the brother, should be disturbed, when he himself, the husband, was perfectly tranquil. No one should ever interfere between man and wife. ... 'She'll be quite all right,' he continued in a more matter-of-fact tone. 'Women are having babies every minute of the day, and nobody thinks anything of it. And she's got one of the best doctors in London to look after her.'

Mr Carrington nodded, as much in answer to his own thoughts as to Ian's remark. He wanted to be convinced that Ian was acting rightly: it was nice to have the boy along with them, but there could be the alternative view, privately held, that at such a time he had no damned business to be there at all.

'I dare say you're right,' he remarked presently. 'It's done now, anyway, and we're going to have a good holiday.' Bending down, he peered out through the companion-way window. 'Soon be in now – there's the north coast line pretty clear already. We'd better all collect near the luggage.'

Ian knocked back the remainder of his drink, cast a regretful glance at the parent bottle, and buttoned up his coat. That was the end of that session, but it was the first of many. All round them there was an increased bustle: the crew marshalled their charges close to hand, the sick and sorry poured out from their retreats and prepared to make the last brave effort – disembarkation without a wayside defeat. Even the sea, under the approaching shelter of France, was taking a moderate turn at last. Mr Carrington, followed by his son, began to elbow his way towards the after gangway. The brandy had done him good in many ways. Now that the holiday was well started, all hesitation and all regret must be put out of mind.

On the upper deck, almost deserted now, Helen squeezed Denys' arm gratefully.

'Thank you for that,' she said, in a softer tone than he had ever hoped to hear. 'You saved my life. . . . I *hate* being cold when I'm on the sea.'

He wanted to say something about doing much more for her, but he knew he couldn't finish the sentence so he didn't start it. She seemed to understand, anyway. She understood everything. She was marvellous.

CHAPTER III

The Schweizer Hotel at Adelboden was deep in its mid-morning silence.

This period of utter stillness was the invariable rule for half the year; for it was during these last few hours that one could count on all the occupants, no matter for what reason they had come to Switzerland, going about their various pursuits and leaving the hotel to itself. There was a general clearing-out, as if a mat had been well-shaken in the sun; the elderly clad themselves in furs and walked sedately down the valley, or along the slow slope to Gilbach: the more active brigade descended to the rink just below the hotel, there to cut an average of one figure every ten minutes and to sneer at their fellow-performers in the meanwhile: and the remainder – expert or persevering or merely laughable – shouldered their skis and made off to the snow-fields. A few perhaps were still in bed, a few more sunning themselves on the southern balcony; but within the hotel a friendly silence reigned, amply confirming its proprietor's description of it as '*un hôtel bien situé pour le soleil et le sport.*'

The proprietor himself, Herr Wilhelm Franck, sat in his little office by the entrance hall, listening to the silence, drinking in the accustomed peace, and drawing comfort from them both. For they meant that the hotel was running smoothly, that it was being used exactly as he intended it to be: voices raised at that hour meant a complaint of some sort, the tramp of feet meant snow too soft for ski-ing or a watery rink, or perhaps even a broken leg up at the Lohneschanze. All of which were bad things, rough and uncomfortable events upon which the management had every right to frown. . . . The morning belonged to silence, had done so for fifteen years, and with the help of God and Herr Franck would continue in that estimable tradition. Nor was there much doubt as to which of the two was the sleeping partner.

A soft step in the doorway announced his wife, and he stood up, prompted by that invariable courtesy which was his second nature. He was proud of her, and she of him: together they had built up the Schweizer Hotel, starting with a little chalet on the lower slopes of the valley, growing grey in the creation of this achievement, and knowing it to be solid and enduring. And was she not the most admirable housewife in all Switzerland? If anyone congratulated him on the perfection of his hotel, he would always point to his wife and say: 'It is she, not I, who has done it all.' It was nearer the truth than many another domestic compliment.

She came forward now and stood by his side, looking down at the many papers on his desk.

'They should be here soon, Wilhelm.' She spoke German, in the gentle blurred way that told of a long exile. 'All is ready upstairs. It will be nice to see them again, our old visitors, our old friends.'

'The good Carringtons ...' Herr Franck nodded. 'To think that this is the ninth year of their coming – it seems only yesterday that they arrived for the first time, so eager and so happy to be here. And they will be just the same, I know.'

'Except that young Mr Carrington's wife will not be with them.' Frau Franck knit her brows in thought. 'I hope she is not ill – she was always so pale, you remember.'

'He would not himself come if she were ill. Perhaps ...' But he did not voice the thought that had occurred to them both. It was none of their business, to question affairs between husband and wife. The hotel, indeed, would have been instantly disorganized had they embarked on such a practice.

'And there is Miss Carrington,' went on Frau Franck presently. 'Each time she leaves us, I wonder if she will be married by the next year. It is strange that she has never married. There must be plenty who would be willing.'

'Always she is so aloof,' answered her husband. 'The young men nowadays are not brave in love. But better to be aloof indeed, than behave as we know some behave.'

There had only been one scandal at the Schweizer Hotel, four years ago, but it had been a resounding one, and the memory clung like an itching skin.

'Though perhaps,' Herr Franck continued, thoughtfully, 'the young man that they are bringing with them is to be her husband. That will be interesting.'

His wife smiled. 'You are too romantic always, Wilhelm.'

'I romantic? Never in my life.' And indeed, in his black suit and shiny wing collar, Herr Franck did not exactly conform to the accusation. 'Except once only, and that,' he smiled, 'was not my fault, God knows. Wasn't it your own mother who said . . .' he stopped suddenly, and listened. 'That's the car – they must be coming.'

Frau Franck patted her grey hair, already superlatively

neat. 'You shall tell me some other time what it was my mother said. And explain also about your one romance, and whether it turned out well.'

She walked out into the hall, followed by her husband, and set the hotel in motion with a brisk sure touch. 'Gaston ... Charles ... The door, if you please.'

Denys, who had been balanced precariously on the small tip-up seat, was the first to step out of the taxi. The snow crunched under his feet, the keen air met him like an advancing wave; and it seemed, as he took a quick glance round him, that he had been set down in some rare country, unique both in its colouring and its atmosphere.

The drive up from the station had been a slow one: the road led a steep and winding course up the valley, and the old Renault taxi, though equipped with chains according to the district law, had to go circumspectly. During the drive, his eyes had been constantly occupied with the scenery: it was something he had never met before, that royalty of outlook with the great sweeping expanse of snow topped by a ring of black and towering rock. And overhead, as he bent to look, the sun shone from a clean sky which had no cloud to spoil its luminous depth of blue. By the wayside, the little chalets, seeming to be unapproachable through the surrounding snow, furnished an added variety: most of them were built of great joists of wood, seasoned to a dark brown or painted some softer shade.

It was novel in every respect: a landscape etched on a bolder theme than ever before, and coloured according to a design freshly conceived and valiantly executed. It had taken his imagination, and to step out of the car now was like stepping into a fairy-tale illustration on which one had looked with longing.

The others followed him out of the car, and a chorus of greeting arose: everyone, it appeared, was looking better than last year, better than ever before, and everyone found an immense satisfaction in the reunion.

Denys was introduced to a small neat couple whom he took to be the proprietors: they both gave him a quick bird-like glance, and shook hands warmly, with identical murmurs of

'It is a pleasure.' In the background the two porters beamed their welcome: other strong men began to unload the luggage and carry it into the hotel: it was as if a brightly-painted clockwork house of call had been set in motion.

And up and down the little street there moved a constant stream of people, manifesting every mode of progress – ski-ing, dragging luges, shuffling along in snow-boots, guiding big horse-drawn sledges. It made a perfect winter's scene, enhanced and sealed by the friendly snow-laden hotel which waited for them. As a first taste of Switzerland it had all the hunger-sharpening variety of hors-d'oeuvres.

'Well, Herr Franck,' said Mr Carrington, when the chatter had subsided somewhat, 'how is business this season? Is the hotel full?'

'Full?' Herr Franck raised his hands in supplication to some *hotelier*-divinity. 'If one was to go down on his knees before me I could not take another guest. We have not even a free bed, even if we had an empty room to put it in.'

'It is you that bring us luck,' his wife joined in. 'You return year after year, like the swallows, and more people come each time. Isn't that so, Wilhelm? Without the Carrington family, we often say, we might as well close our doors.'

'People know how well they will be looked after,' said Mrs Carrington kindly. 'So don't let's talk of luck, when you know it's nothing of the sort.'

Helen turned slightly to one side, bored with these annual civilities. 'Like it, Denys?'

'It's grand.' He was looking at the slope behind them, where two skiers, coming down at a tremendous pace, were weaving with their tracks a pattern like an immense plaited rope. At the bottom they turned swiftly, as if on a pivot, and came to rest within a few yards of each other. 'Those chaps look damn good.... Is it as easy as all that?'

'It is not.' She laughed gaily. 'Just wait till Ian starts putting you through your paces. Then you'll know what it's like to fall through space with six-foot planks on your feet.'

From beside him came Frau Franck's gentle voice. 'Are you expert at the winter sports, Mr Wilder? Or is it your first time out in Switzerland?'

He turned towards her with his young diffident smile.

'It's my very first time. I was just wondering whether I was going to be any good at it. There must be a lot of things to think about, besides keeping your balance.'

'But of course you will be good. It is always so: people come out here, beginners like yourself, and in one, two days they are going about on skis as if they have been born to them. You will see for yourself. And now,' Frau Franck turned back to the party, 'if you will come in, you shall see your rooms. They are the same as before, as we promised, and we have put Mr Wilder just opposite. I hope that will be convenient.'

There was nothing remarkable in her tone of voice, but for some reason Denys found himself looking straight at Helen, and meeting her eye blushed vividly. She gave no answering sign, but only preceded him through the doorway. That was rather sweet of him, she thought: if he had been a few years older he would have worn a very different expression, to suit a very different train of thought.

Denys paused at the foot of the staircase and looked back. 'Aren't you coming up, Ian?'

'You go on, old boy – I know my room.' There was a girl in the bar, leaning against the counter, just raising a glass to her lips. It was rather early to be drinking cocktails. Perhaps she would be interesting. Ian hung up his hat, and went along to join her.

Lunch also was a time of reunion, on a grander, more full-blooded scale. Many people returned to the hotel year after year, as did the Carringtons, and there was thus much journeying from table to table, much raising of glasses, much hearty salutation.

Mr Carrington was in his element, standing up suddenly with an exclamation, bearing a loaded glass to every corner of the room, calling out greetings in passable French and execrable German, smiling, winking, waving his knife and fork. ... He hardly got a bite to eat, though there were five courses and a huge variety of cheese. But he did not seem to mind. To be labelled a good mixer was worth going hungry till dinner-time.

Mrs Carrington greeted, more decorously, a wide

acquaintanceship; Ian, who came in late, was questioned so many times as to Cynthia's whereabouts that he became irritable and subsided into silence. There was an extremely noisy family at the next table, hailed *en masse* as 'the Jacksons' and appealed to, on some point or other, half a dozen times in as many minutes; they were, together with the Carringtons, the hotel's oldest inhabitants, and many obscure allusions, backed up by loud laughter, passed between the two tables.

Mr Jackson, a large florid man in ski-ing trousers and a yellow polo sweater, came and sat at their table for some time, eating a peach with one dripping hand and patting Helen's knee with the other drier one; it was obvious that later on he would run Mr Carrington neck-and-neck as the life of the party, and as far as necks were concerned he had a good red fleshy start.

Helen remained aloof throughout the proceedings, eating with a concentration she rarely gave to her food and talking only to Ian; clearly she did not like the Jacksons, and as clearly she disliked her father's widespread and indiscriminate *bonhomie*. It made the meal an over-public function. It was like lunching at a hotel with the head-waiter.

Each year she had this same sense of shyness, and each year she made up her mind that she must speak to her father about it before they came out again; there was really no reason why he should behave in this odd manner, when at home he was always so conservative – except (she supposed) that after being preoccupied exclusively with making money for eleven months of the year there was something to be said for really breaking out when you spent it on the twelfth. ... But was it essential to his enjoyment of the trip? and was his enjoyment the sole and paramount consideration? There were five people to be catered for; and, as usual in a family, it was a question as to how many members were to have a satisfactory holiday, and how many an unendurable one. And surely, taking the average level of inclination. ...

Denys, too, felt a certain embarrassment at the publicity which surrounded him. He had never suspected that Mr Carrington, the keen and forceful business man, would blossom out in this fashion. But the food was extremely good, and the lager so eminently drinkable that he was able, to a great extent, to exclude the outside world altogether. And after all, Mr Carrington was paying for everything; and this generosity surely permitted him to call his own tune as well as to dance to it. To be old and poor was inexcusable: to be old, rich and generous entitled one to a certain latitude of behaviour as well as of girth.

Lunch over (and topped off, as a special occasion, by a Grand Marnier each), they all adjourned to the lounge, where introductions of a more formal nature were effected. They revealed a surprising range of assorted humanity – some half-dozen nationalities, some score of social contrasts; and typical of the wide appeal made by the Schweizer Hotel was the fact that out of a total of about sixty guests there were not more than fifteen English people.

It was refreshing to find a foreign hotel that was not like an extension to the Strand Palace; and pleasant, too, to listen to the variety of language, and to know oneself to be a part of the pattern.

Denys, shaking hands with complete strangers, all of whom appeared to be amazingly glad to meet him, concluded that there was, after all, something to be said for Mr Carrington's method of approach: it was a reasonable alternative to silent instinctive hatred, it did at least ensure a vast improvement on the graveyard atmosphere of an English hotel lounge.

Presently Ian took him out to arrange for hiring his skis and boots, and that afternoon Denys had his first tentative introduction to the art.

It was, as Frau Franck had prophesied, easier than he had expected: at the outset the skis seemed too long, the ski-sticks unmanageable, and balance a matter of god-like agility, but he could glimpse, far ahead, a time when he would be able to tell where his skis were going in time to imitate their lead and postpone disaster. He looked eagerly towards that time – a worm's-eye view of progress.

Ian, who was an expert, ranged further afield as soon as he saw that Denys might safely be left to experiment; although whenever he toiled up the slope again he could always count on finding Denys lying on his back, in process of deciding which leg to move first. Occasionally things would come to such a pass that he would ask to be sorted out and stood afresh on his feet: and towards the end of the afternoon he had collected a greater weight of snow than seemed to constitute a fair human load. But obviously he was enjoying himself thoroughly, and there are not many modes of enjoyment which only require enthusiasm and two slightly bent pieces of wood.

They missed tea, and came back, both stiff and tired, some time after six, in time for a glass of sherry in the hotel bar. This was, at the moment, deserted except for themselves: dinner-time was drawing near, and there was always a certain amount of competition for baths at the Schweizer Hotel, even at the advanced and rather spurious price of nearly half a crown each. As they sipped their drinks:

'It's a damned good sport,' said Ian presently. 'In fact I think it's the best in the world.'

Denys nodded, leaning forward against the bar, trying to find a position which would rest his aching back. 'It's certainly easy to be keen on it, even at this stage,' he agreed. 'I hope a fortnight will be long enough for me to pick it up properly.'

'Oh yes – you'll be breaking your neck in comfort, in two or three days. ... By the way,' he went on casually, 'you won't mind my going off on my own, will you? You don't need me around, and I'd like to get up to Hahnenmoos – that's the main ski run – sometime tomorrow.'

'Of course. Do whatever you'd be doing if I weren't here. I'll be quite all right.'

'That's fine. You'll have lots of fun, experimenting: and there are beginners' races, every now and then, which you can go in for. No one's terribly good here, you know: all the real experts go to Klosters or Scheidegg. But it suits the family, and I don't mind the bar, and there are some very good runs.'

'It's a pity Helen doesn't ski,' said Denys after a pause.

'No, she's never liked it. But she skates very well – as well as the pro here, which is saying something. Sometimes they give an exhibition together: it goes down rather well.'

Ian stretched idly. 'Skating's something I've never managed to become interested in: everyone down at the rink is so darned efficient, and if you get in their way or skate round at all fast they give you black looks and try to get you barred from the ice. But as you see, no one minds how badly you ski – there's plenty of room, and it isn't looked on as a matter of life and death if you hit someone. In fact it's considered pretty eccentric if you don't.'

Helen came in, already changed for dinner, in a black frock which set all doubts at rest.

'Hallo, you two boozers,' she began amicably. 'I knew you'd be here. Are you giving him bad habits, Ian?'

'Only sherry, darling – not the sort of rum-and-Rough-on-Rats that you're so fond of. Why dressed so early? – you'll never beat father to the hors-d'oeuvres.'

'I had my bath first. And if you want to use the parents' bathroom, now's your chance.'

'Oh, can we do that?' asked Denys.

'Sure – the hotel prices for everything else are so fantastic that we have to sting them some way. So we pay for one private bathroom, and all use it.' Ian swallowed the last few drops of his sherry. 'I'll toss you for first go, Denys. The winner has the benefit of Helen's high-water mark.'

'No, you go ahead. I can change in about seven minutes.'

Ultimately Denys was late for dinner. But nobody minded very much; and Mrs Carrington was relieved to see Helen in such good spirits.

Afterwards the hotel gave itself over, in the wildest sense, to dancing and games. The band was a negative affair – piano, violin and a drummer with more enthusiasm than finesse and more sheer strength than either; but Herr Franck bustled to and fro and eventually whipped up a Paul Jones, wherein Denys, by the customary evil juggling with fortune, danced every dance with Helen and still gave the illusion of joining wholeheartedly in the fun.

It was a most curious roomfull; the surrounding balcony held only the most blasé or decrepit, for everyone else worked with might and main to expend their surplus energy. They all whirled round – fat and sweating Germans, dried up Dutch officials from the East Indies, a dyed and enamelled Frenchwoman or two, a sprinkling of Swiss lads in soft silk shirts: the band ground out its lamentable melodies, the hum of conversation coursed backwards and forwards in great increasing waves: Mr Carrington shouted to Mr Jackson, Mr Jackson waved his emptying glass and exhorted him to show the young ones a thing or two. . . . It was all in the best style of the village hop on New Year's Eve: at any moment, it seemed, the Vicar might strike a gong for silence, and bestow the spot waltz prize. Except that silence would have been unobtainable, gong or no, and that he might at the same time have had something distinctly clerical to say about the amount of alcohol in evidence.

Helen danced well, with a controlled grace which needed no versatility to sustain it: her movements supplied the rhythm, as well as the exhilaration, that the band lacked. But the atmosphere of the hotel worried her: it was difficult to conduct a civilized relationship when one was involved in such alien surroundings; it was difficult, indeed, to have a private life at all in face of such boisterous intrusion. As usual, she was irritated by the crowd, and something which came under the 'jolly throng' category as well, and behaved as such, was enough to defeat her altogether.

Presently, when balloons made their appearance, and her father had donned a paper hat of the shape affected by Napoleon when in battle, she stopped dancing and drew Denys to one side of the room.

'This place is getting on my nerves. Let's go somewhere else.'

Denys laughed. He had had some brandy after dinner, for the first time in his life, and it seemed to suit him admirably. Now he could say: 'I like a glass of brandy after dinner.'

'That sounds very London-ish,' he answered her. 'Is there somewhere else to go? Do you really hate this?'

'In its present state, yes.' The flow of dancers whirled past them, noisier than ever, trailing great lengths of coloured streamers. Mr Jackson, beribboned like a May Queen, was dancing a sort of Highland schottische with a fat Dutch banker from Amsterdam.

'I'm not just being blasé about it, but it *is* getting rather like a Christmas romp, isn't it? Let's go down the street to the Bar-Français – it's a sort of cellar, all very smoky and unhygienic, and last year it had a marvellous little orchestra.'

Denys fell in love with the suggestion. But he nodded towards her parents, who were at last sitting out on the balcony. 'Will they mind?'

'Good Lord, no – father's in his element, and I suppose mother will get him off to bed sooner or later. And Ian's gone out long ago. . . . I'll just go and tell them: stay here.'

The street, unexpectedly, was full of people, and as the two of them clumped slowly down it in their snow-boots they received a variety of friendly greetings. It was an odd crowd: most of them young men, skiers who had come over the pass from Lenk, or who had been all day on the snow-slopes at Hahnenmoos: they stood about in their business-like clothes – blue plus-fours and white stockings, fur caps, Canadian lumberjacks' jerkins of gaily-coloured blanket-cloth – talking and laughing with each other, sure of themselves, of their tradition and company, with their skis shouldered or leaning against the near-by houses.

A light powdery snow was falling, through which the lamps gleamed hopefully: the little street became a shaft of light cleaving the darkness, and the trodden snow, cut and cross-cut by ski tracks, reflected the glow from a million tiny facets. So the two of them progressed down the street, arm in arm, leaving deep footprints, calling 'Grüss Gott,' or 'Bon soir,' or 'Good evening' to the murmuring groups: the snow settled gently on their shoulders, the sickle moon lit the roof-tops, and a calm sky looked down on this new creation – this minute and close concentration of dark shadow and gleaming light set deep in the valley, for human beings to come upon secretly.

The contrast between this, and the gloomy profundity of the Bar-Français, was a sharp one, moving to laughter or expectation. Originally designed as the cellars for the village wine-shop, the room was low-roofed and full of odd corners: in the hot and smoke-laden atmosphere, the few lights seemed to increase rather than dispel the attendant murkiness. But for a certain mood – the mood of Helen and Denys at that moment – it had a distinctly inviting air: the accordion band was playing a soft discreet tango, the voices never rose above a lulling murmur, there was no harshness and no hard surface anywhere, only a dull golden light and the promise of secrecy. Certainly, thought Denys as he followed Helen across the uneven floor, she had been right in preferring this to their own hotel.

They found a table, tucked away underneath an arch of the roof and lit by a solitary swinging lantern; there they sat down, and, following an earlier and somewhat rash decision, ordered Frankfurters, *Sauerkraut* and draught Pilsener. . . . Almost immediately Denys caught sight of Ian, dancing with a young woman whom he remembered having seen at the Schweizer – dark, pretty enough in a rather obvious fashion, with a determined face which somehow contradicted the lissomness of her figure. He looked away again hurriedly, uncomfortable in his observation: they were dancing in a manner too closely suited to their surroundings for him to care to watch them.

Now suddenly it was all spoilt, now the music disturbed instead of soothed him. ... Was it silly of him to be shocked? Was he right to be taken aback at seeing Ian there, so obviously and so conventionally enjoying himself? Was it merely sentimental that his mind should flash back to Cynthia lying at home, awaiting the birth of Ian's child? He took a long draught of his lager, and then stared down at his plate. Was he, in actual fact, having a good time? And had he really got to eat that revolting mess?

By his side, Helen spoke suddenly: 'There's Ian – I thought he might be here. I wonder who that is with him. ... Let's ask them over here.'

She raised her arm, preparing to wave.

'No!' said Denys suddenly. 'Don't do that. Let's – let's just keep this table to ourselves.'

Helen turned to him, smiling into his eyes. 'I thought you said you weren't sentimental. ... All right, we'll be exclusive for a change.' Privately she was surprised at Denys' voicing his wish so straightforwardly; hitherto she had been sure of a wall of diffidence separating them. 'And now,' she continued gaily, 'we have to demolish these things somehow or other. Shall we race, or just plough our way through slowly?'

Denys smiled in his turn, recovering quickly from his depression. From one point of view it was none of his business what Ian did, and in any case there was nothing much wrong in dancing cheek to cheek with a pretty girl. That was what one did with them. And besides, there was Helen here to comfort him. ... He leant towards her, touching her shoulder, becoming her partner again.

'This *Sauerkraut* looks a bit of a problem for the dainty eater,' he said smilingly. 'Let's dance first, and work up an appetite.'

Ian, hailed suddenly from a distance of three feet, was at first embarrassed, but quickly he noted Denys' mood, and responded to it at once. They danced round the floor, the four of them in companionable proximity. The girl's name was Jill Collier, and she used rather a lot of rather intriguing scent: she also was the least bit embarrassed to start with, so presumably (thought Helen) Ian had been talking a bit of this and that. ... Not that it mattered how he enjoyed himself, and Cynthia must be pretty awful to live with; but the Collier girl looked tough, and it was just as well not to put too many cards down. ... Helen had the sudden thought that it might be because of this girl that Denys had not wanted Ian to join them, but she rejected the idea immediately. He could not be so impossibly sensitive. And besides, her first thought was much the more attractive one. ...

Tonight, she had no scruples about her own manner of dancing: she allowed the lights and the persuasive atmosphere to make their obvious appeal to her senses, and did not hesitate to include Denys within the range of this moving erotic force. Soon he too was possessed by it, experiencing for the first time in his life a deliberate generosity, exploring the tide of young desire: soon he forgot to be astonished that he was behaving like this, that he should have set aside all his old restraint: it seemed a miracle that she should be so kind, so acquiescent in all his wishes, and he abandoned every reservation that shyness and inexperience had built up in him.

She kissed him as soon as they returned to their table – the first truly-awakened kiss he had ever exchanged; and later their walk back to the hotel, through the snow and the silent village, became a sweet and loving progress from shadow to shadow.

He had tip-toed after her into her bedroom – so much she had decided to allow; and now, with the door still ajar, they sat on her bed, giving each other a lingering good night.

'I've enjoyed the evening, Denys.'

'So have I – more than anything else before.'

'And there's lots of time, a whole fortnight still to go.'

'Let's dance every night.'

'You'll get tired of it.'

'How could I when you're so sweet to me?' He frowned into the darkness. 'But why weren't you like this before?'

'We've never met, really.'

'I suppose not. . . .' He moved restlessly, his arm tight about her shoulders. 'I'll dream of you tonight.'

She kissed him. 'You're young – and so sweet. You must go, Denys darling.'

'All right.' He stood up, without hesitation, straining his eyes in the darkness to see her face. 'Good night. I'll never thank you enough.'

'There's no need, now or in the future. Till tomorrow, my dear.'

'Till tomorrow.' Her lips were warm, and soft as down. His own clung to them longingly; and then, hardly conscious of frustration – for he had never thought of possessing her – he crossed the passage to his own room.

He lay awake a long time, striving to recreate her image deep within his mind, thinking amazedly of his good fortune: fitfully, into the wild tumult of his thoughts, there kept drifting the remembrance that Ian, unless he had been impossibly quiet, had not yet returned to the hotel. But the knowledge could not remain for long with him: already it was Helen who possessed his whole living consciousness.

CHAPTER IV

There followed three days of confused development. The hotel shook together, welding itself into a working unity; the period of readjustment necessary between acquaintances who have not met for a year or more ran its course and produced its pleasant train of good humour. Conversation gradually became less stilted: people talked even over their honey and rolls at breakfast, no longer taking refuge behind a heavy-eyed misanthropy and the *Berliner Tageblatt*: the bar did, if not a roaring trade, at least a briskly clinking one. And there were other, more solid, signs of progress.

The evening games now took on a ritual significance, so that a wide fame attached to the various champions at table-tennis, bagatelle and tests-of-memory; and even such futilities as blowing a ping-pong ball across the floor of the ballroom (disastrous alike to lungs and trouser-knees) had their place in the accepted competitive hierarchy. The party, on the threshold of Christmas, got going in real earnest, and cunning, or misanthropic, indeed was the individual who contrived to escape its net.

Herr Fanck, who was of necessity sensitive to these changes of rhythm, was well pleased that this, the most important season of the whole year, was thus fulfilling its promise: it was not always so, for he could remember dreadful Christmasses just before and just after the war, when half the guests were not even on speaking terms with the rest – in nineteen-thirteen the sight of binoculars was enough to set the hotel in an uproar of spy mania, and once an entire French family had left because '*Faisan rôti Allemand*' appeared on the dinner menu. . . . But this one clearly was to be a success – there was much laughter, much friendliness, a great *kameradschaft* throughout the hotel. Indeed, it seemed that in certain quarters this *kameradschaft* was likely to overreach itself, becoming something quite different and not nearly so commendable. . . .

To his analytical, true-Teutonic mind there were observable

three flaws which disturbed, or might in the future disturb, his present peace: the situation in the kitchen, where Alois the head-waiter was paying far more attention to the little Viennese chambermaid than was good either for his work or her prospects, the fact that the Karlsbad Hotel, and not his own, had been chosen for the Downhill-Race prize-giving, and lastly the strange state of affairs within the Carrington party.

He marshalled them in that order, for in that order they might be resolved. Alois would see reason (or else Alois' wife, one of the three cooks, would give him a sizable glimpse of it), and the chambermaid might be exchanged to another hotel; and the Karlsbad had clearly bribed (i.e. overbribed) the Sports Committee, and would later find that it did not pay. For the appetite grew with what it fed on, and sports committees the world over were notorious for turning nasty if nourishment were withheld. That affair would adjust itself. But the Carringtons....

A good hotel proprietor watches no one and sees everything; and Herr Franck, first-rate member of the brotherhood, was as well aware of the tangled situation within their party as he would have been had he been one of the protagonists. Purged of fantasy and the taint of rumour, it resolved itself into this: Young Mrs Carrington was at home, having a baby; her husband, who should have been with her, had come out here instead and was running after the Collier girl in 47; and lastly, Miss Carrington was infatuated with the young Mr Wilder, who (it appeared from the *carte de régistration*) was eleven years and four months younger than she was.

That difference of age might not be important in some respects: for a light-hearted affair, for a mere holiday flirtation, it was nothing; but there seemed to be an element of seriousness in this case which would make for future unhappiness, if for nothing more dangerous. Nor was this a matter of guesswork. For it had chanced that in one of the hall mirrors Herr Franck had seen her kiss Mr Wilder, when they were alone in the writing-room, and to his mind there had been nothing light-hearted, nothing of the experienced woman condescending to a young enthusiasm, about that. Such an affair was surely unhealthy for them both; and, if it ran its true course, might become a genuine peril.

It did not seem possible that her parents knew about it, and were doing nothing. That was not the English way. Without doubt they thought such an idea ridiculous, they thought of the boy as far too young to cause any disturbance. ... Should they be enlightened – by a word, by a respectful hint of some kind? For although (thought Herr Franck) it was none of his business what happened within the Carrington family, yet this sort of thing made for unrest, and unrest was, as every hotel keeper knew, an infectious phenomenon.

The other matter – young Mr Carrington's affair – concerned him much more closely. For that was a SCANDAL – or would shortly become one: nearly everybody knew by now that his wife was at home, having a child (that kind of information spread more quickly than anything else on earth, as if it were a disease to be labelled 'vicarious maternity'), and very soon everyone – instead of just half the hotel, as at present – would recognize that the attentions he was paying to Miss Collier would have been more than significant in an unattached bachelor.

Miss Collier. ... Herr Franck, who was in his office, reached forward on an impulse and took from its pigeon-hole her registration card. 'Collier, Miss Gillian: Clifton Street, London, S.W.1. British subject by birth: Independent.' Independent – *selbständig* – a word of significance: it told that she was able to take care of herself, and able also to achieve a width of experience denied to her more homely sisters. She was out here alone, she liked young Mr Carrington, and she was *selbständig*; it was a combination which certainly promised ill for the conventions. And his hotel lived by the conventions, cherished them passionately, and would if necessary die for them. *Ach*, love! thought Herr Franck, and turned with a sigh to his accounts. A pity that 'doubt and anxiety caused' could not be added to the bill, to round it off into a fatter total.

For Denys the three days had furnished an odd contrast of long solitude and unforgettable companionship. From the very beginning, when Ian remarked casually after breakfast: 'I'm going to ski up at Hahnenmoos with Jill Collier – you'll be all right, won't you?' he had been left to his own devices during the day-time; Helen skated with graceful industry, the two parents circled the rink sedately or sunned themselves on the balcony, Ian took his lunch with him and was no more seen. . . . The plan of that portion of the day was complete and immutable.

But with the coming of dusk, Denys' life seemed to be transformed: during the day he struggled valiantly with his skis, daring the hazards of the nursery slopes, twisting his ankles, wrenching his knees, burrowing deep in the snow, and gradually acquiring a sense of balance and direction; with nightfall he slipped back into a different world. Before there had been cold, discomfort, a measure of danger; now there were only soft lights to welcome him, music to soothe and caress his senses, Helen close by his side to bear him company. The contrast was a sharp one, and that did not make it any less sweet.

For Helen was still with him, in the most agreeable sense of the phrase. He had been half afraid that after that first night she would retreat, that she had acted on impulse alone and would relapse into her former non-committal attitude; of the few girls he had kissed, at dances or after cocktail parties, most of them were inclined to have an edge on their tempers at the next meeting – the prettier they were, the more nonsensical were their ideas about making themselves cheap. When one rang them up in the morning the conversation petered out into a cold accusing hum, as if miles of wiring were busy making a cage for virtue. And Helen might have been the same, for surely she had every right to cling to her superiority.

Helen was not the same. She had come into his room early next morning, had scraped some snow off the window-sill and tried to put it on his chest, had kissed him happily and played hell with the eiderdown; then they had shared her tea, and he had known that she was neither angry about the preceding night nor inclined to regret it, but simply glad that they had discovered a method of amusing themselves which suited them both so very well. He was ready to worship her at that moment: all his daydreams concerned precisely that kind of intimate feminine generosity, and to have it accorded to him thus unexpectedly seemed a marvellous stroke of luck.

Nor had that luck faltered. They danced again that night, they ranged further afield to the Grand Hotel, and on to the little Ratskeller restaurant – it was like the Bar-Français on a less savoury scale – and she behaved towards him as on the first evening, making herself approachable without hesitation and without question as to his ultimate motive. And there was now the added thrill of becoming excitingly accustomed to each other, in the sense not of habit but of initiation; given a certain movement or a certain turn of phrase they each knew what to expect, and each could count on the other's generous reactions under all circumstances.

Throughout those three evenings they were lovers in all but the ultimate technicality; and he did not ask for more only because, quite apart from her point of view, the ideal of complete chastity until his marriage was still the strongest force within him.

There were flaws, of course. Even Helen's sweetness – dancing with him, walking back through the crisp moonlit snow, saying good night at the door of her room – could not entirely prevent the growth of an anxiety about Ian. There had been no news from London, and no word from Cynthia: and it was as if Ian had walked clean out of his normal life into something entirely different and entirely unworthy. He breakfasted with Jill Collier at her table, he was out ski-ing with her most of the day; she sat at the Carringtons' table if there was dancing after dinner, and invariably they went out together after the parents had gone to bed. Denys had seen them dancing more than once, and could not fail to notice their degree of concentration; and the hotel, awakening to a piquant situation, was taking a lively interest in every phase of the affair. Both Helen and Denys were worried by it, though for almost diametrically opposite reasons: Denys was shocked by Ian's callousness, and Helen merely wished he would be more discreet.

Neither Mr nor Mrs Carrington had given any sign that

they had noticed the strength of this new development. In fact occasionally, in moments of depression, it seemed to Denys that he was surrounded by a ring of half-blind or wholly indifferent people, and that he alone viewed the affair through normal eyes and with normal instincts. But such a mood rarely lasted long. He simply did not feel that he was in a position to interfere or even to criticize. And of course he had Helen.

High up on the blue-shadowed snow at Hahnenmoos, six miles from Adelboden, Ian and Jill rested at the halfway mark of the last strenuous run. Together they had come down the hill-side, using the Slalom, the great sweeping stem-turn that alone could check their speed: they were the first to cross that slope after the previous night's snowfall, and the fresh tracks of their skis were the only marks on all the great expanse of white. Wherever they turned, a shower of powdery snow was thrown up, glinting in the sun: their skis hissed like a continuous scythe stroke, the air rushed by them, the passing of their shadows was swift as a storm-cloud before a gale. At the bottom of the slope their failing speed seemed to have an infinite sadness in it, like the death of some great ambition.

Now Ian knelt at her feet, chipping the ice from her ski-bindings and undoing the buckles. His gauntlets lay in the snow beside him, his hands steamed as the moisture encountered their warmth; he breathed fast after the effort of the run, rejoicing to do her a service while he was thus spent with fatigue.

Jill shook her feet clear of her skis and stood aside, flexing her knees gently to relieve their tension. 'That's better – they need a rest.' She too was breathless, so that her low voice was hardly audible. 'We came down that pretty fast: it's far the best ski run in this valley.'

'Cigarette?'

'Thanks.'

When they lit their cigarettes the spirals of smoke, intensely blue, drifted away from them slowly, as if partaking of their own languor. They stood in the shadow of an old timbered cattle shelter, close to the Adelboden road. Ian, leaning back, stared at the long valley and the figures moving on either side of it, and found in them the complement of his own inanimation. There was an intense peace in the air: the cowbells sounded faint and lost among the high open spaces, the occasional voices had no strength, only a lazy unsubstantiality.

'We must be starting back soon,' she said presently. 'You were late for dinner again yesterday – your family will be getting restive.'

'That doesn't matter much.' He was not self-consciously off-hand: the answer was a true and exact statement of his outlook.

'I don't believe you've got any conscience at all.' She looked sideways at him as he leant against the barn, his handsome head and black hair outlined against the snowy background: having no conscience herself, her voice was without reproach. 'You leave your wife when she's having a baby, you ignore your parents entirely, you ruin my reputation, you make Denys miserable.'

'Denys?' He turned towards her, his eyebrows lifting. '*Denys* miserable? What makes you say that?'

'Haven't you noticed? It's rather pathetic. Whenever he sees us together he always looks as though the sins of the world were on his shoulders, put there and strapped on by us. It's natural, I suppose.'

Ian snorted. 'Natural. . . . What's it got to do with him how I behave? He can't think he's my keeper at that age.'

'Well, he's Cynthia's brother, and he sees you carrying on as though you were a nasty old bachelor again, and he doesn't like it – for her sake. And the younger one is, the more essential it is that one should reform the world, if possible by the end of the week.'

'He'd better not try to reform me, all the same. That's something I couldn't stand. And besides,' he smiled, raising his eyes to the sky, 'technically I'm still faithful.'

'But you think it's only a matter of time?'

'I hope so.' He turned towards her again, searching for some clue to her mood. 'It is, isn't it, Jill?'

'You take a lot for granted.' Her voice was attractive, musically true: her flushed face under the little blue ski-cap seemed for a moment less determined than usual. 'We've progressed pretty fast, I know, but that doesn't mean that I'll do everything you want. After all, Ian, you *are* married: and I have some scruples, even if you haven't.'

He sighed. 'But I've told you so many times . . .' he began.

'I know how things are between you,' she interrupted. 'But don't you see that it's so hopelessly ordinary: everyone seems to get tired of marriage – if what one hears is true, no single wife understands her husband when they've been married more than three years. . . . Just because you want a change, it doesn't have to be me that gives you one.'

'But it's been going on for so long,' Ian protested. 'And the last few months have been absolute hell. This sort of thing was bound to happen sooner or later.'

Her chin went up. 'In fact, you're just filling in a square with the first thing that comes to hand – with me? What do you think I am – just a nice tasty meal for any hungry gentleman that likes to dine out?'

There was a silence between them for a space: she angry, and he trying to find words to convince her. At length:

'You know that's not true,' he said quietly. 'Darling, please don't spoil this – we've had such fun already, and I don't want to badger you into something you don't care to do.' He touched her shoulder, suddenly bored with words, attempting with sensuality a short cut to her good humour. 'You're not really annoyed with me, are you, Jill?'

'Furious. . . .' But she smiled now, her anger dissolving; Ian could be exceedingly persuasive when he wanted to. 'Sorry I snapped, but as far as most men are concerned, when they start talking about their wives you just know what's coming.' She laid her hand on his, rubbing it with her cheek. 'Sorry again.'

'That's all right: you know you're always free to say what you want. But the fact remains that I'd be behaving like this even if everything were quite different: it isn't just difficulties with Cynthia, and living on edge the last few months, that makes me want you.' He was himself almost convinced of the truth of this. 'Now kiss me, and we'll forget all about it.'

She returned the pressure of his lips warmly: the world round them retreated, the sky faded out, the force of reason was defeated. They clung together, Ian eager for the primitive comfort which it seemed she alone could give him, Jill stirred by a like urge and knowing now that her surrender could not be long delayed. Presently she looked up, and smiled into his eyes.

'For how long do you suppose we'll forget about it?'

'That's your fault,' he answered her breathlessly. 'How can I be distant and respectful when you look and feel like this? What is it that makes you so horribly attractive? Experience? – or original sin?'

'Experience, certainly.'

'And may I not add to it?'

She slipped from his arms, and bent down to restrap her skis. From there she spoke, her voice muffled and almost inaudible.

'That depends. ... I don't want to get too tangled up, I don't want to make anyone unhappy when there's no need. But original sin can be very strong, can't it? Let's go down this next slope as fast as we can.'

CHAPTER V

Helen, thinking of Denys as she waited for him in the bar, took stock of her position and found it inexplicable. Examine it how she would, she could see no clear way to regain surer ground.

It was all very well to dismiss the affair as a holiday flirtation, as she had tried to do, but already she was certain that there was more in it than that. There was more in it for both of them, too, which was the disturbing part: a one-sided relationship, with Denys the adoring swain and herself the gracious idol, would have been *vieux-jeux*, pleasant, and entirely manageable, but that she should be deeply involved herself was more than she had bargained for. Yet it was so:

apparently everything had been taken out of her hands and she was being borne along by his will and his initiative: she was now the helpless passenger instead of the immutable scenery. It was a feeling which she hated, and not only for the surrender of dignity which was its essence: for if she must be helpless, it should be by choice, not through her own weakness: that was how it had always been before, and it was late in the day to reverse the process. Particularly as behind it all there lurked that cruel (though not particularly applicable) phrase: 'Old enough to be his mother.'

Sipping her drink, unconscious of the stares of the girl behind the bar, who knew all about the whole thing from the waiter in the lounge, who kept his eyes open, Helen reviewed the history of the affair from her own angle.

It had come upon her out of the blue: the impulse to be nice to him had been followed so swiftly by the urge to win his favour that she had been taken unawares. Certainly that first evening had got entirely out of control: she had intended nothing more than a few dances and a drink with him (because they had been such complete strangers before, and she hadn't known he was so sweet), and then suddenly it had become quite imperative to explore further and to find out very quickly what he was like, to be kissed by him and told that she looked pretty and felt desirable. And that was no sort of a way to behave: at least, not when they were really so different, when they were hardly of the same generation.

That was the queerest part of it. Hitherto he had been merely a schoolboy whom she saw four or five times a year – at family teas when he was home for the holidays, at Christmas theatres; he had no mother, and his father was virtually a hermit, but it did not seem that he needed any parents to help him: and since he shared a flat with one of his many cousins, and had innumerable friends, he was very seldom to be seen at the Carringtons' house. And now, at one stroke, from being a normal eighteen-year-old just finished with Eton, he had caught her up and become an individual personality; from that first moment on the Victoria platform she had had to see him through different eyes, and to recognize him as a tangible force with which she would have to contend. And so far all she had done in the way of contending was to come near to being seduced by him, without thinking it anything out of the ordinary. So much for the gap between them, so much for her aloof superiority.

And what was to happen now? She did not want to draw back, she certainly did not want to take things to their logical conclusion. Yet, if he asked her, as it seemed he must do soon, it would be difficult to disappoint him at this stage: there was something about him – his unassuming manner, his sincerity, his clear good-looking face – which had captured all her will.

Finally, she could not conceivably marry him: he still had to get started, to find himself a job and begin the business of living, and eighteen was, in any case, a faintly ridiculous age, whether measured against her own or not. Thus had her emotions, and his attraction for them, brought her to a dead end.

Her thoughts were also brought to a dead end at that moment by Mr Jackson, who strode into the bar, stamping snow off his boots and calling out: 'A whisky and soda, for God's sake,' while still on the threshold. Helen sighed, recognizing *bonhomie* thirsty for a victim, and summoned her strength to meet the assault.

'Why, hallo, Helen!' He wheeled round, sending a liberal shower of drops over her table. 'Have a drink – a little one with me? How's the skating getting on?'

'Quite well, thank you.'

'That's good, that's fine. You ought to ski, though, if you want some real exercise. How about that drink?'

'I've still got one, thank you very much.'

'Well, swallow it up then – that's the only way to get rid of it.' With a gesture of immense energy Mr Jackson swept his tumbler on high, and then downed half its contents at one gulp. 'That's better: that's what I needed.' He sat down on the bench next to her, and inevitably his hand descended on her knee. 'Well, how's my little Helen today? Enjoying your holiday?'

'Oh yes. ...' Her tone of voice had a brilliance as sparkling and as bogus as chromium plate. 'I hope you are, too.'

'Well, I'm not as young as I was, you know.' He paused

momentarily, but a denial not being forthcoming he continued in a voice only slightly subdued: 'Still, I always like it here, and there's plenty to do, one way and another.'

His grip of her knee tightened, and he looked at her roguishly. 'Put me right if I'm wrong, but I'm told that you're finding plenty to do, too.'

Helen stared, uncertain whether to snub or to misunderstand him. Finally she chose the latter.

'Yes, I'm skating nearly all the day,' she answered coolly. 'And it really is quite strenuous exercise, you know.'

'Skating, is it? Ha, ha! that's good. ...' Mr Jackson dissolved into peals of enormous laughter, so that the girl behind the bar looked at him in consternation. There were strict instructions from Herr Franck to permit no extensive drinking until after dinner: if in doubt or under duress, she was to call him immediately, playing for time with a reluctant corkscrew. ... But though she was new to the job it did not seem possible that one whisky and soda should serve to induce this overwhelming mirth. And Herr Jackson was, she knew, one of the oldest guests – she compromised by clapping the stopper into the whisky bottle and returning to her book with an air of finality. Time, the Great Revealer, would show whether she was right or not.

Helen joined politely in the laughter, without making her contribution audible. She was well aware that she had not nearly disposed of the subject, and was curious to know exactly how far Mr Jackson would go in his eagerness for knowledge.

It was, of course, inevitable that the hotel should be talking about herself and Denys: sin at second hand was less a luxury than a staple diet. Nor could she forget how year after year the same people, the same speculative men and crowing women, sandwiched in their conversation with her the semi-inquisitive, semi-malicious question 'And when shall we hear of *you* getting married?' or 'How many times have you been a bridesmaid?' or even made reference to Mr Right – that broad-beamed, tweed-clad figure perennially suspended in some clean-living fourth dimension, always Coming Along and yet never quite showing up. ... But it was rare for gossipers with something tangible between their teeth to come to the fountain-head for their facts. Mr Jackson, however, seemed to believe in first-hand information, for when he had recovered somewhat:

'Skating's all very well,' he wheezed heavily, 'but it doesn't take up twenty-four hours, not by a long chalk. There's a sort of whisper going round that you do a lot of dancing nowadays.' It seemed that only by a miracle had he avoided reference to a little bird. 'And with one young man in particular. ... How's that?'

'Quite true,' she answered equably. 'But he's in our party, you know: isn't it natural that we should go about together?'

'Now who said anything about anyone in your party?' he exclaimed in enormous triumph. His hand gave her knee an excruciating wrench. 'Caught you there, didn't I? Got a guilty conscience already, Helen?'

'Not in the least – it's just that Denys is the only person I've been out with at all.' She smiled angelically. 'So it wasn't very difficult, was it?'

'Ah well, we're only young once.' This seemed an evasion of the point, but she let it pass: to get an idea into his head was a Herculean affair, and to get it out again was approximately half as feasible. He regarded her with an interest somewhere between the pert and the heavy-weight, being still a shade too ambitious to accept the role of father-confessor. 'He's a nice chap, young Wilder. ... And that brother of yours is having a high old time, too. What a family, what a family. . . . What does father think about it, hey?'

'I don't think he pays much attention to what we do.'

Mr Jackson set down his empty glass with a clatter. 'Come on now, the old 'uns aren't quite blind, you know. Give us credit for seeing beyond the end of our nose.' He fingered his own, which was large and uncertain in shape: ridiculously Helen found herself surveying hers in the wall-mirror. It did not seem very far to be able to see. ... 'But still,' he continued, 'holiday time makes a lot of things all right. You can't expect to keep it up all the year round – it isn't human.' Though he did not specify what was inhuman. 'Give it a rest – have a drink.'

'No, really, thank you.'

'Oh well, there are drinks and drinks, aren't there? I suppose you're waiting for someone, eh? Now I wonder who that could be.' Mr Jackson regarded the pools of water which the melted snow had formed under his feet. These pools were to be observed alongside every chair and sofa in the hotel, the staff of which spent a substantial portion of their working day mopping them up. 'I wish I knew a pretty girl who'd wait for me as long as this.'

'I'm not waiting for anyone,' said Helen coldly. Her patience was not going to outlast the interview, even when massaged with compliments as weighty as this.

'Just sitting here, on the off-chance, then?' Mr Jackson was in a mood at once so romantic and so dogged that he really deserved a consolation prize of some kind. 'Ah well, you never know, do you? And he can't be very far away, can he?'

At this moment Denys gave extreme point to his observations by entering the bar precipitately and apologizing for being late. Helen was sufficiently glad to see him not to mind the guffaw of laughter with which Mr Jackson signalized his triumph.

'Well, young man,' said the latter, 'we were just talking about you – or rather Helen was doing the talking and I was listening.... Will you have a drink with me?'

'Thank you very much, sir – sherry, please.' But though he accepted the drink politely, Denys looked from one to the other in some bewilderment: where Helen was concerned he could be rendered nearly frantic with jealousy by the most ridiculous things – a greeting shouted to her in the Bar-Français, a ritual dance with Herr Franck, the skating instructor's arm round her waist – and to find Helen sitting here with this fearful old man, apparently drinking away as if it was quite normal, was just the sort of thing to spoil his entire evening.

She smiled secretly at him, knowing the signs of danger and striving to soothe his temper, but for some little time he returned only monosyllabic answers to their conversation; and Mr Jackson, when finally with a mammoth display of tact he left them, carried away some very confusing impressions of the course of true love. As he remarked later to his wife, eager for details: 'Some of these young chaps nowadays have about as much go as our kitchen clock. . . .'

Helen and Denys sat in silence for some minutes after Mr Jackson's departure: he was remorseful about his boorishness, and she was disturbed to find herself almost in panic lest he should be truly annoyed with her. For it really was ridiculous: whichever way one looked at it, she oughtn't to get into this state – she wasn't a cat aching to be stroked, she wasn't a schoolgirl propping the wall at her first dance, smirking hopefully at all comers. . . . And yet over this little thing – the difference between a smile and a frown from Denys – she could become so stupidly, so *overwhelmingly* worried – she stared at the bright array of bottles behind the bar, searching for some form of words with which to bridge the gap, and yet not reveal too frankly her anxiety of mind.

Finally he spoke for her: 'I'm sorry, Helen: it was stupid of me to be rude like that.' He took her hand, and with immense relief she clasped it tightly. 'But I never could stand that man for more than twenty seconds at a time – he is so unbelievably hearty – and somehow the sight of him sitting there drinking with you made me angry. Why does he always paw you like that?'

'Paternal affection, darling.'

'He must do very well out of it. . . .' But their handclasp had disposed of the matter. 'What have you been doing all day?'

'Falling down and pretending I hadn't hurt myself. How was the ski-ing?'

'Much the same. I was down on the Grüben slope. Good snow, and I did a Christiana turn, of a sort.'

'Good for you. I must come and watch some day.'

'I wish you would. I could do with company during daylight. . . .'

'Oh. . . .' She turned towards him, struck by the loneliness in his voice. 'Poor Denys. Were you all alone again?'

'Yes.' He paused, staring idly at the rim of his glass, watching the cigarette smoke curling round it. Behind the bar the girl, an imperfect linguist, held her breath, certain that she was hearing a romantic declaration of unmistakable moment. 'Yes. . . . I don't mind much for myself, but – Helen, what *is* Ian doing?'

She was on her guard immediately, recognizing a certain danger: she had to serve two camps, and still did not know which was the stronger loyalty.

'How do you mean?' she asked at length. 'Ian's just normal, isn't he?'

'You know that isn't true.' His voice at first was quiet. 'What's it all going to lead to? He's never with us, he's always going off somewhere with Jill Collier.' Denys broke out suddenly, on edge with conflicting emotions. 'Why is he doing it – he must know it's wrong.'

Helen pressed his arm comfortingly, trying to forestall the onset of tension. 'Darling, aren't you exaggerating just the least bit? There's nothing *wrong*, surely, in taking her out now and then – he can't just sit in the hotel moping while we enjoy ourselves. After all, that's the way the party splits up: Mother and Daddy, you and me, and Ian and someone else. Why shouldn't he go about with her?'

'Good Lord, you too?' Denys shivered suddenly, as if touched by a cold hand. 'I thought you might be on my side, against the others.'

She stared, for a moment sincere. 'But that's silly. There aren't any sides – no one's thought about it at all except you. You mustn't imagine things like that, in fact you must forget all about it. Everything's perfectly normal, and it only makes for endless difficulties if you try to interfere.'

'Difficulties?'

'Yes. Ian can do what he likes, and it's his own look out entirely.'

'But it isn't. It concerns all of us. And you all back him up, you all behave as if Ian was – was free.' Savagely conscious of his isolation, Denys came to the crucial point, where before he had held back. 'What about Cynthia? Hasn't she got any rights in this?'

'Naturally.' There was a subtle change in Helen's voice. 'And as she is the only person who can exercise them, she must take care of her own interests.'

'But she can't. That's why I want to do it for her. Do you think I can sit quietly and watch while Ian does just what he likes?'

'Why shouldn't he? We're not back in the Middle Ages, you know.'

'What's that got to do with it?'

'Apparently everything. Denys, you must understand—'

So they talked, each sentence adding something to the distance and the shadow between them: it was a question concerning which they should have had some common ground, and apparently they had none.

To complicate matters, the bar began to be populated: people said good evening to them, smiled knowingly, and sat down as near as was practicable. To defeat the encroaching audience they lowered their voices, thus adding enormously to the weight of evidence against themselves: to the watchers it was quite certain now that something was afoot, something with the spice of unhallowed romance in it. Why else should anyone want to whisper, in such a gay companionable place as a bar?

As between themselves, they were truly on dangerous ground. Each was nervous of estranging the other, each was driven by a prior claim of loyalty to try to justify their point of view; and yet, through fear of using some damaging or cruel argument, neither could effectively convince the other. Denys was shocked at her callousness, but still certain that she was not really like that – she was Helen, his own Helen, and she could no more condone unfaithfulness than she could be unchaste herself. ... Eton had taught him many odd things, but it had not persuaded him that the marriage bond could ever be qualified: to such of his contemporaries as subscribed to this view he usually replied that they would grow up to something better – a reversal of the common procedure the humour of which had not so far occurred to him.

But really, he thought as he stared round the bar, sometimes he could not understand Helen at all. She must know, as everyone did, the difference between right and wrong.

She, too, found herself in some perplexity. She was certainly falling in love with Denys, and his fresh ideals – the right ideals, as her instinct if not her reason told her – were most attractive; but when they became liable to put her brother in the wrong it was easy for her to relapse into her old cynicism and decide that Denys was a juvenile moralist who must be laughed out of his nursery standpoint. For Ian was still her closest companion, as he had always been; and when it became, as now, a question of supporting him against Cynthia, the only person who had ever come between them, her path was doubly indicated and doubly welcome to her. She had resented that marriage, and the changes it had brought within their family, and she had a fierce sense of fulfilment whenever it threatened to go wrong. She might be in love with Denys, but that could never make her let slip a chance of striking at Cynthia, the supplanter, in any way she could.

Then Ian and Jill came in, obviously in a fine state of exaltation.

The temperature in the bar rose perceptibly. Here were the other pair, to complete the scandalous picture: and as a final stroke they were going to sit down at Miss Carrington's table, and what would the young Wilder boy say to that. . . . The fat Dutch matron who was nearest to them drew her daughter aside majestically: it was all very well for the grown-ups to be in the vicinity, but little Griselle must be shielded from such turpitude. And little Griselle, who thought Jill was marvellous and had kissed Ian in the ping-pong room the year before, was forced to sit in mutinous isolation on the other side of a pillar.

The silence which had fallen dispersed gradually, when it was seen that there were to be neither blows exchanged nor even voices raised; only a trio of young Austrians remained leaning against the bar and staring at the hotel's main point of interest, wondering why they had been taught to look on the English as a race of frigid and prudish bores.

The young Wilder boy suddenly found himself in a murderous temper, without much inclination to keep it under control. The expansive way in which Ian and Jill had come into the bar, as well as the expectant hush which greeted them, had caught him on the raw; and Helen's smile of welcome for the new arrivals seemed the last stroke to complete his discomfiture. He could tell now for certain that they were all ranged against him and Cynthia, all of them banded together in an instinctive devilish alliance: Ian didn't care a damn what he did, Helen was his sworn partner, and Jill the willing instrument of his treachery. ... Cynthia lay at home, while her husband abandoned every consideration of decency and did his utmost to win another woman. And Helen – Denys' own Helen, whom he had thought so dear and clean and loving – she had sneered at his ideals and was even now entrenched in the opposite camp. ... He stood up very quickly, and nodded to her.

'Sorry, I must go.'

He was out of the room almost before they had taken in his words.

Jill bit into an olive. 'You see,' she said gently to Ian. 'He *is* rather mad about it.'

CHAPTER VI

With so bad a start, it became a leaden evening. To such an extent indeed that even Mrs Carrington, presiding at dinner over the lower end of the family table, wondered why everyone seemed so glum. She usually ignored minor attacks of group-sulkiness, but this one was something out of the ordinary. What had gone wrong? Not a word out of Helen, not a word out of Denys – usually the two most cheerful people at meals: and all Ian did was to answer his father's questions as shortly as he could and keep looking round at that horrible girl on the other side of the room.

That horrible girl ... the words could not be qualified. Mrs Carrington had a very good idea of what was and what was not done, an idea which had not altered for forty years, and she was extremely worried over Ian's behaviour; a little fun on holiday was all very well – Henry had often had a little fun on holiday, and (as far as she could judge) no harm done – but really Ian seemed to be carrying it rather too far. Why, the two were never out of each other's sight.

Mrs Carrington had discussed the matter with no one, she did not know what her husband thought about it: she simply knew that it was wrong, and, with Denys there, extraordinarily embarrassing, and that sooner or later a MOTHER'S ADVICE would be given, whether it was asked for or not. The holiday was not going to be spoilt just because Ian wanted to behave like any common young man at the seaside.

Not being subject to outside atmosphere, Henry Carrington was unaffected by the prevailing depression. He talked to Ian, he conversed at ten yards' range with Mr Jackson, he dealt faithfully with titanic helpings of grilled sole and chicken casserole; this was dinner, just like any other dinner, and one had to keep one's strength up, to be in good form for the dancing afterwards. Though in point of fact it wasn't just like any other dinner, for Jackson seemed to be a bit queer this evening: he kept winking and nodding his head at something, he kept calling out 'Got a bit of a story to tell you afterwards – great joke' and then going off into roars of laughter.

Mr Carrington didn't care for it much: Jackson was a good fellow, but occasionally he did things that were in bad taste. If he really had a good story to tell, he ought to keep quiet about it. One didn't advertise these things: one kept them for the bar or the smoking-room, at a decent distance from one's womenfolk.

Ian, glancing blackly now and then at Denys, wondered whether he should speak to him first or wait until he apologized. Cheeky young devil. . . . Not that it mattered much, except from the point of view of keeping the kid in order: he didn't want a quarrel with anyone at this moment, he just wanted to get away to Jill, who (after what she had said at Hahnenmoos) would surely be marvellous tonight. Weighed against that prospect, what did it matter if Denys was a bit above himself? Everyone was, at that age.

Helen, depressed and angry, thought: 'Why is Ian such a fool? He's so obvious, he'll have the whole hotel cheering in a minute. ... If he'd only keep quiet I could square Denys. It's spoiling everything for me, too.'

Denys hardly ate a mouthful, and thought of nothing save how to bring things back to normal again. Reaction had come almost as soon as he left the bar. It had been frightfully rude to rush off like that, and Ian must think him an awful little fool: no one in their senses tried to show people ten years older than themselves how to behave, no one ever thought of making a scene in public like that. Perhaps if he said that he had felt sick. . . .

Even Alois, the head-waiter, seemed subdued this evening. From his usual place behind Mr Carrington's chair he surveyed the room with a blank expression; his mind wasn't on his job, and though far too good a waiter to splash soup or drop plates he had been making mistakes over sauces and jugs of cream such as would have disgraced a fifteen-year-old *commis*.

His trouble also was the current male-and-female one: unaccountably, Else had disappeared – packed up and left without a word to him, all in an afternoon. Herr Franck said that she had been offered a post at Zurich, and had taken it without even giving notice. But it wasn't possible, just when things were coming along so nicely – and after he'd promised her that silk blouse, too.

Sugar-sifter in hand, Alois meditated gloomily on the cunning of hotel-proprietors and the ungratefulness of kitchen-maids: it was sacrilege to treat a head-water like that, it wasn't natural at all.

There is a term to all situations, and Denys had his chance, and took it, immediately after dinner. Ian was waiting for Jill in the hall, and their eyes met as Denys came out of the dining-room, where he had been lingering with the others. It was even made easy for him, for Ian, now perfectly restored to humour, nodded in the old friendly fashion.

'You were in rather a hurry, weren't you?'

'Yes. I remembered I had to get my dinner-jacket brushed. I'm sorry if it looked rude, Ian.'

'That's all right, old man.' He put his hand on Denys' shoulder and gave it a good-natured pressure. 'But tell us what it's all about next time.'

'I will.'

And that was that. It was a climb down, but anything else was out of the question: the roles had had to be restored, for he was in no position to criticize Ian, in this or any other matter. But it did not help that at that moment Jill came downstairs, and that she and Ian went out arm-in-arm, laughing gaily at nothing in particular.

And there was still the matter of Helen, which would not

resolve itself in so casual a fashion. Ordinarily the two of them would themselves go out a little later, ordinarily they would laugh as happily and (he frowned in resentment) kiss as eagerly as did the other pair: but this was no ordinary night, and he could not bring himself to speak to her as he had done to Ian. For she ought to have been different: he had thought that he had a special claim on her sympathy, that she was his natural ally, and she had instead shown herself to be on Ian's side. (For there *were* sides, however much she scoffed at the idea.)

He had no need of her forgiveness – it was rather she who should apologize for so betraying the spirit of the last few days. Thus he did not seek her out, then, or at any time during the evening, but spent the time playing ping-pong and lounging in the bar; and not till eleven did they meet, just as he was thinking of going to bed. She came near to him without hesitation.

'What's the matter, Denys?' They stood alone in the hall, and she faced him squarely, the light overhead making odd shadows under her cheek-bones, as if she were wasting with despair. ... 'Where have you been all evening? Have we quarrelled?'

'Well, *have* we?' For no reason at all he felt completely in command at that moment – for the first time since the new relationship started: he would hear her side of the affair, and judge for himself, without any reference to her old superiority. 'P'raps not a real quarrel, but there are one or two things we don't seem to agree on.' He paused, then repeated foolishly: 'We don't seem to agree on.'

She saw that he wasn't quite sober, and might make a scene, but she faced the subject. 'You mean Ian?'

'Yes. We talked of it before, I know, and I still haven't changed my mind.' As he spoke, and his mood became more evident, he saw the line of her jaw stiffen, and the little shadows change shape and grow less, but his session in the bar had done him a lot of good, and he thought: 'she can take it or leave it – I'm sick of bowing and scraping to these people ...' 'You must see, Helen, that the way he behaves is bound to look queer to me, you must make some allowance for what I feel.'

'Perhaps I ought to.' Helen really had no idea how to treat him this evening: she could not see the importance of the affair under discussion, and so she temporized, wanting to risk nothing over it. But risk there certainly was: for though Denys was rather sweet when he'd had a few drinks – even one or two made a difference to him, loosening his tongue, by-passing his self-consciousness – he was dangerous too, in the sense that his irresponsibility could effect a real rift between them.

She went on cautiously: 'But even so, should you try to take a hand in it? Everyone has a right to their own sort of life, as long as they don't make a nuisance of themselves to the people round them, and if Ian wants to have a rather adventurous holiday that's a matter between himself and Cynthia.'

'But you don't approve?'

'Of course not.' She might be forgiven a lie in a good cause. 'But that's a very different thing from trying to influence him one way or another. I never believe in interfering unless it's in something that affects me personally. And this certainly doesn't come under that heading, for – for either of us, does it?'

'I suppose not.' He felt himself grow dispirited, aware that he was waging war not against Ian's conduct but against his own outlook and limited experience. He might be wrong about the whole thing: he might be out of date, out of the true, out of focus altogether. 'But it *has* something to do with me, after all,' he added, almost to himself.

'Not directly, not enough to make it necessary for you to get involved in it.' She wondered afresh at his change of mood, and rejoiced in it: with her voice and glance she tried to press home the advantage. 'Let's leave it, Denys darling – there's nothing to be done, and it will probably straighten itself out without our worrying. And we've wasted enough time this evening already.'

He smiled, and took her hand. 'You're so good to me. You're never difficult. Even when I'm really sulking, you put up with it, and wait for me to come back.'

'I like it. . . . Let's go out, or dance a little bit here, and then – then you can come up to my room and say good night properly. All right?'

'You're so good to me,' he repeated.

'I thought we'd lost each other.'

He was near to winning her that night, but regret for his bad temper made him gentle and diffident, and his young humility was an effective check – the most effective human check of all. And he still differed from her, root-and-branch, in thinking of seduction as a wrong done instead of as a benefit conferred – which was the way her thoughts were shaping themselves.

Mr Carrington, being a good Conservative and a champion of orthodox economics, was reading *The Coming Struggle for Power* with frequent pauses and a certain amount of concern. The Marxist diagnosis was, as usual, persuasive: these fellows could always talk the hind leg off a donkey, and Strachey was no exception – he seemed to know exactly why everything had happened, or had nearly happened, or had not happened at all, and that was certainly impressive, even though a lot of it was simply a matter of being wise after the event, which even a Liberal could be fairly adroit at. ... But it couldn't be true, thought Mr Carrington, that things really had to take this course: there must be a compromise, a good old English compromise, which would let everything go on as before and of course give the businessman a free hand. If you wanted to socialize something, there were all sorts of things – electricity and coal and such – which might be made to work: but not the banks, never the banks – they and the stock-markets couldn't be touched without ruining the country. And yet this Strachey chap seemed to think.... It was all very puzzling.

The idea of inescapable class-warfare worried him as well – in fact he wouldn't have been reading the book if he hadn't promised a chap at the club that he would do so. ... But thank God he had never gone into politics: it wasn't a gent's game any longer, but simply a matter of backing the right horse, and there was a damned sight more coin to be picked up doing that in the city than at Westminster.

Politics was so much tougher nowadays, too, with its reds and blacks and greens: not like the old days, when the true-blue ticket was good enough for anyone, and the only problem was that of dishing the Whigs. But then everything was the same: all his world seemed to be vanishing, swept away by forces which had surely become far more urgent than when he himself was young. Everything was the same: whatever happened, it was always blamed on the wrong people: there even seemed to be an idea that there was something scandalous or immoral about Private Enterprise. . . .

He read on, hunched up in bed, while his wife made her usual infernal clatter in the bathroom. Mrs Carrington did a great many things before retiring for the night, and thirty years had accustomed her husband to the ritual; but tonight he could tell from the especial downrightedness of her movements that she had something on her mind, something which she would shortly expect him to listen to. It interfered with his concentration, this knowledge of argument just round the corner; how could he judge (and the judging was clearly imperative) whether 'the men who ran away' in 1931 were Social-Democrat time-servers or saviours born out of their time, when the constant rattle of bottles and jars and tubes gave warning of a far more inviting problem.

Gradually, inevitably, he paid less attention to his book, and more to his wife's progress through her toilet; and as, without actually watching her, he became aware that the face massage had yielded place to the meticulous folding of clothes, and this in turn to the breathing exercises, and the touch-the-toes, and the rose-water for the hands, so he withdrew bit by bit from the political arena and entered the domestic one. Marx must wait: the wife and mother clearly would not, and only in the most class-conscious of homes would she have been expected to.

And presently, when his wife, fairly girded with tonics and skin-foods and the costliest of greases, had Time sufficiently at bay to climb into bed, he shut his book and laid it aside with no great regret. For he had a fair idea of what was troubling her, and he had also his own views and speculations on the subject, pleasantly ripe for the airing.

'Something the matter, my dear?' Some backwash of an old forgotten ecstasy always made him gentle at bed-time. 'You seem worried.'

'Worried? Not at all.' But they both knew that this was

merely automatic, part of the convention of their exchanges. 'Why should I be worried?'

'Well, things are sometimes a bit difficult. ... Is it about Ian?'

She took him up quickly. 'Then you've noticed something?'

'Noticed? Well, no. ...' He drew back at that, much as witnesses of an accident cross over the road or retreat into doorways, rather than risk having to give evidence later. 'But I'm not altogether happy about him. It seems to me that—'

'*Happy?*' She was ready to join battle now, the formal passes having been made. 'Happy? I should think not, indeed. Henry, I think it's disgraceful, the whole thing: and if you're not going to speak to him about it, I shall.' She breathed heavily, as if at the exertion of speaking her mind; and indeed it was more than she was usually accustomed to, a luxury of fortitude.

'You mean—'

'Of course I mean that.' They were unable to put it into words, as yet: probably they would never do so, throughout the discussion, but would continue to rely on pauses or the most elegant circumlocutions. 'He's behaving abominably – even if he weren't married, I should be ashamed of him. And at a time like this – oh, I can't believe he would be so cruel.'

'Cruel? Aren't you exaggerating a little? After all, we know nothing – he's on holiday – he's come out here to enjoy himself.' His voice tailed off, confronted by the vision of his own dangerous tolerance. Not on such quicksands as these was the Empire founded. . . . Then he finished, uncomfortably: 'There's no real harm in it, is there?'

Mrs Carrington shook her pillow with furious energy. 'Of course there's no *real* harm.' With that, they dismissed by agreement the possibility of adultery. 'But everyone in the hotel knows he's married: and everyone can see he's making up to this – this horrible girl. It puts us in quite a wrong position. And there's Cynthia to consider, too. He oughtn't to be able to think of such a thing for a moment.'

The issues were confused, they both realized: there were appearances to be considered, there was faithfulness to be upheld, there was a real heart-break to spice the problem. It was true that they had their own position to think of, but they were not the real losers in the affair. That was Cynthia's place, reserved and unalterable: she was a long way away, and she needed their help, for far more cogent reasons.

'Well, I'll have a word with him, if you think it's best.' Henry Carrington was tired, and could have welcomed darkness and sleep; but this was his wife's hour, by custom long continued, and he wanted to put her mind at rest. 'I dare say it's just thoughtlessness – he'll understand when I put it to him, he'll settle down and be a bit more careful. You know he's a good boy.'

'Very well.' Partly mollified, Mrs Carrington lay back, contemplating the backs of her hands. The rose-water was excellent stuff, expensive stuff, but cold winds and melted snow might be winning the battle after all. 'I never thought he should have come out here, in the first place: it isn't at all usual. And if, on top of it all, he's going to behave like this, well, all I can say is—' she shrugged her shoulders, and let the sentence die. She had gained her point, and her habitual hesitation was returning, shrinking both her vocabulary and her spirit to their accustomed domestic insignificance.

'He needed a holiday – you know that.' This had been the basic argument of the last three months, and it could still serve. 'Cynthia will do well enough – as it is, he's better out of the way, if I know anything about it.' And Henry Carrington, who *did* know something about it and had made himself an infernal nuisance at the birth of each of his children, smiled reminiscently. 'He might get over-excited, you know.'

'Very possibly.' Mrs Carrington knew by experience that it was only too likely. 'But that has nothing to do with how he's behaving here – that doesn't excuse it at all. An open flirtation at this time ...' she was in danger of becoming breathless again, and if her pillow had not been particularly comfortable she would have started battering it once more. 'Think what it would mean to Cynthia if she ever found out. And there's Denys too, poor boy.'

'Do you think he's noticed anything?'

'Of course he must have done.'

'Well, personally I don't.' The mention of Denys' name

recalled to Mr Carrington another worry, more clear-cut in his mind, 'If you ask me, he's paying no attention to it at all.'

There was something in his tone which made his wife look across at him closely. 'What do you mean?'

'Jackson said a most extraordinary thing to me after dinner ...' Mr Carrington paused, as the discomfiture of that moment renewed itself. 'You know the sort of jokes he makes.... Well, he was remarking on that Van Geysel girl, saying how pretty she was, and then he looked across at Helen and said: "Of course, I know which my choice is – and so does young Denys, doesn't he?"'

Mrs Carrington frowned. 'Whatever did he mean?'

'He wouldn't say, for a long time. And then he came out with some extraordinary tale about Denys and Helen being in love with each other, and the whole hotel knowing about it and enjoying it.... That's what he said: "the whole hotel's enjoying it".'

Mrs Carrington drew a scandalized breath, and sat up sharply.

'What?'

'That's what he said.'

She burst into words. 'It's disgusting.... Really, the gossip that goes on in these hotels is past belief. They seem to have nothing to do but – Denys and Helen? – why, the idea is preposterous.'

'So I told him, at first. But he said it was obvious, said I must be blind not to have noticed it. And come to think of it,' he fingered his chin, as if feeling the growth of the seeds of evil, 'they *are* together, those two, the whole time, aren't they?'

Mrs Carrington, now some way from any thought of repose, exploded again. 'Together? Of course they are. What else would they be? What have they come out here for, if not to enjoy themselves together? If two people can't go dancing without every busybody in the hotel.... Why, it's as bad as that woman on the boat.'

'What woman on the boat?'

'Some silly creature – you didn't meet her. I tell you, the whole thing's ridiculous.'

'Well, I hope so. We don't want any complications of that

sort.' He turned swiftly to the fresh hare. 'This woman on the boat – what did she say? Had you met before?'

'There won't be any complications – the idea isn't even worth considering. Helen is difficult enough sometimes, I know: but she's always been so sensible about that sort of thing.'

'Maybe.' And Henry Carrington, who privately thought that his daughter was at times rather too sensible for her own good, prepared to let the matter drop. 'I might mention to Jackson what you think about it.'

'You'll do no such thing.' It was Mrs Carrington's last sally before she went to sleep, and she brought it out with fine determination. 'You know what people will think – that there's something in it after all and that we're afraid of gossip. Far better to ignore it altogether.'

'Very well, my dear. Er – about this woman on the boat . . .'

'Oh, don't fuss, Henry. I've said it was nothing. Good night.'

He pulled his pillow into shape, blew his nose vigorously, and clicked out the light. But he did not go to sleep at once. Instead he spent some time making a firm resolution – to keep his eyes a little wider open in future. For it was only at night time that he deferred to his wife's authority as he had been doing: tomorrow morning would be different, tomorrow morning he would become the head of the house again, able to take his own strong line.

And if there *should* be anything in Jackson's idea, or if Ian carried on the way he was going and didn't slacken off to a more reasonable pace – well, as the head of the house he really would take some unspecified step that would put everything to rights. It only needed resolution: in home affairs not ripeness, but firmness, was all.

CHAPTER VII

Jill Collier counted it a good Christmas, and, knowing how near she had come to making it a bad one, was correspondingly grateful to fortune and her own intuition. For she had almost decided to stay in England – to yawn her head off in London, or to join the relations at Guildford and work through the whole round of too much food, walks with the dogs, games with the children, and too much food again.

That was what it usually amounted to, and that was what she had been prepared to do: and then had come that sudden discontent with London – damp and foggy and dispirited – and with her current escort, who seemed to mirror the climate in his own person, and a sudden longing for the sun and for movement and, probably, a quick refreshing love affair. It was a matter of probability because she liked men, as people like exciting books or good-looking furniture: to have something on hand, a mild flirtation or its usual development, gave her an interest, gave her a background for her life to move against.

It happened naturally that she treated men as the currency, large or small, of her existence; they were the means of enjoyment, the customary vehicle for her desire: of necessity they were human beings, of habit they became the marionettes of her own whim. She was kind to animals, because she could see when they suffered and was moved by it; but unconsciously she was damnably cruel to human beings, because she used them up quickly, and they were always more entangled emotionally than she was. When, to her way of thinking, a thing had lasted long enough, that was its natural termination: the subject itself, man, woman or dog, could hardly be expected to have a say. ... She was not strong-minded; just lazy and self-centred and miserly in her method of enjoyment; and when she had said to Ian, 'I don't want to make anyone unhappy,' she had meant, 'I don't want to be responsible for anything – I want the tune, but I don't want to pay the piper's bill at the end.' She had paid one bill in twenty-five years, and this affair was certainly not going to spoil that remarkable average.

For, above all, as far as Ian was concerned, she was not the 'other woman'. She was a little in love with him, as she usually was with anyone new and attractive; but for her, being in love was a matter of physical reaction, of hands and mouth and soft skin, touching her emotions very little and her brain not at all.

She was prepared to sleep with him, because they would both enjoy it and it was the obvious thing to do; but the idea of making it a triangle, of coming between him and his wife, never entered her head. For it didn't matter to that extent, it wasn't as important as that: it never was, and saving some outstanding change of heart or conversation of habit, it never would be. To have sexual intercourse was something you did because you wanted to, like switching on the radio or lighting another cigarette: it had no latent significance, it was not tied up with honour or duty or convention, it was not a sin any more than enjoying the tang of good sherry was sin; physically it was a great deal, but mentally, morally, socially it was nothing.

So she was able to enjoy herself, while celebrating a premier Christian festival. She liked the hotel, she was fond of ski-ing, and she was glad of Ian – glad of his eagerness, of his good looks, of the vague air of frustration he had brought with him. She fenced with him as a matter of habit, and to satisfy that faintly remembered legacy of her upbringing – the instinct not to make herself cheap. But one of these nights, sooner or later, she would surrender – a rather ludicrous word which she still used occasionally. She would enjoy it and it might continue in London: that depended on a lot of things – things to do with her, not with him. As usual, the reins were lying loose in her hand, ready for her sole manipulation.

Oh yes, it was a good Christmas. When she met Ian at breakfast – she had kissed him good night approximately four hours before – she had felt in especially good form: he was smiling, he looked as if he were in love, he had a little package in his hand. . . . And if that was not enough to explain her good humour, perhaps it was the atmosphere which was serving them so well. That was part of the charm of Switzerland, of course – the amazing quality of the air: one could ski all day, one could dance (or, as she well knew, do a lot of other things) most of the night, and one still woke up feeling like a king – one of the old-fashioned kings with neither a conscience nor a care in the world. . . . When opened, the package exhibited a little slim diamond bracelet: and as she slipped it on – eyed by the waiter, stared at by people at other tables –

and realized the trouble he had obviously taken to get it for her (he must have telephoned to Berne or Zurich), she knew that the matter of her 'surrender' had been settled there and then. She had no habit or convention which was proof against persuasion of this sort.

'Darling, how very sweet of you.' She turned her wrist this way and that, letting the morning sunlight glint on the many facets, appraising the jewels in terms not of money but of devotion and humility. He must be very eager – she would enjoy that eagerness . . . 'What a lovely thing it is – you must have had lots of practice at this sort of surprise.' Aware of the whispering round her, she looked up again, smiling. 'But you shouldn't have done it, really you shouldn't. There'd be a riot if your family knew.'

Ian smiled in answer. It was early in the day to revel in atmosphere of any sort, but the little scene, with its blend of scandal and publicity and secret understanding, seemed entirely suitable to a Christmas morning, from any but the strictly orthodox angle.

'I've already had part of that riot this morning,' he told her softly, charmed by her nearness, her implicit availability. 'My father woke me up, far too early, to point out that you and I are a public disgrace.'

'Your father?' Her eyes sharpened suddenly, so that for a half second the truth peeped out of them. Parental control was a good talking-point, but the game was never worth any sort of official hubbub. . . . 'What do you mean? He knows nothing – there *is* nothing.'

He touched her hand reassuringly. 'Of course there isn't, and he didn't put it like that at all. He simply said that, though of course he knew there was nothing between you and me, I ought not to make you quite so conspicuous.' Ian smiled. 'Like I'm doing now.'

She sighed with relief: for a moment complications had seemed close to her. . . . 'Well, if all he's worrying about is my reputation. . . . What did you say to him?'

'Nothing much. I was half asleep, and feeling rather happy anyway.'

She sipped her coffee, eyeing him over the rim. 'Happy?'

'Yes. You've been so sweet, and I'm enjoying this holiday so much, and—' but at that he stopped. He could have mentioned the bracelet, which had seemed to him then, as he saw it lying on his bedside table, the final and undeniable element which would bring him what he wanted. With its help her generosity was virtually guaranteed. . . . But as a simple matter of tactics he kept silent on that point. 'I just told him there was nothing in it, and that I liked going about with you, and it was far more fun ski-ing with someone you knew than by yourself.'

She nodded slowly, ironically. 'All very true.' Taking off the bracelet, she let it swing to and fro on the end of one finger, catching the sunlight, glittering with a certain wicked allurement.

A couple at the next table pursed their lips, estimating the scene at something near its correct significance, persuaded finally that to speak of national characteristics was an international delusion. English women weren't frigid – they were warm, scandalously warm and free with their favours. Ian stared at the jewels, letting their glitter signal and beckon to his senses; they were his ambassadors, doing his work for him, discreetly procuring his heart's desire. And apparently he was right to rely on them. . . . 'There's nothing certain,' Jill went on deliberately, as if answering his thoughts. 'You know I can never make up my mind. But I'll wear it tonight, and we'll see, shall we?'

Ian smiled: 'Were we talking about that?'

'No.' She stretched suddenly: the ring of fire in her hand swept upwards, the sunlight splayed over her breasts as they lifted. 'But it's easy to think of it when you're as sweet as this. And as I've forgotten to *buy* you a Christmas present. . . .'

He felt happy on the instant, so happy that he could not bear to pursue the scene further. Affairs between them were at a stage of delicious fragility, and it seemed that if touched too closely the half-promise would melt away, and he would be left forlorn once more. He sat up briskly, and poured out his second cup of coffee.

'What shall we do today?'

She considered. 'I'm tired, I think. And we're sure to be

late tonight, what with overeating and everything.' Having committed herself, she wanted no failures, nothing less than sensual perfection. 'Let's just practise, below the hotel. The snow's soft enough for a telemark, and that's by far our worst thing.'

Ian nodded. He too had no sort of inclination to waste his energy, on this day: man had been granted reason and foresight for just such occasions. . . . 'Very well. We can stay in to lunch, for a change.' He looked round, and then up at the clock. 'I wonder where Denys is. He might like to come with us.' The suggestion was perfectly sincere: approaching triumph made him the friend of all men.

It was not yet ten o'clock and the sun had hardly climbed above the encircling ridges; but already Denys had passed the six-thousand-feet mark, and was still plodding upwards, his skis bound with skins to prevent them slipping, his chest open to the cool air, his rucksac pulling at the muscles of his shoulders.

He had caught the seven o'clock bus out of Adelboden – the first bus of all, filled with travellers and sleepy-eyed enthusiasts: it went up as far as the inn at Geils, and from there one set out to the great sweeping snow-fields of Hahnenmoos, two thousand feet above. He was very happy, as young children or healthy animals are happy in their exertions: this was what he wanted to be doing – leaving all care behind in the valley, mounting upwards to the silences and the embracing sunlight above, thinking of nothing save the next wary step and the steep escarpment below him.

It was the first time he had made the trip – the best one that that part of Switzerland had to offer, the goal of keen skiers for many miles around – and he knew it would be a severe test of nerve and balance and endurance: the downward run could be taken in one section, two thousand feet of swift turns and unexpected drops, and this he meant to do. For he had already learnt to control his skis, and he loved the swift delirious breath-taking movement; and it was Christmas Day, and the sun promised a brilliant sky till evening came again. This was the setting he wanted, this was the day and time he had chosen for himself. He lacked nothing now save the fulfilment of his small ambition, and this would be added to him.

They had all started out level from the inn, a dozen of them welded into a gay party by the drive up and the anticipation gripping each one; but Denys must have been the only beginner among them, for already he was some way behind, already he had the slopes to himself. At the moment he was traversing one side of the valley, going up half forwards, half sideways, digging the edge of his ski into the snow-crust, shifting his weight quickly, pulling up the other leg and planting it a few feet in advance. It was tiring work, and it called upon unaccustomed muscles and untutored sinews: occasionally he paused, and leaning on his ski-sticks gazed across the valley at the gleaming slopes opposite.

The sun was stronger now, piercing the morning haze, so that within the dwindling shadows the snow seemed tinged with blue by contrast. Far below a single moving speck broke the expanse of white – it was a peasant's sleigh, heavily-laden, making the slow climb by another pathway. Probably it was the same one that their bus had given a tow to, for a couple of miles on the way up; the man had looked pathetically grateful as the bus had slowed down and he had been able to rope his sleigh on behind, and then sit, half-triumphant, half afraid, as they bumped and slithered their way up the snow-crusted road. Now Denys could just make out the man's bobbing head as he tugged at the shafts and laboured to gain a few feet at a time.

The sight gave Denys a momentary feeling of discomfort: the life led by himself and others like him seemed so easy, so artificial, by contrast. Though the division might be necessary, it still disturbed him. That was the other side of Switzerland, of course, the other class living hard and dying miserably, as surely cut off from the cosmopolitan world as a colony of lepers. They might represent the bedrock wealth of the country, but they never saw their toil accorded its due reward. On the one side was easy money, on the other a pitiful and sweating drudgery; and if you were not numbered among the angels, you felt and earned no more than the lash of their wings in passing.

But for the moment, thought Denys as he took up the trail again, this was just as hard work as any brand of farming yet invented. The excuse was a specious one, but it served its turn. His contentment returned.

It was eleven o'clock before he came in sight of the hut at the top of the pass: the sun was high, the snow blindingly white, and other skiers from the later buses had caught him up and passed him; but he was well content, and when at last he stood at the summit, and saw that within his view was the winding slope down to Lenk as well as the Adelboden valley behind him, and that around him stood new peaks and new gleaming vistas of rock and ice and sunlight, then he knew that the toil had been nothing compared with this reward.

He took off his skis, leant them against the side of the hut in a row of others, and sat down on the fenced-in terrace, drinking in the warmth, letting the sun play down on his face and the open neck of his shirt. Round him was peace: a young man waxing his skis with a little instrument like a blow-lamp, a girl munching an apple, a drowsy murmur of voices as his neighbours also took their ease: peace, and a gathering of energy for the real test and crux of the day.

Presently he roused himself, and entered the hut in search of something to drink. He liked the little place immediately, as an adjunct and a contrast to the world outside: it was so alive, so crammed full of colour and vitality, so essentially an extension of the vivid snow-scene. There was only one room, with a diminutive counter sandwiched into a corner of it, and a door leading to the kitchen: round the walls were benches and rough tables, and at these sat or stood a jumble of people, laughing, talking, overflowing into the next party, opening their rucksacs, exchanging food or frankly scrounging....

The noise was tremendous, the competition to get near the kitchen door intense; and to add to the attractive confusion there was an amazing contrast in accent and language as well – the quick pattering French, the lovely German cadences (how stupid to dismiss this language as 'guttural'), the Dutch which did not seem like a language at all, the odd bastard tongue in which the Swiss guides addressed each other. And yet, within those few square yards, the warring nations sank as well as demonstrated their national differences: in a score of ways – a feather in a hat, a queer salute, an eccentric way of wielding a fork – was the wide variety of the world proclaimed: but over it all was that good-humour and good-fellowship which might one day supply the sinews of the world commonwealth. It was even worth a moment's Utopian day-dream, a gentle looking-forward.

There was in that room, set on a snow slope seven thousand feet above the sea, a sort of tangible brotherhood, so that for the moment it seemed that the little hut was the meeting place of all nations, the coming order of the universe in miniature – foregathering in intelligent comradeship and envying their neighour nothing; it might owe much to the noise and the heat and the steamy windows, or to the clean Swiss air and the sun and snow beckoning from outside, but it would travel well, it need not always be confined within these frontiers.

These were the sort of ambassadors that the world needed – young men and women of good-will, travellers of reason and simplicity, ultimately concerned with enjoyment a little, with conciliation and equity a lot, with power, prestige, and the burden of possessions not at all....

Denys spent some twenty minutes procuring his cup of coffee: he was no match in weight for some of the competitors, and there was in front of him a determined young woman in a white beret and a cute all-green ski-suit, who simply would not understand that today's dish was hash, nothing but hash, and that the menu permitted no variation. Possibly she was on a diet – one that did not include 'No' for an answer.

Outside in the sun once more, he found himself sharing a bench with an enormous blond young man – Danish or Swedish, probably – who was wolfing his food as if half-starved and drinking (most inadvisedly) lager beer. Any intoxicant, at that height and after such a climb, was liable to play queer tricks with one's balance. However, that was *his* worry. . . . Presently, stowing with no sort of hesitation half a crusty roll into one corner of his mouth, the young man turned and said with a smile:

'English? You like ski-ing?'

'Yes,' said Denys. 'I like it very much. I'm rotten at it though.'

'Please?' His accent was clipped, and he groped for each word as if he had a bandage over his eyes.

'I'm not good at it. I've only just started.'

The young man smiled again. 'It will learn soon. You will not fall always.'

'I hope not.' Denys looked at the other's business-like heel-springs. 'You're an expert, I suppose.'

He was indeed an expert – a ski-jumper, and a member of the Norwegian Olympic team of the year before. (No wonder, thought Denys, he allowed himself a glass of beer.) At the present moment – the story came out laboriously, with many odd expressions to confuse it – he was making a round of the ski-jumping competitions: Abelboden was staging one on the following day, and from there, later on, he was going on to Feldkirch in Austria.

It seemed an attractive way of spending a holiday, and he looked amazingly well on it – bronzed, flushed with the keen air, lazily sure of his strength. He seemed, too, to know a great many of the people round them: there were frequent greetings as newcomers reached the hut, and occasionally he would jump to his feet to salute some girl or other – usually a remarkably pretty one. (Was there actually much point in saluting any other?)

'I come here very many times,' he explained presently. 'I make many friends. You make many friends, too?'

'Not many,' Denys answered him, and smiled: 'I'm English, you see – I don't know how to.'

The other shook his head. 'That is not true. I have journeyed in England. It was happy. And all the English were kind to me. They were ready to be friends always.'

'It's different when we're abroad. Then we become really English, and think it's wrong to speak to strangers.'

The young man frowned, unsure whether to take Denys seriously or not. 'But you speak to me? It is not forbidden?'

'That's because it's Christmas Day.'

Once more he frowned. 'An English joke, perhaps?' But clearly he would never understand the rather feeble point, and

Denys, feeling rather small, switched to the safer topic of soft snow and the Telemark versus Christiana controversy. That at least was of international significance.

More and more people arrived: the slopes around them were dotted with figures, practising turns or taking a tentative run in the direction of Lenk; and looking down the valley towards Adelboden one could see a winding procession of people – black against the snow, seeming motionless unless one took some other landmark to measure them against, making the ascent at a slow plod. Denys was reminded of an old film of the Klondyke gold rush which he had once seen – there was the same vast expanse of white, the same blinding uniformity, the same chain of humans stretching back till they were hidden by the Levigrat shoulder.

The hut, the Mecca of their pilgrimage, was swarming with people: skis were waxed, bindings adjusted, jerkins buttoned up against the speed of the descent: here and there were little forests of skis and ski-sticks, upright in the snow and topped by a pair of gloves or a gay scarf, looking almost too like the advertisements to be of accidental grouping. And inside of course, nothing was obtainable save friendly greetings and elbows in the ribs – the nations in conflict, with no casualties and (as ever) no hope of reward.

Denys finished his lunch at the same time as the Norwegian, and it happened naturally that they both began, side by side, to put on their skis again. The first to be ready, the Norwegian smiled down at Denys, still struggling with a refractory heel strap.

'Which way are you going?' he asked. Then without waiting for an answer he pointed onwards to a ridge slightly higher, across the top of the pass. 'The Kummi slope is good – more interesting than going straight down.'

Denys nodded. 'That's the way I was told to go, as far as I remember. Is it easy to get across to it?'

'Oh yes. We go down together, then?'

'I'd like to,' Denys answered hesitatingly. 'But I'm so slow. I don't want to keep you back.'

The Norwegian spread his hands widely. 'It does not matter. I have been down this morning – two times.'

Denys stared. 'Twice already? How long does it take you?'

'The full run? About four minutes and a half.'

Four minutes and a half – for a drop of two thousand feet, and a winding drop at that. Denys stared at the other man again, wondering if he himself would ever approach that figure. It must mean going straight down even the steepest bits – no stemming, no long traverses to avoid a sudden falling away of the slope. It must mean perfect control, and balance, and above all nerve. . . . He smiled and shook his head.

'I'd spoil it for you,' he answered regretfully.

'Please. . . . I can show you the way, and help you. Also I am lazy now, after the beer. You will see – perhaps I will myself fall down at the first slope.'

'I wouldn't mind watching that,' Denys laughed. 'All right, we'll start off together. But please go on ahead if you feel like it. I'm not in the four-and-a-half minute class – nor the fourteen and a half, if it comes to that.'

A half-hour's gentle ascent brought them to the top of the ridge, by now well-trodden and cut about with ski-tracks. There were half a dozen people on it, and just as Denys came to a standstill, resting on his sticks, one of them set off – straight down, leaning forward slightly, feet close together, one ski a little in front of the other – in perfect style, and at an immense speed. He disappeared in a flurry of powder snow over the next drop. One after another his companions followed, at half-minute intervals: they all took different tracks, and the one farthest to the left fell badly – the sound came up to them as he tried a Christiana – a harsh scraping followed by a thump.

'Ice,' said the Norwegian briefly. 'A bad part – I found it this morning also. One need not find it like that.'

But the man was up, and off again in a flash; and already, far down below, Denys caught sight of the one who had started first – a tiny figure dropping swift as a bird into the valley, the only moving speck against the universal whiteness. Once, twice, the sun glittered on his back – probably it was the buckle of his rucksac – and then he was out of sight again. Three others followed, and then there was a pause. The other two must have fallen, and given up trying to make a fast run. Certainly the leader had set a tremendous pace.

'That looked pretty good,' said Denys admiringly. 'Did you know any of them?'

The Norwegian nodded. 'That was the Oxford team. They are on ski-tour – they go to Murren next, I think. Yes, they were good, except for the third: he was too much bent. You see how he went over the hill – as if he had a pain here.' He tapped his stomach. 'It is taught like that in some places – they call it the Arlberg crouch. In Norway they call it bad style.'

Denys laughed. 'It's difficult to know what to believe. . . . Shall we start?'

'You are rested enough?'

'Oh yes, I think so.'

'Very well. I will go first, to choose the best way. Keep close to my tracks – not in them, just by the side. And if I go too much straight, you make a Slalom – a stem – and take the slope sideways. We have plenty of time, you understand.'

'All right. ... Ready.' He faced the slope, and drew a deep breath.

That run down, those two thousand feet of snow and pouring sunlight and great mountains, made up the finest experience Denys had ever had. Trusting the Norwegian implicitly, he followed him slope for slope and turn for turn: it was a faster pace than he had ever tried before, as well as a longer run, but though he fell three times – each one an over-adventurous attempt at going straight down – he never felt in the least inclined to stop. This was real movement, real sensation: he sped downwards between the crusted drifts, across the small valleys – now skirting a rise, now turning swiftly to delay the immense pull of gravity; and always a little ahead of him was his guide, slowing up on the level to let him catch up and then gliding off down yet another slope, past yet another grim-looking cornice. The wind whipped his face, the snow hissed past or sprayed over his knees: and all the time he was dimly conscious of the splendour of his surroundings – the ring of towering peaks, the lovely shadows on the hill-side, the clumps of trees each glistening with its white filigree of snow.

Once he crossed a patch of ice, and marked the cruel lacerating sounds his skis made over it – unpleasant to fall there, but with a rough twist he was safely past; and half-way down he paused for a few minutes, to get his breath and drink in the scenery and watch the Norwegian do an astounding jump-turn over what looked like a minor precipice. That, he decided, was not part of the regular course. . . . Then at last they had reached the bottom; and as he felt the ground become level again, and his speed slacken and die away, and the noise of his skis become no more than a soft murmur, he felt a moment of sadness, knowing he was never likely to touch such an exhilaration again in his lifetime – it could not be given him a second time to make such a run on such a peerless day.

The Norwegian waved as he approached: the former's greater speed had carried him on some way. 'Well done,' he said, as soon as they were within ear-shot of each other. 'You followed well. In a few seasons you will be good.'

'That was marvellous.' Temporarily exhausted, as if he had run a terrific half-mile, Denys bent over his ski-sticks and relaxed. 'That was *marvellous*,' he repeated. 'God, what a sport it is. . . . I only fell three times, too.'

'That is nothing.' The other man looked at his wrist watch. 'From the top we took just nine minutes.'

Still breathless, Denys glanced up. 'That's not so good, is it?'

'For the first time? It's very good. To come down in one piece is a great strain too, when you are a beginner.' He turned and pointed to the Geils inn, a hundred yards away to the left. 'Shall we drink to it – your first Hahnenmoos run?'

'Yes, let's. We go back by the road, don't we?'

'That is easiest, yes. I have done enough for today.'

Denys straightened up slowly, conscious of back muscles which would be aching by bedtime. 'So have I, certainly. But it's been wonderful. I don't think I've ever enjoyed anything so much.'

'We have plenty more time. We can do it again tomorrow. Hahnenmoos is always there.'

CHAPTER VIII

When he got back to the Schweizer, after bidding the Norwegian good-bye and arranging to meet him later that night for a drink, the head-porter handed him a letter; and as he recognized Cynthia's handwriting on it, and the thoughts and fears accompanying the recognition returned to him, his good humour dropped away like a shed skin.

Supposedly it could not be helped, but it was beastly to be brought up thus sharply, after such a good day, and after a walk back full of anticipation for the coming evening; he had been thinking of Helen and the splendour of her kindness, and now he must think of Cynthia, and something very different. For Cynthia was hard reality, and her coming child a stinging reminder of Ian's treachery: he had wanted tonight to be a real Christmas celebration, with the added joy of his answered love, but the letter, even though still unopened, had brought him the certainty of unhappiness, a warranty of the outside world's encroachment. Whatever was in it, it meant a change of mood, and that could only be for the worse.

He walked through the hall, greeting half a dozen people on the way: through the lounge door he saw Helen sitting at their tea table, preparing to pour out for herself and Ian and Jill. Oh yes, they were all there, the strong entrenchment of the other side: he himself might be forgetful and lose his cares out on the snow-fields, but these people never relaxed their alliance, their plotting, their evil intrigue. . . . As he hesitated, unwilling to join them, Mr Carrington's voice made itself heard through the opening front door.

'Hallo, Denys. Had a good day, old boy?'

Denys turned back to him gratefully, as he was grateful for any show of friendliness. 'Fine, thank you,' he answered. And to Mrs Carrington: 'Have you been skating?'

'Only walking, I'm afraid. We're getting so lazy.' She smiled up at him, and he knew suddenly from the warm quality of her smile that she was the only one who saw the thing from his angle – who realized, indeed, that he had any part in the current of affairs. 'But the sun was lovely,' she continued. 'Have you been up to Hahnenmoos?'

'Yes. It was the first time I've made the run. I loved it.' For a moment a breath of that loveliness came back to him, and the swish of the snow under his skis could be faintly heard, like a dwindling echo. If only all life could conform to that measure. . . . 'I met an Olympic ski-jumper, too – a Norwegian. He came down with me.'

'And you raced him, hey?' asked Mr Carrington boisterously. 'That's the way. We'll be having you in the championship class in no time. There's no holding you young fellows, once you get started.'

From behind him Helen called out softly: 'Do you want some tea, Denys?'

He turned and smiled at her momentarily, pondering a possible move. It would be rather fun to go over, to sit down between her and Jill, to open Cynthia's letter with a great crackling of paper and begin reading out loud. It might start something really worth while. . . . Then, as she smiled back, he pulled himself together.

'In a minute,' he answered. 'I want to get some of these clothes off – they're stiff with ice and they'll flood the place out when they start melting.'

'Where were you ski-ing?' asked Ian.

'Hahnenmoos,' Denys answered briefly. The bare information was suitably non-committal. ... He turned and went on upstairs. Everybody took a great interest in him – when they bothered to remember his existence.

Upstairs in his bedroom, in locked security, he opened the letter: it was short, and rather ill-written in pencil, and he could guess the physical distress which had left its mark on the scrawled characters. The letter (she wrote) was just to wish him a happy Christmas. Her present would be waiting for him when he got back to London. She hoped he was having a good time, and not spending too much money. London was rather cold and wet. The baby was due in about a week: perhaps on New Year's Day, which would be rather fun. And then, at the end:

'How is Ian? I haven't heard from him – I suppose he is

too busy. You might mention that you've had a letter from me. With much love, Cynthia.'

'I haven't heard from him' ... Denys frowned, hardly taking in the words, and sat down on his bed: automatically he began picking the ice off his socks and loosening the ties of his trouser-ends. Then his vague surprise at the significance of the phrase was followed, swift as the onset of a storm, by a fit of blind rage that Ian could be so cruel. It was more than cruel, it was monstrous. . . . Couldn't he even write to her, couldn't he spare ten minutes and a sheet of paper and a thirty-centime stamp? ... Surely there was something barbaric in that sort of behaviour. . . . Surely Ian realized that he had made certain contracts, that his loyalty and his concentration were already mortgaged, that the bargain had been made and there was no turning aside from it? And if he didn't realize it, wasn't it high time that the basic facts were demonstrated?

Denys knew himself to be still subject to the twelve-year inferiority of age: but he knew also that the inferiority would not long survive treatment of this sort. He might be Ian's junior, but he was still his brother-in-law, still Cynthia's brother, with a special position of his own which should be clearly demonstrated.

So his thoughts strayed hither and thither, as he exchanged the more weather-beaten of his garments for something suitable to the evening's decline. He mustn't let things slide any longer: he must go downstairs, he must take Ian aside and ... He shook his head. No, that was quite impossible; he hadn't sufficient weight, he simply wasn't tall enough to make a scene. ... Perhaps it would be best if he tried to enlist Helen's help again: she had been difficult enough when the subject was broached before, but in face of this evidence she could hardly line up on the wrong side this time.

But it was a long time before he summoned sufficient determination to go downstairs: he delayed every move, he pretended to himself that he must change his clothes completely even for tea, he wrote in his diary and counted his money (a progressively easier business) and stared at the darkened deserted rink outside. And when finally he reached the lounge again the immediate problem had solved itself, for Jill and

Ian had disappeared, Mrs Carrington was having her rest, Mr Carrington was playing bridge....

Helen remained. She greeted him smilingly as he sat down, calling for more tea and saying she had missed him in the same breath: she had been aware of some tension at the earlier encounter and she wanted to make up whatever ground was lost. As he settled himself in one corner of the sofa:

'What's the matter, Denys?' she asked gently. 'Didn't you enjoy yourself up at Hahnenmoos?'

'Hahnenmoos was fine. . . .' He faced her squarely, ready to meet all attempts at evasion. 'The run down was the most wonderful thing I've ever been able to do. And now I'm here.'

She waited, leaning forward. 'Well?'

'Here it's rather different.' Once again he was nerved by his indignation, once again he was strong in his conviction of right. 'Here it's just the old story once again.'

'What do you mean?'

'Ian and Jill, as usual. You remember having tea with them, don't you? . . . I've just had a letter from Cynthia.'

'Cynthia?' Helen came to attention sharply. 'Why? I mean, had you written to her?'

'Yes. Just for Christmas. I thought someone ought to.' But he couldn't handle sarcasm properly, and the words missed-fire, becoming an ordinary almost apologetic explanation. 'She was wondering when she would hear from Ian.'

'Oh, I see.'

He tried to attack again, he tried to keep the scene flowing his way. 'What did you think had happened? That I'd been reporting back to her?'

'Don't be silly, darling. What is there to report?'

'Enough to have prevented him writing, obviously.'

Helen turned away slightly, frowning to herself. 'Nothing *prevented* him. Why do you twist things round like that? You know he's on holiday – you know how difficult it is to write letters here. That's all there is in it.'

Denys sighed. Would she never see his point, would she never admit what her conscience must tell her was a matter of fact, not of opinion? It was Christmas, Cynthia was Ian's wife: and even discounting Christmas, the fact that she was going to have a baby made his obligation as clear as daylight. He set down his cup again and leant over.

'But you do understand, don't you? – that he should have written to her? You would have written, in the same circumstances: and you know what your parents would say about it.'

Helen stirred restlessly, shaking her head. 'I've told you before, it doesn't concern me, or the parents, or anyone else except Ian. It's his responsibility, and his look out, and he can take care of it alone.' She touched Denys' hand. 'Why do you worry? It can't do any good, it can't make any difference. Let's concentrate on ourselves instead.'

'But Cynthia wrote to me. I must do something to help her, if I can. I'm the only one who's on her side.'

As usual she seized on the last word, the easiest to resist.

'There you are, you see – you *will* think of it as a kind of battle, where you have to choose one side or the other. It's nothing like that at all: no one tries to fight or to interfere like that nowadays. And anyway there's nothing extraordinary in the circumstances: people just do behave in that way, and you can't do anything to change it. In fact you haven't any right to try.'

He clung obstinately to his point. 'But Cynthia asked me to. She wrote to me about it.'

'She would have written to you, anyway. It's Christmas, isn't it?' Helen could not resist the dig, though her instinct warned her against it. 'And what actually did she ask you to do?'

He frowned, and took out the letter again. 'Well, as a matter of fact ...' Then, reading between the lines, he essayed a lie. 'She asked me to remind him to write.'

'Well, that's easy enough, isn't it? Why all this fuss? Shall I do it for you?'

He frowned. 'But you know that's not all.'

'It's all she wants you to do, isn't it?'

'But if she knew the *truth*....'

'There's no truth. He's forgotten to write, that's all. You're spinning something out of facts that aren't there.'

And so the little scene continued – uncertain, difficult,

horribly inadequate. He understood, as easily as if Helen had said the very words themselves, that she thought there was only one difference between them – his age compared with hers: that there was virtually no other point at issue, that she counted on his outlook being the same as her own in a few years' time. That gave the encounter a depressing background, for he could not be sure that she was not right: she had said that this was the way people behaved, and supposedly she should know, she should be the surer authority. ... But above it all, and whatever the truth of the matter, he was conscious of his own resistance stiffening: this time he had something more tangible to go on – he had been watching Adelboden only, but now here was Cynthia's letter as confirmation from the other end. And, age difference or not, he knew where the stronger loyalty was. ... So it came about that they parted on a high note, leaving fewer loopholes, if any, for a later sympathetic understanding.

'I don't care how stupid and how interfering I'm being,' he said finally, when they had explored each other's prejudices for half an hour and were further than ever from reconciling them. 'You can say what you like, but I still think Ian's being frightfully unfair to Cynthia, and that we ought not to help him like this.'

'No one's helping him – that's where you're being so crazy.' The rejoinder came with spirit, proof of a new impatience. 'He's just doing what he wants, and it isn't our business. I'll remind him about writing, if you like: but I won't do any more, and neither should you.' She was adamant now: a little earlier she had made a gentle bid for tolerance, seeking to recall to him their own new relationship, and it had not worked – he had brushed it aside as irrelevant, or, worse still, had not noticed it at all. That was something which for the moment she could not forgive: to be generous, and then to have that generosity entirely overlooked, brought a sense of personal cheapness most unwelcome.

If he didn't want her in a loving mood he would find something very different in its place. ... 'You know it'll only make him even more dissatisfied,' she went on crisply. 'You'd better leave well alone.'

'What do you mean, dissatisfied? He was all right until he came out here, until Jill got hold of him.'

'Was he?' Helen gathered up her things and rose, smiling not very pleasantly. 'I don't think you see as much of him as I do. You must keep up to date, you know. His home life isn't exactly exciting.'

He stared up at her. 'You're being beastly.'

'I'm being grown-up,' she said, and left him. He watched her go, impotently furious. She had had the last word, and it was the one which clinched every dispute and would always do so, into the far unglimpsed future.

But Helen was hardly more sure of herself than he was: she might win an argument, but she knew that she was losing something more tangible and far more precious. Once again it had been a choice of evils – either to admit that Ian was in the wrong, and keep Denys by her side, or to stand up for Ian and (as now) make certain of a quarrel. Hitherto she had been able to sit on the fence and get away with it; but now she had had to choose, and it seemed that she had lost in the choosing. ... Ill at ease, and with the vague idea of trying to retrieve her position, she went upstairs and sought out Ian.

He was in his bath, but ready to talk. For him, the day had gone well: there had been some lazy practising in the morning, watching ice-hockey in the afternoon, the usual intimate six o'clock drink at the Bar-Français: and there still remained the evening, Christmas evening, when that companionship, mingled with a sweet anticipation, could be continued, developed, fulfilled. ... He smiled up at Helen as she came in.

'Hallo. Want to be useful? Soap my back, then.'

But she was not to be delayed by charm, least of all by the brotherly brand. She went straight to the point. 'Listen, Ian. Denys has had a letter from Cynthia.'

Ian stared. 'What of it? Didn't she put the right stamps on?'

'No, this is serious. She said you hadn't written to her, and Denys is pretty worried.'

'Oh Lord, I suppose I haven't.' He put a soapy hand up to his chin. 'Damn. I'll write tonight.'

'Couldn't you have done it before? Why make things so difficult?'

Ian looked up. 'How do you mean, difficult? You know I never *can* write letters when I'm out of London. It's such a bloody nuisance collecting ink and paper and everything. ... And what's Denys got to do with it?' He frowned at her. 'He's not going to make a fool of himself again, is he?'

'Not if I can help it. But you might take a bit of trouble yourself instead of leaving it all to me. You know how young he is – you know what he's bound to think.'

'He can think what he likes.' Ian lolled back, and a cloud of steam enveloped him. From its midst he declaimed heroically, like a juvenile Colonel Blimp: 'By gad, father, Lord Dessicate is right – I have my own life to lead now – I'm grown up – you don't realize that. ...' He rolled over again, and cocked an eye at her. 'What's your worry, anyway? It doesn't affect you.'

'In a way it does. I have to explain everything to Denys, I have to try to keep him quiet. And ...'

'And what?'

'Well, it's a nuisance,' she finished lamely, 'and I'd rather things were made a bit easier.'

'All right, I'll send some sort of letter tonight.'

'You ought to – considering it's Christmas Day,' she mimicked Denys irritably. 'I suppose you couldn't go slow with Jill – in public, I mean. That might make it easier still.'

He laughed, splashing water over his chest. 'You're taking this pretty seriously. How do you know I'm not going slow?'

'Good God,' she flared up, 'how can anyone miss it? You've been going about like a cat that's got at the cream the whole of the last two days. ... Do you sleep with her, Ian?'

'No, not yet. That's tonight, I think.'

'Well, for the Lord's sake be careful how you go about it. They wouldn't sling us out, but they might be rather unpleasant to her.'

'I'm not going up there in nailed sea-boots, if that's what you mean. ... Anyway, no one cares in these hotels, as long as you don't make more than the essential noise about it. I must get out of this bath, darling – it's late already. Anything else you want?'

'No, I don't think so.' She laughed suddenly. 'It's late in the day to give you the facts of life, but don't forget you've got one child nearly here already.'

Ian smiled in answer, preparing to heave himself out of the bath. 'I hadn't thought of that. ... Can one buy christening mugs by the half-dozen?'

Denys had not been sure about his date with the Norwegian – he might have gone out with Helen instead – but now he found it easy enough to keep. He was in a bitter mood, which the horribly festive Christmas dinner did nothing to dispel: he had been expecting great things from Cynthia's letter – surprise on Helen's part, a real feeling of remorse from Ian – and now between them it had been frittered away to nothing, it was no longer a weapon of any sort.

That wasn't the way to get things done, that was the path of compromise and retreat and ineffective bargaining: he knew he had a case, he knew he was in the right, and yet half an hour had been enough to bring his plans to nothing. Pretty meek, whichever way you looked at it. ... Of course, it wasn't half an hour really, it was Helen's twenty-nine years against his own eighteen, it was the usual assumption of superiority ... His determination to do something towards breaking that superiority drove him out of the hotel immediately after dinner, ignoring Helen's surprised look and implied invitation. No, he was damned if he'd stay in to amuse her. She wasn't going to have it both ways: if he was too young to hold his own point of view then he was certainly not old enough to dance with her. And anything else was positive cradle-snatching on her part.

There was, too, at the back of his resolve the wish to revert to his old standard – it now seemed that dancing with Helen, 'in that way,' kissing and being kissed by her, was somehow second rate, and he wanted to leave it all behind him. The effect on him of her attitude was a reaction to his original guarded forbearance, the forbearance which he had only surrendered for her sake: he had known all along that his was the best idea; justified, cured, convinced, he would go back to it.

He made for the Grand Bar at the other end of the village, and there he found the ski-jumper already installed in an armchair and his element, surrounded by a tableful of friends and almost as many empty glasses. It was by now about nine o'clock, and the place was steadily filling up with that gay and vaguely disreputable crowd which made of it a regular haunt: it was like the hut at Hahnenmoos, only on a more intimate scale – fewer draughts, more drinks, music if you cared to listen, and nothing to tempt you outside.

Denys was attracted by the contrast in dress: there were a few dinner-jackets, a few smart frocks worn by those young women whose only other luggage was a toothbrush and a bottle of scent: but for the rest, flannels, ski-ing trousers, jerseys, scarves, students' hats, shirt-sleeves: while many people, making the best of both worlds, were dancing in their ski-ing boots, which lent a certain ponderous dignity to their movements, and made the floor look correspondingly silly. The atmosphere was still tolerable, and the band, having been well cooled down, just beginning to warm up.

Sketchily introduced to half a dozen people, Denys quickly found himself one of the centres of interest: for there were fewer English visitors than usual in the village that year, and to his companions – the lean guides, the inquisitive Frenchmen, the Spaniards who only seemed to wake up at night – he was a major curiosity and fair game for any number of questions. So, in quaint perversions of his own tongue, the questions came, like burrs thrown with gay intent and uncertain aim: was England always contented, was justice not to be bought, were there truly no pretty girls in London. . . . Whatever he answered, his words were taken up, translated into half a dozen languages, questioned afresh, frankly disbelieved: Denys found himself inventing or lying freely and at will, and enjoying it enormously, and, with a pint and a half of lager inside him, was in far better humour than he had been earlier on. This was the best of Switzerland – the free internationally-minded side – and one could hope that it was the most enduring, though many of the discussions left an odd taste of despair behind them; there was so much that only time would show, there were so many things wherein the common man could only guess and hope and walk blindfold, while others dug the pits and held (unyieldingly) the stakes.

The Norwegian talked in spasms and would then fall silent, sitting aloof – a being from another world, a modern Viking strayed into Europe; in those moments he seemed to reflect his country's own standpoint, withdrawn from the storm-centres, watching and waiting for friendlier times. Out of his silence his blue eyes stared straight ahead, seeing that steep snow runway and the immense drop which he would face on the morrow.

A Frenchman by his side was trying to get him to talk of Socialism, but to no purpose – politics were *kaput*, and only the smooth beer and tomorrow's mile-a-minute leap were realities. Occasionally he caught Denys' eye, smiled, and raised his glass. '*Skohl!*' he called out, and drank it off with the true Viking zest. Possibly this was as good a contribution to the evening's progress as any other.

Later on, about eleven o'clock, Ian and Jill looked in for a moment, found it not to their liking – the room was getting rather boisterous, a poor market for lovers – and disappeared again. They did not see Denys, and he found himself able to regard them with a certain detachment: they were enjoying themselves, but so was he, much more, and that seemed to permit of his resentment having a holiday. . . . Brief as it was, however, their appearance did not escape comment.

'I like that one,' remarked the Swiss lad next to Denys. 'Pretty, hey? And English, too. Perhaps you meet her in England?'

'Oh, almost certainly,' said Denys. 'It's a wretchedly small place.'

'A hot stuff,' one of the Frenchmen conceded. He leant over. 'And always with the same man. You know who she is?'

'No,' answered Denys. 'I've seen her before though.'

'She is Miss Coll-ee-er. She stays at the Schweizer. With that man, I think. You must walk in your sleep, and see.'

'How do you know her name?'

'I follow her and ask the head-waiter. ...' With legitimate

pride the Frenchman nodded sagely. 'She is pretty, yes? Naturally, one must make inquiries.'

'Well, well,' said Denys vaguely. He really couldn't think ill of anyone tonight. 'Have a drink on it. It'll stand a good many.'

The evening progressed: the air became thick with smoke, the windows steamed over: no breath of the intense cold outside could disturb them. Denys danced once, rather uncertainly, with a Dutch girl who had smiled at him from further down the table, but it was one of those whirling Viennese waltzes, all vertigo and perspiration, and his partner was too strenuous to be intriguing, though that may well have been her intent.

Then presently the band stopped, and out of the haze a man got up and made some annnouncement: he made it in five languages – French, German, Dutch, Swiss-German and English – and when it came round to Denys' lingual turn he found that it was simply to say that tonight, Christmas night, was the band's benefit, and that the hat was coming round. (Of course, the band had a benefit every night, but this was clearly to be a good expensive one.) And by and by the drummer did come round with it, and stayed at their table, talking and laughing, for some time – *he* knew eleven languages altogether, in different stages of the embryo, picked up from various visitors and various travels over the past twenty years. That, Denys felt, was true education: to be able to talk to the world, and laugh with it, and spread a many-sided goodwill, that was a distinguished ideal to aim at; though perhaps, in a competitive and ultra-nationalist world, the drummer, glad to see them and everyone else, had been born out of his time, and would discover the fact before he had run his full course.

They made him very welcome, however, and he departed with three full glasses and a jingling pocket.

More talk, more international gossip, until it grew late, and the lights were switched out one by one, in coaxing proprietorial fashion, and they prepared to take their leave. There were many hand-shakes and formal good-byes: but they would meet again on the morrow, most of them, out on the great snow slopes seven thousand feet up, and that was something to look forward to, something to dwarf and take the sting out of any parting.

Presently Denys found himself walking slowly down the street, arm-in-arm with the Norwegian; a light snow had begun to fall, and instinctively he kept looking back at their tracks – it meant a new surface for the earth, a clean sheet, there in the very centre of Europe, for anyone to make what impression he chose. It was late in the day for symbolical speculation, but one could hope for the best, even in a world ruled by the unruly. . . .

The Norwegian had drunk far more than he should have done, considering the effort he had to make on the following afternoon: and Denys himself was pleasantly uncertain of his stance, so that when his snow-boots slithered down a slope it was difficult, and somehow tantalizing, not to abandon everything and follow their lead. They passed groups talking, and greeted them, trying each time to find a legitimate version of 'Grüss Gott' – 'Grüsse,' 'Grüss es,' 'Gru' es,' all in that soft drawl which the natives used; they passed couples like themselves, intent on their balance, and late skiers clattering through the village, and girls laughing with powdery snow in their hair. And then, within a few yards of the Schweizer, Denys became aware that the pair ahead of them – arms entwined, pressed close together – was Jill and Ian.

He checked his step, and in doing so slipped and fell full length, bringing the Norwegian down with him, and by the time they had sorted themselves out and were on their feet again the other two were out of sight in the hotel courtyard. That was satisfactory, thought Denys, brushing the snow from his trousers and collecting his gloves and saying 'sh'' to the Norwegian, who was loudly cursing the state of the road; he couldn't be angry with Jill and Ian, not tonight, not on this one night when he had enjoyed himself so much, but he didn't went to meet them, he just didn't want to be hanging about in the hall at the same time and getting in the way. . . . He gave a final brush to his coat, and then turned to the Norwegian.

'Where is it you're staying? A long way up the street?'

The Norwegian shook his head vaguely. 'A little way. A

little chalet. A little path. Down here, please. Mind the step and wipe the feet.'

'I'll come with you.'

There ensued a long argument as to which of them was seeing the other home, but Denys gained his point, and had the satisfaction of guiding his companion across two fields and through a singularly ill-garnished farmyard to a little house which turned out to the wrong one. It was to be hoped that the latter's sense of direction would have improved by the time daylight caught him up. ... When at last the mistake had been put right, and Denys had got on to the road again, it was well past one o'clock.

The hotel was silent, the porter sleepy and vaguely resentful. (Of course it was fairly late, but damn it, he *was* paid to be on night duty.) Denys wandered slowly upstairs, counting each step, aware of weak knees and a rocking head: he had only been drunk once in his life, and he wasn't nearly as bad (or good) this time, but that didn't make the journey any easier. Seventeen, eighteen, nineteen, twenty – Room Eleven – key – lock. ... On the point of entering, he turned round and glanced at Ian's door. It was ajar, and there was no light inside.

Denys frowned to himself and then dismissed the matter. Probably he was talking to Helen – or even saying good night to Jill upstairs: it didn't make much odds. What did make rather too much odds was the fact that he couldn't really find the light – or his bed – or any of the things he really wanted so tremendously.

CHAPTER IX

Alois, the head-waiter, surveyed his breakfast-room on the following morning and found it particularly interesting. This was often the case after a festive night: there would be grave faces, and bored faces, and faces pink with health or grey-green with over-indulgence; and sometimes there would be quarrels to be noted, or some new alliance promoted by the preceding night's gaiety. Alois himself was in a good mood, unprofessionally speaking: he had got over the little kitchen-maid's defection (what was a kitchen-maid after all? a mere snipper of an affair . . .) and matters between him and the second floor chamber-maid were already eminently to his taste: from the vantage point of personal satiety – the most effective eyrie of all – he could survey the world about him and judge whether it was as good as his own private one.

But talking of the second floor – his eyes went round automatically to Miss Collier, and he gave her an appraising glance. That was a fine girl – and, if his new conquest was to be believed, a bold one also. For he had been given a queer bit of news last night, something that he could depend on: little Anna, who was on night duty, had left him about three and gone down to her post again, and then had come up almost immediately to say she had seen Mr Carrington – young Mr Carrington, ha! ha! not the old boy – leaving Miss Collier's room and returning to his own. Now there was a nice state of affairs.

Alois had not the same horror of scandal as had Herr Franck, but still he thought there ought to be certain decencies observed. For was it not these people who were meant to set an example to the rest of the world? And if they did such things as this, how could a waiter – even a head-waiter – be expected to keep to the path of virtue? Surely a certain minimum of discretion would not be out of place? Alois shrugged, and set a knife straight, and swept some crumbs away, all in one quick series of movements. What a world. And what a hotel, eh?

Oh yes, it was a fine roomful. There was little Fräulein Hochmeyer, sitting there as demure as you please, and yet last night – dancing in the bar, kissing in the passage, and one didn't know what besides. . . . And old Freiherr Novak – drunk as an owl he'd been – it was a wonder he'd come down to breakfast and a miracle that he stayed to eat it. And come to think of it, young Mr Wilder did not look too good this morning, he was pale, he wasn't eating, and his hand when he drank – pouf, it shook like a leaf.

Miss Carrington was as usual, perhaps a trifle pale also: and it looked as though there had been a quarrel there – she didn't usually come down to breakfast, and this morning she had done, and yet the two of them sat there without saying a word. She ought to take a leaf out of Miss Collier's book – or perhaps that was the trouble. One never knew what to think – it was the quiet ones that gave you the biggest surprises.

He laughed softly, remembering. The quiet ones. ... Like the mad clever Englishwoman with the dog, for which she refused to pay the boarding fee. No one had known how she fed it, for she was much too mean to buy food outside the hotel: but he had taken to watching her closely – he had been second waiter at the time – and he had discovered this. At each meal she brought into the dining-room a sponge-bag, and in it a little tin bowl; this she filled, very discreetly and cunningly, with the scraps from her plate – she always took more than she needed – put it in the sponge-bag again, and walked out, pretending it was her reticule. ... No way could be found of circumventing this, but happily the dog had died of over-eating within a fortnight, and Herr Franck had charged her two pounds for disposing of the body. It took a good deal to get past that old one. ...

And with that Alois, seeing that there was really no more to do, made for the service door again. He would like to see Anna before she went off duty and up to bed: he wanted some more facts about last night, if it was possible to get them.

The first of the early sunlight played through one of the windows, setting the dust dancing, shining on to Mr Jackson's head as it bent in confidence towards his wife's. At the sun's touch he looked up, shading his eyes against the glare.

'Another good day,' he said heartily. 'That'll be nice for the ski-jumping.'

His wife shook her head. 'I'm sure I don't want to see those nasty things again.' She was a massive woman, but she spoke occasionally with an affectation of nervousness which seemed hopelessly insincere, like an elephant complaining of a draught. 'Remember the last time, when that poor man was nearly killed? I thought I should faint.' It had been a minority opinion.

'Got to take the hard knocks sometimes, those chaps have.'

'Well, you won't get me down there, not if you dragged me.'

'No one need go that doesn't want to. You know that.' And

then, as Denys passed their table on his way out: 'Hallo, young Denys! Going to watch the jumps?'

'Yes, I think so.' Denys, conscious of an aching head, spoke with care. 'I know one of the men going in for it – I'd like to see him.'

'That ought to be interesting.' Mr Jackson put his head on one side and looked at him closely. 'How are *you* this morning? Bit shaky?'

'I've a bit of a headache, yes. I was up rather late.'

'Up rather late. ... Ha! ha! ha! Just listen to that. Up rather late, eh?' His laughter wheezed out of him, like a barrel of water slopping over. 'And what kept you up late? Not the traffic, I'll be bound.'

'Poor boy,' said Mrs Jackson maternally. 'Leave him alone, Charlie, he doesn't want your jokes this morning. . . . How's your sister, Denys? All right?'

'Cynthia? Oh, she's fine. I had a letter from her yesterday.'

'Really?' A question hovered on Mrs Jackson's lips, withdrew, and then surged forward. 'And the baby? When shall we hear the good news?'

'In about a week, I think.' This was the precise kind of discussion which Denys loathed most in the world, but there was no escaping it: Helen had gone on ahead, and he felt unequal to the task of changing the subject. The glamour of the near-obstetric must hold its accustomed sway.

'A week, eh?' Mr Jackson achoed. 'That's good, that's great ... I suppose Ian will be going home soon, then?'

Denys was conscious of both their glances suddenly concentrating on his face. Would Ian stay? Was the new attraction strong enough to keep him? That was what they all wanted to know: and whatever he said now would be taken as the official bulletin. For a moment he had a wild idea of lying, of giving the day and hour of Ian's departure and leaving him to face it out: but it opened up a vision of endless complications, and he braced himself against the temptation.

'I don't know what he intends to do,' he said slowly. 'We arranged to stay the whole fortnight, you see.'

A silence fell, a reflective silence in which each of the trio examined this answer and considered its implications. Mrs Jackson was first with her comment.

'Well, of course, you didn't know when the baby was due. I expect he'll want to go home now.' Denys was suddenly aware that she was looking past him and straight at Jill Collier on the other side of the room. 'I mean, it's only natural, isn't it?' she concluded without conviction.

Her husband struck nearer the knuckle. 'Of course, if he's having a good time – I mean, if you're all enjoying yourselves, it seems a pity. . . .' He smiled with great heartiness. 'Switzerland is a great place, isn't it?'

Denys answered shortly: 'I like it a lot, yes: I think we all do. But I really don't know what Ian's plans are.' Aware that he was being both rude and ineffective, he turned to go. Then across the room he caught Jill's eye and knew that she must have overheard some of the conversation, for she grimaced in that intimate way he had noticed her use towards Ian, sympathizing with his difficulty. Denys found himself resenting it fiercely: it was a false signal of allegiance, he wasn't on her side at all. . . . He turned back to the Jacksons and proceeded with mischievous care to undo whatever good he had done. 'I don't suppose,' he went on, 'that Ian would go home, anyway. It would be a pity to cut his holiday short, just for that.'

'Just for that. . . .' Mr Jackson repeated the words on a rising note. 'Nothing important, eh? When you're a bit older, young man, you'll think a bit differently, I'll be bound. Having a baby is quite an event, you know. It's a turning-point in anyone's life.'

'Oh yes.' He turned round, to glance at the other two across the room: Mr Jackson's eyes followed his. 'Obviously it must be,' he concluded spitefully, and left them staring.

Mr Jackson was the first to recover. 'Well, I'll be . . . So that's what he thinks of it, is it? Cheeky young devil. When I was his age I had more sense of respect.'

'Poor boy,' said Mrs Jackson. 'Can't you see how worried he is? I wonder if he knows anything. . . .' She pursed her lips. 'Mark my words, somebody's going to get into trouble before very long.'

'Trouble? What trouble? Just a pack of gossip, that's all it is. These hotels are all alike – smile at a girl at breakfast and you're divorced from her by dinner-time. Ian's decent enough, you know that.'

'That may be, but his place is with his wife, and no one can say it isn't. And instead of that he's carrying on – well, look at that, for instance.'

Mr Jackson looked, and drew in his breath sharply. The little tableau at the other table was certainly arresting: it might have been specially staged to give the lie to any counsel of discretion. Ian, facing Jill, had her hand in his and was playing with the ring on her finger: he was speaking softly, leaning over towards her, and on both their faces shone that soft illumination born of the acknowledgment of desire, which one may sometimes see if one comes upon lovers suddenly. It was intensely revealing, and it lent extreme point to Denys' parting remark.

'It's a bit thick, I must say.' Mr Jackson's voice was uneasy, instinct with the eternal accents of respectability on the watch. 'Behaving like that when everyone in the hotel knows how he's placed. If I was old Carrington I'd have something to say about it.'

'Something to say about it. ...' Mrs Jackson's astonished gasp indicated both her dismay at old Carrington's forbearance and the spate of words which she herself would have let loose under the same circumstances. 'I should just think he ought to have something to say about it. It's ridiculous – it's *criminal*, to let things go on like this. You don't know what harm may be done. And that poor child. ...' She nodded towards the door by which Denys had left. 'He's suffering, really suffering.'

'Oh, Denys is old enough to take care of himself, I should think.'

'Nothing of the sort. He's just a boy, and he has to stand by and watch that sort of thing.'

Their eyes went round to the other table again, and once more the little tableau had its effect, like a slap in the face from a curling wave.

Mrs Jackson rose to her feet, gathering her bag with a

crisp decisive gesture. 'Mark my words – Master Ian hasn't heard the last of this. He may be chirpy enough now, but he'll pay for it later, that I do know.'

She stalked across the room, her head held high, her eyes steadfastly on the doorway, while her husband, with something of the air of a discredited mastiff, trailed in her wake. Their departure should have been deeply significant, but was in point of fact unnoticed by anyone save their waiter, who thought he was to blame and trembled.

Ian was deep in remembrance of the previous night. Gazing over his coffee-cup at Jill, he could see her only as she had been a few hours before: naked and welcoming, clenching her strong, athletic body to his, melting to him, surging and shuddering on a crest of desire which had driven him on to greater heights of ecstasy than he had ever known.

'You are,' he said softly, 'as sweet as I could ever wish for, deserve, obtain, lie about, or lick the lips over. Last night was the sort of thing I've only dreamt about. Tonight will be the same.' His eyelashes flickered upwards. 'Tonight *will* be the same, won't it?'

Jill smiled lazily, feeling his desire play over her like warm sunlight. 'As long as you can keep your strength up,' she answered, 'I shall be there to enjoy it.'

That was all it meant for her: a kind of after-hours extension of the Austin-Reed service. But Ian, drugged alike with memory and with anticipation, was very far from taking note of what was exactly in her mind.

Denys hung about the nursery slopes: solitary, angry, increasingly aware of his isolation. He found that it was becoming stronger than ever, that feeling that he alone was normal in his instincts and saw through unclouded eyes; clearer thinking might have told him that, if it came to counting heads and adding chances, the Jacksons for a start were certainly on his side, but since the breakfast encounter he could only view them as inquisitive spectators, who were watching and therefore enjoying his embarrassments.

And as he plodded up the hill or slipped and slithered down it, practising his stops and turns with a sort of fatalistic determination, grandiose schemes of revenge kept parading themselves before him: if Ian could behave in this manner, and be so careless of public opinion, he himself could also have a good try at something in the same line – he wouldn't always keep quiet, he'd make people realize he was there, present and not particularly correct – he'd get drunk in the hotel and disgrace the whole family, he'd pick up some woman and take her about, he would hit at each and every one of them by some unpleasant or undignified display....

He remembered an occasion, long ago, when a trifling but unfair rebuke had made him hate his whole family, from his father down to his nursemaid, with a clear insensate rage: and to score off them he had purposely wet his bed six nights in succession, until he judged that things were evened up and honour restored. ... He laughed at the remembrance – it had been a prodigiously uncomfortable affair – and then frowned again: how good, how intensely satisfying it would be, to discover the adult equivalent of this former protest, and put it swiftly into practice to the same confusion of the enemy. And how gladly he would bear any discomfort or embarrassment, if it gave him a chance of levelling the score....

Then his train of thought was interrupted by a sudden cry of '*Attention!*' behind him, followed by a clatter of skis and a sharp blow in the small of his back: he came down heavily, unable to break his fall, and then found himself, with an inconsiderable weight on his chest, gazing up at a girl's face a few inches from his own – a face very young, perfectly oval, glowingly coloured. He laughed, and the girl laughed too, embarrassedly, for she was very young, not more than sixteen, and she was lying on top of him in an attitude deliciously indecorous, with her long legs across his stomach and her arm about his neck: nor was he much less embarrassed – in fact both of them were breathing fast, and covered with snow, and inexperienced enough to feel very shy of their proximity.

After a minute Denys heaved himself up and disentangled their skis, and then they laughed again, and she began in French a halting apology which he did not need, but which he enjoyed because it gave him time to collect his thoughts and look at her and watch her lips moving.

She was probably the prettiest girl he had ever seen: her colouring and the symmetry of her features alone were enough to decide that. Hers was a static beauty, independent of expression, and though her face – and indeed her whole body – had a sweet immaturity about them, yet he would not have had them changed, he would never want her to grow older, to emerge from her untried state.

Denys found himself quite unable to take his eyes off her: she was so young, and her eyes so large and violet, and her skin so clear – and then her hair, and the astounding oval of her face – of course she would have to grow up sooner or later, and be a woman and married and entirely spoilt; but just at this moment, as she stood there in her grey ski-suit flecked with snow, and her red scarf, and the whole thing topped by a little forage cap corded with green, he need share her with no one. . . . Presently, still marvelling, he found his tongue, and cut short her protests in clumsy schoolboy French.

'It doesn't matter at all,' he said. 'I've knocked down lots of people – it's understood that one can't help it.'

'But . . .' She put her head on one side: silhouetted against the snow slope she might have been Hans Andersen's goose-girl straying southward to enchant Europe. 'You are a beginner, too? You must be better than me. This is my first season.'

'Mine, too.' He smiled, trying to put her at her ease. Perhaps quick movement would do the trick. 'I'll race you down to the hedge,' he suggested, 'then we can see who's best.'

'All right.' And she was off in a flash, rather unfairly, but he caught her half-way down. They landed in a friendly and exciting heap at the bottom of the hill – another good reason for prosecuting the acquaintanceship.

She came from Alsace, she told him: she was at school in Strasbourg, which apparently was not a very exciting place, and she was in Adelboden with her father, who was very strict and liked skating. (Denys could just imagine him, standing on the rink and glowering at anyone who got in his way.) They were here for another fortnight, staying at the Bellevue, and she was very lucky to have such a holiday, because nearly all the girls in her school only went away in the summer, and not at Christmas at all. ... All this came out very solemnly, during the intervals for rest, in a voice low-pitched and almost apologetic: it was obvious that by her father's standards she should not have been talking to the *jeune étranger* at all, but rather shunning all mankind and assiduously practising her turns. But perhaps he needn't know, just for this once. . . .

It was for Denys one of the sweetest interludes he had ever experienced, having all the necessary attributes of romance – an unconventional meeting in strange surroundings, a companion rendered intriguing by her nationality as well as by her loveliness, a secret to be guarded from the grown-ups; altogether it provided some measure of compensation for the difficulties of the last few days. He, too, had his excitement, his own breathless enjoyment which was now a match for anyone's. And there was one little phrase of hers – or rather, one small intonation – which he carried away with him like a traveller's charm, which kept recurring to him later, which he found himself repeating. He had asked her where she had been the night before, meaning, had she been dancing somewhere: and she had looked at him and answered rather primly:

'*J'étais au lit.*'

It wasn't really the words which took his imagination, it was the way she said them and the way her lips moved when she spoke the last two – forward, to be kissed, on the '*au,*' back to a smile on the '*lit*' – he found himself watching her mouth eagerly in case he could catch that movement again.

For a moment it opened another train of thought – the warmth of her bed, the sweet young limbs curled up, the boyish sort of pyjamas she would probably wear, the smooth oval of her face against the pillow; but standing there in the snow and the crisp air he found it impossible to hold on to the idea for more than a moment – it was alien, it was swamped in freshness and carried away by the clean searching breeze. She was too young for that, she would be left alone for a long time yet, and he was inordinately glad of the fact.

Before they parted he tried his hardest to arrange another

meeting, and succeeded at last, in face of all her objections, in winning a provisional fixture. (Had he but known it, it was her first assignation of any sort.)

The preliminary obstacles came thick and fast. She couldn't go with him to watch the jumping because she had to have a rest after lunch (the strict father once again), and tonight she had to play bridge with some relations who were calling at the hotel. Tomorrow she and her father were going away for some days to visit friends at Zurich. It was uncertain when they would return. But perhaps – here Fate relented, the delayed sun topped the horizon – if he were waiting at the Bar-Français on New Year's Eve she might slip out – it would be difficult, but her father might be less stern on such an occasion – she would make some excuse, she would really do her best. . . .

With which promise, and a lovely smile, she shouldered her skis and left him; and he went back to lunch with a new gaiety lighting his face – he now had at least one consolation, one person on his side to balance the increasing odds against him.

CHAPTER X

The little track leading up to the ski-jumping ground rather appealed to Jill. It commanded variety, it was never at a loss for fresh contrast, it was a vast improvement on human nature. . . .

It dipped and swung its way through fir woods, across valleys and streams, and up steep hillsides glistening in the afternoon sun, as if it were a fairy-tale pathway, the kind the Babes in the Wood took on their ultimate excursion; and though she and Ian could by no stretch of imagination qualify for this latter role, she felt nonetheless a part of the enchanting picture.

She strode along, her boots picking up square clods of snow and throwing them a few paces ahead, her gloves swinging at the end of a long cord from her waist, her cap cocked on one side to advertise the feminine rather than the workmanlike mode; and behind her Ian, carrying four skis and two sticks and dragging a luge as well, made an effective advertisement of another sort – a proclamation that she was desirable, that simply by being a shapely young woman she could get young men to involve themselves in the most maddening drudgery, that people were glad to serve her in any capacity, however stupid or inexplicable, just because she was Jill Collier. . . .

In the present case she had not really wanted the luge, except perhaps to sit on while they were watching the jumps, since the way back, over the other side of the valley, was one of the finest runs in the district and she had every intention of using it; but Ian had been there, obviously adoring her, obviously ready to do anything in or out of reason, and it had been quite impossible not to implement, to its fullest extent, this store of romantic humility.

As was usual with Jill, their partnership was one of signal inequality, both in strength and in purpose: she already had a clear ascendancy, with the balance tipped far in her favour: though he was as yet quite unaware of the fact, she couldn't be hurt by him, because she was not emotionally involved, and so she had no more to do than fill in the time by making use of him. He was good-looking, but he was under her thumb, and so she could be sure, in a politely sadistic manner, that she would enjoy herself without anxiety.

As a natural corollary to this she was now in a mighty fine humour. Circe, excepting when she was crossed, was probably a good-natured tomboyish creature with the merriest of laughs.

Moreover the ski-jump meeting made it a busy pathway, and the number of strapping young men in exhilarating or fantastic clothes who, overtaking her, strode past, stared sideways, and smiled at her, was a most agreeable tonic. Good ski-clothes could set off the male figure exceedingly well, and the endless procession, diverse in nationality, in looks, in technique, seemed to her a most satisfactory decoration, like some frieze of paintings conceived in desire and executed with aphrodisiac fervour. The men that this town collected were to her mind the prime attraction: they were good-looking, tough, agile, and presumably experienced in indoor sport as well, and she reacted to this as if it were sunshine, or some superior kind of massage.

Ian might supply the true and warrantable commodity, but the feel of their surroundings was infinitely important, and, in a way, he was only the spearhead, the personal projection of this large-scale masculine attack. Though of course the head of the spear sees most of the action, and indeed initiates it.

As they neared the end of their journey the pace slowed up to a crawl: at the top of the hill had been set a turnstile, with a man selling tickets backed up by two policemen, and there was now in progress one of the periodic mass-efforts to save gate-money by slipping over the hedge or sneaking through the woods. It led, inevitably, to a fine chaotic scene: the ticket-seller roared out threats and bounced in his seat, the policemen whistled and swooped, the honest citizens betrayed their fellow-men at the tops of their voices: in fact the whole thing, thought Ian as he dutifully paid over his five francs, was in rather bad taste, and it annoyed him to see Jill laughing at the efforts of one young man to get past by an elaborate series of feints and false alarms. That wasn't in the least funny: it was simply dishonest, it was a typical Damned Foreigner's Trick, and Jill was quite wrong to encourage it. Her encouragement should be a reserved and rationed product, in any case.

But in point of fact nothing, not even the suspicion that Jill had an incorrigibly roving eye, could today affect his mood for long. For however catholic her interests, she had given him tangible evidence that his position was established; she might smile at other men, she might reflect their personal interest like a little swinging mirror, but by the supreme measurement, the good old-fashioned test, he was first and the rest nowhere. ...

It did not occur to him, or rather he dismissed the idea as not worth dwelling on, that Jill was entirely untrustworthy and would drop their affair as easily as she had picked it up; he had got what he wanted, and he did not even wish to see the wood when the trees were so entirely to his taste. He was content to live in the moment, not knowing that the moment was evanescent.

As they emerged side by side on to the wide snow field, her eyes went up to the jumping platform towering above them, and she drew in her breath.

'It looks so high up – I don't know how they don't kill themselves. They must have the most amazing nerves.'

'Or rather, none at all,' Ian answered her. 'Probably there's something lacking in their make-up, something which results in a kind of unawareness. If they knew, really knew, what an insane game it is, and what fantastic chances they take, they'd never start at all.'

Jill laughed. 'Why spoil it for me? I've got them fixed in my mind as death-defying heroes, and you say it's all due to their being half-witted. I suppose they *can* read and write, after all.'

'Just enough to fill in the entry forms. ... But it *is* a crazy sport, Jill: it has no calculable limit – you can go on building bigger jumps, and you can go on getting people to ski over them, if you make the prizes big in proportion – you kill three men, and then one maniac happens to keep his balance and the record is advanced by so much. But it's plain murder, in effect, and instead of getting the bloodhounds out they sell tickets for people to watch it. That's probably the luckiest part of the whole thing.'

'They seem to have sold a lot of them today, at any rate.' Jill looked about her, smiling vaguely, setting her cap crooked with practised fingers. 'Even though half of them are gate-crashers, there's obviously money in murder.'

It was at once an animated and a peaceful scene. Crowds surrounded the field where the jumpers finished their course, lines of figures straggled up the hillside, stationing themselves as nearly opposite the fifty-metre mark as they could – anything beyond this was, on this course, an exceptionally good jump; and high up, level with the take-off, a stand had been built which was already crowded with people.

Banners and flags, in the familiar red-and-white, supplied the final touch of colour. But it was the snow and the ring of great hills around about which set the pace of the scene; no human exertion could affect their aloof majesty, for they were asleep, they set over everything an indestructible peace. High up there, one knew that the air was still, the trees motionless, the silences unbroken: men might throng and murmur in the valley, but their tiny clamour could not reach the immutable guardians above.

Two hundred feet up, at the top of the run-way, a group of figures had gathered, dwarfed by their surroundings to an insignificant stature, so that one could distinguish only the separate bodies and the white numbered placards on their chests; and even as Jill watched a flag swept downward, brilliant in the sun, and one of them turned swiftly in his tracks and set off down the hill.

Silence fell, as all eyes watched that crouching swoop. Down he came, arrow-swift: momentarily he was out of sight and he appeared suddenly in mid-air – erect, arms outstretched, poised in flight like a hovering seagull. For a second he seemed to hang in space, then he plunged downwards, the smack of the snow as his skis met it sounding clearly all over the valley, to be followed by a prolonged 'Ah . . .' from the crowd and a burst of clapping.

It appeared a good jump: and a moment later the board went up with '47' on it to tell them that it was so. Perfectly balanced, perfectly controlled, the man sped on across the field, finishing up with a Christiana that sent up a shower of snow over the watchers. Then he looked back at the board, and smiled, throwing back his head with its great mop of yellow hair, as if to say: 'That's not the best I can do, but it's pretty good for a first jump.'

Probably he was a local man, for from the ring of stamping blue-nosed sleigh-drivers there came a guttural cheer, to which he waved in answer.

'Do you notice how these chaps dress?' whispered Ian as the man slid by them on his way up again. 'Just any old clothes, with one of those night-caps on top, if they bother to wear anything on their heads at all. It makes the ordinary visitor look pretty silly. In fact, the worse skier you are, the more smartly you turn yourself out. That puts you pretty near the danger-line, Jill. And as for this . . .'

Close by them, an immaculate young man in a pearl-grey

ski-suit fitting oh-so-snugly at the waist slithered a little way down the hill and then collapsed in a heap with a wail. Jill laughed.

'How did you know that was going to happen?'

'I've had my eye on him for some time. ... He reminded me of those photos of mannequins dressed for the Twelfth – you know, sitting in a fake butt made of cotton-wool, surrounded by dead birds with the price tickets still on – immaculate tweeds, hat with an emu-feather in it, and holding a gun as if it was a vacuum cleaner.'

'Hey!' said Jill. 'That's exactly what I look like when I go north.'

'I don't doubt it. But then no one imagines that you go north for the shooting.'

Another silence as the second jumper started, another poised split second in mid-air, another sharp crack and a rustle of clapping from the crowd. This time the man nearly lost his balance, and he wavered first on one foot and then on the other, going all the time at a tremendous pace. Finally he rocked to a safe standstill. The board said '43', and the jumper, also a local man whom Ian knew by sight, looked black as thunder. Publicity had its drawbacks on occasions such as this.

'I want to go nearer,' said Jill suddenly. 'Let's climb up to the take-off.'

'That's too close,' said Ian, who was comfortably settled on the luge. 'You hardly see anything of the jump from there. Why not stay here, and get the proper view?'

'I want to see what they look like as they go over.' Jill got to her feet, stamping the snow from her boots. 'Come along. We'll leave the skis and things here, and pick them up on our way back.'

It took them twenty minutes to complete the climb up to the platform: the proper pathway was reserved for the jumpers, and the slope was very steep, so that progress could only be made by traversing the hill in zigzag fashion and digging hard into the snow with every step. Jill kept stopping, too, as each of the jumpers went by: she was thrilled by their terrific speed as they hit the ground, and thrilled also to be so close to them, close enough to feel the wind of their flight, the trembling of the air before their onrush. But presently the two of them were level with the take-off, and by smiles on her part and some adroit pushing on his, they got to the front of the crowd and looked about them.

Jill was surprised to see how narrow the run-way was – it was really no more than a banked-up path of snow, about four feet across, and that meant that there was precious little margin for a mistake. The take-off platform itself was made of rough boards, covered with bracken and then with beaten snow: with a flag at either side as well as a row of spectators, it was presumably sufficient target for the heroes above.

Nearby the flag flashed once more, throwing a swift shadow over the heads of the crowd; and up above them one of the jumpers jerked to attention and slipped on to the run-way. He gathered way at an amazing speed: it was possible now to see how critical these first few moments were, and how small a slip would send him off the track and into the crowd. Jill held her breath, fascinated by his approach. He crouched over his skis, plunging down towards them like a comet: his body grew, his features became clearer, the sound of his skis could be heard: and then suddenly he had reached them, had straightened up, had braced himself for flight.

The sight of his face at that moment photographed itself on Jill's brain. The man was young, tall, fair: and as he left the ground and launched forward into the void his lips opened and he grinned, to reveal white teeth bared to the gums and tightly clenched. There was something especially significant about that grin: it seemed the sign-manual of the heroic tradition, marking the wearer out as one of a new race of men, strongest and toughest of all, without chink of fear, virile conquerors of space; and thus the image of him was left in her mind – teeth and jaw set, arms delicately balanced, chin and head and shoulders thrust forward in a brave determined line. ... But that was all she saw, for he landed out of her sight, far below, and the board went up with '51' on it, likely to be the best jump of the meeting.

'That was marvellous,' she breathed. She was rapturously excited, as if at a glimpse of heaven. 'They must be amazing people – hardly human beings at all. Did you see how he smiled? – so unafraid, so sure of himself, as if he had invisible wings.'

'It's just practice, really,' answered Ian, slightly piqued. There were other things besides hulking great yokels jumping 51 metres. 'If you did this sort of thing three times a week from the time you were seven or eight years old, you wouldn't think much of it.'

'You always try and spoil it.' Jill looked at him critically. 'Why don't you volunteer? – they're always glad of a little comic relief. ... Personally I think it's a damned brave thing to do, and obviously it doesn't get easier as you go along – it gets harder, and if you had one bad fall it would be enough to put you off it for life.'

'I only meant that they develop a special kind of nerve.'

'I dare say. But presumably they start with some sort of pluck.'

Annoyed, she turned away, seeking some new counter-poise to his short-coming, and found herself looking straight into the eyes of Denys, who was standing next to her. She smiled brilliantly.

'Hallo, Denys! Have you been here all the time?'

He smiled back. He would have smiled at anyone. He was at peace with all the world, thinking only of his little Alsatian girl. 'Yes. In fact I was standing where you are, until you elbowed me out. I wondered how long you were going to continue cutting me. What do you think of these jumpers?'

'I think they're grand, but Ian says they're so stupid that they don't know it's dangerous.'

'I only said ...' began Ian peevishly.

'Now don't start it again,' she cut in. 'I've clumped all the way up this hill and I'm going to enjoy myself, whether we're watching heroic genius or raving lunacy.'

'Hear, hear,' said Denys unexpectedly. 'The stuff's the same whatever the packing.'

Another competitor shot past them, taking them by surprise. This one didn't grin, Jill noticed: in fact he didn't do anything except jump superbly: his face was expressionless, almost bored, as if he were going down the club steps after an indifferent lunch party. But bored or no, he cleared fifty metres and she was prepared to love him for it.

'I like watching their faces as they go over,' volunteered Denys presently.

'So do I.' She turned towards him and they smiled again, linked by this preference of connoisseurship. 'It's much the most interesting part of it, the real human element. There was one that smiled. ... I don't think I should see the joke, on the edge of a fifty yard drop.'

'I dare say the rows of gaping faces look pretty fatuous.'

Jill giggled. 'That may be it, of course. In fact the temptation to put one's tongue out at them must be enormous.'

It was so surprising not to find Denys vaguely hostile that she had warmed to him immediately: they had never been as friendly as they were now, they had never approached so close to each other. She liked it: indeed she could understand now what it was that was having such an effect on Helen – a train of events which she had been watching with a certain detached amusement. Now she herself caught the echo of it in Denys' manner: there was about him an openness, a guileless deference, a rather sweet humility. . . . She smiled to herself: of course she wasn't competing, but he certainly *was* a nice kid.

Denys looked up the hill, shaded his eyes and exclaimed suddenly:

'There he is! I know the man coming down now. We were on a party together last night.'

He examined his programme swiftly. 'Number nine – Hans Jorgensen. ... This is the first time I've been able to discover his name.'

'Oh, it was that sort of party, was it?'

'Doesn't sound too good, does it? But you don't get many regular introductions up at Hahnenmoos – or at the Grand Bar, either.'

While he was still speaking the Norwegian swept past them, hair loose in the wind, bronzed face tense with the effort of concentration: for the moment he looked particularly godlike, and it was that demeanour which stuck in Jill's brain, rather than the shattering fall which followed.

Something must have gone seriously wrong with his balance,

for when he landed he hardly stayed on his feet for a moment before falling sideways, losing a ski, and rolling over and over down the hill. A shout went up from the crowd – the fall looked an ugly one, as if a leg must be twisted; but he got to his feet and shook off the snow and waited for his ski to be brought to him, without making anything of it or seeming in the least perturbed. As his bearing was noted a small sentimental cheer made itself heard: the Roman crowd cheering the Christian instead of the lion, while in no way curtailing the odds on the latter.

Jill joined fervently in the clapping. 'That's what I mean,' she said excitedly. 'A fall like that must be terrifying. Imagine going up to the top again and waiting your turn for another jump. Personally I should always have a suitcase parked at the bottom, and slip quietly away to the next town.'

Denys smiled meditatively. 'You know, I feel a certain responsibility for that fall. If we hadn't stayed out quite so late he might be in rather more athletic form. You can't train for this sort of thing on beer and chewing-gum.'

'Was it a good party?' asked Ian. 'He looked a tough sort of chap to go on a blind with.'

'Oh, nothing very special. But we didn't get to bed till about one, and he didn't exactly stick to his training.'

Nothing very special. ... That was another thing which Jill decided she liked: he hadn't yet got to the stage of boasting about the amount he drank – to her mind the most sickening male usage. So many of her contemporaries found it quite impossible to sustain a conversation without embarking on that fatal sentence: 'God, I was drunk last night ...' a fact which in her stratum of society, and many another, might surely be taken for granted.

'Where did you go?' Ian asked him.

'The Grand Bar.' Denys hesitated for a moment, and then forgot his embarrassment. 'You and Jill came in for a moment, but I don't think you saw me. I was up at the far end with a whole gang of people.'

A silence fell, involuntary on his part, rather strained on theirs: all three of them suddenly became aware of the situation, and of the precise kind of cleavage which the history of the preceding night typified. Jill felt a momentary pang of regret, recognizing the dishonesty of being so friendly with Denys when only twelve hours before she had been sleeping with Ian. We're connected by adultery, she thought to herself: and for once did not find herself amused by the idea. It was a faintly cruel one, and she didn't want to hurt him: he was so young and gentle, he almost came within her kindness-to-animals category. . . .

'Yes, we looked in for a moment,' she remarked presently. 'But it was rather noisy – just the place for you rough skiers, of course, but we wanted to dance in comfort.'

At that there was another silence, of which Denys caught the full significance almost immediately. He had a sudden vision of two happenings of the previous night which he had not before connected, but which now fell into place. First there was Jill and Ian walking back close to each other through the snow, just ahead of himself and the Norwegian: and then, when he had gone to bed, there had been Ian's door still open, with no light inside the room. 'We wanted to dance in comfort. . . .' And later, make love. Of course. That was it. Silly of him not to have seen it before. Last night then had been *the* night. No wonder Jill looked satisfied, no wonder Ian was so pleased with the whole world. They were in the middle of their honeymoon.

He looked down at his feet, quite at a loss for the next word. But, oddly enough, he did not feel himself to be as shocked and hurt as he had expected: once again, of course, it was the little Alsatian girl coming to his aid – in her gentle way she had armed him for such an encounter as this, she had given him a loving protection which would carry him through the days until he met her again. How could he judge anyone harshly when he had so soon to meet the scrutiny of those wise young eyes? . . . Or, if that seemed to be placing too high a value on their meeting, it must be something else as well: perhaps he had changed since he had arrived in Switzerland, perhaps he had been too Puritan-minded before: perhaps people just *did* do these things, and he was coming to realize it properly.

At any rate, standing there among the friendly crowd and

aware of Jill's warmth and attraction and Ian's good-fellowship, he found it impossible to condemn them outright. He must have leisure to think it over, he must try not to exaggerate concerning facts and ideas which he understood very little. He must play for time, since time – in terms of growing up – was obviously the vital factor.

But in any case he was saved from having to produce some comment at that moment by a loud hail from behind him, a hail which demanded attention, which would not be denied. It was the Norwegian, toiling uphill again with his skis over one shoulder, disdaining the reserved pathway: he appeared none the worse for wear, and his unabashed smile as he greeted Denys seemed to disclaim all knowledge of his recent lapse from grace. His arrival dissipated the tension of the party. Denys introduced him, Jill looked at him with her biggest eyes, and Ian asked, with a faintly ludicrous concern, if he had hurt himself.

'Hurt?' He smiled largely, waving away the possibility with his free arm. 'No, the fall was nothing. I blame myself only: I was not paying attention: my head was wrong. One cannot hope to stand up if one holds oneself like a ballet dancer. And also,' he gave Denys' shoulder a friendly pat, 'if you and I had not stayed out so late last night, I might have given a better performance, this fine afternoon.'

'I tried to get you home,' said Denys plaintively.

'And all the time I thought it was I who was trying. . . . Never mind – I have two more jumps, and there is no need to fall again. Watch for the next one: I will set myself to show you how we manage these little affairs in Norway.'

'Tell us more about it,' said Jill eagerly. She liked talking to him: there was a glamour surrounding him, a reflection of that tremendous fall through space which he had just accomplished 'Is it very difficult? Does it need a lot of nerve?'

'No, it is nothing like that.' He looked at her with grave courtesy, wondering how Denys came to be in the company of the colourful Miss Coll-ee-er of the night before. He must be clever. This young one. . . . 'You see, I have been doing it since I was a child, and I know that if I make certain movements, and hold myself in a certain fashion – just so – I will not be hurt. And the better I do this, in this perfect way, the faster I can move and the further I can jump. It is only sometimes that one forgets, and then it is too late to correct the mistake. Very much too late. So I try always to concentrate, in spite of late hours and my English friends who lead me on such pathways.' He smiled, and then looked up to the top of the hill. 'But I must go, I think. It is near my turn, and if I am late they will fine me, and God knows I cannot afford to lose points, after such a spectacle.'

'Well, good luck this time,' said Denys. 'And how about another drink, one of these evenings?'

The Norwegian nodded. 'Yes, we will have that. I will present myself at your hotel. And this time I need not be so careful about staying out so late. It is difficult to rejoice, when one has an anxiety like that.' He smiled once more, bowed to Jill, and resumed his way up the hill again.

Viewed from where they stood, he looked an almost uncannily romantic figure as he plodded up the slope: boots heavy with snow, blue ski-ing trousers, white sweater across great broad shoulders on which the skis were balanced, fair hair outlined and gleaming in the sunlight: and then above him, like a triumphal arch, the tree-tops and the high sloping mountain-side which crowned them. For once, the Nordic was the Heroic as well: and the three of them, and indeed all the rest of the crowd, seemed miserably earth-bound by comparison.

'Nice chap,' said Ian after a pause. 'I didn't know you had such exalted friends, Denys.'

'We met up at Hahnenmoos, as a matter of fact, and he guided me down. He's in the Olympic team.'

Said like that, casually, it had a most satisfactory ring about it. And when, a little later, the Norwegian brought off a truly matchless jump to tie for first place, Denys felt that nothing could really damp his good humour. He might be only eighteen, and they mightn't think much of him within the Carrington menage, but outside it he was the familiar friend of the great.

CHAPTER XI

To prosecute an attractive acquaintanceship and to annoy Ian, Jill elected to walk back with Denys, who had come on foot without skis; and thus when the jumping was finished they set off together over the shoulder of the hill, leaving Ian to collect the luge and go round the other way. Both of them had some sense of the novelty of the situation, like opponents at bridge who find themselves, at the end of a long evening, suddenly playing together for the first time; and Jill especially was eager to make up the ground she supposed herself to have lost during the previous estrangement.

She had no idea why Denys had so swiftly changed his attitude: she hoped that the change was permanent, she could not know that he had suspended criticism with regard to the whole world, that he was merely being universally tolerant while he recollected his thoughts and applied them to the problem. Nor could she know about the Alsatian girl, by far the strongest element of his contentment.

'I'm frightfully glad your Norwegian friend won,' she remarked presently, as they began the long descent to the main road. 'He deserved something after that fall.'

Denys laughed. 'He was in good training for falls, at any rate. He came down the most awful crack on his way home last night: we both did, as a matter of fact, trying to stand up in snow-boots on ice.' He paused. 'That was just after we'd seen you and Ian – you were a bit ahead of us.' Which, he added privately, was true in a good many senses.

'You saw us?' She tried to cover her embarrassment with an air of carelessness. 'Where was that? Outside the Grand?'

'No, by the hotel. You were going in.'

She nodded, relieved. Ian and she had kissed now and then on the way back, sometimes drawing aside into the shadows, sometimes not bothering (since the whole street was full of couples provoked to a like carelessness), and though it wasn't vitally important that Denys shouldn't have seen them –

because it surely wouldn't have told him anything he didn't know before – yet it made things easier if he hadn't.

'We'd been at the Bar-Français,' she went on evenly. 'Ian loves that place, though for me the charm is rather beginning to wear off. I hate having to peer through the smoke and guess who I'm with and what I'm eating. Still, I enjoyed last night.'

They walked on in silence for a few paces; along the pathway couples and odd groups were gathering, drawn by the approach of twilight towards the friendly town. The sun was now well lost behind the hills, and it was much colder. Their silence persisted, almost unnaturally: indeed, it seemed to Denys as if Nature was conspiring to make of their walk home the concluding passage of the subject in hand, as if it had been ruled that discussion of it was to cease with the advent of darkness: and he found himself unwilling to leave it – just for the moment he was able to view it objectively, and all his instinct told him not to miss a chance of learning the truth.

So, after a pause, and an effort to find a reasonable opening: 'I suppose Ian's pretty fond of you,' he began again thoughtfully. 'You've been about a lot together, and he seems to be enjoying himself.'

'We both are, I think,' she answered him, without hesitation. Tonight she had less than her usual caution: Denys was so sweet that it was impossible to think of him as an enemy, just as one could never wholly dislike a sincere priest or an attentive head-waiter. 'There's no harm in it really: we just like doing the same things, and actually there's no one else for him to go about with. Of course I know he's married and everything, but that doesn't mean that he's got to stay locked up for the rest of his life.'

'I suppose not.' The words came naturally, but he was depressed by her answer: it did not accord with his own view, he knew that she was somehow missing the point, skating round the real issue. Again he hesitated, wanting to ask her definitely whether she and Ian were lovers, and not daring to. Their companionship was novel, their truce too recent. . . . But, as it happened, she saved him the trouble.

'I didn't think he was happy,' she volunteered suddenly. She turned to Denys, and laid her hand gently on his arm. 'I'm not blaming your sister – marriage is terribly difficult sometimes – and you mustn't blame me. I wanted to help him, if I possibly could. He was too – too tightly wound up. I thought there was some release that he could have. I tried to give it him.'

'Do you mean you . . .'

'Yes.' Jill had no clear knowledge why she was telling him this: certainly it was no triumphant proclamation, it was not one of her usual possessive boastings. But she had been taken suddenly with the idea of putting an end to the awkwardness between them, of laying everything on the table and enlisting his sympathy on her side. And the first thing to do was to clear up his doubts with that kind of adventurous frankness which she had frequently used in parallel cases. People who were taken into your confidence were very often flattered by it into supporting you, even against their habitual principles. 'Yes,' she repeated. Then: 'Does it mean anything to you? Do you mind much?'

'I don't know.' But he knew well enough, and at her words he had withdrawn completely within himself, prompted by the beginnings of a clear disgust with the whole thing. 'It's something I'm not sure about.'

They were nearly at the hotel.

'Well, don't be angry with me, please.' She squeezed his elbow slightly. 'I want to be friends with you. It needn't make any difference, need it? Look, we're here. Do say it's all right. It *is* all right, isn't it?'

'I don't know,' he repeated. He dropped back as they reached the doorway, and when she would have lingered he motioned her forward with a gesture half formal, half impatient. From behind her his words came mumblingly: 'It's rather a surprise. I hadn't thought that Ian would. . . . But don't worry – I won't tell anyone.'

She knew then that she had made a mistake, that her tactics had proved wrong; and it disturbed her that she had put a weapon into hands whose strength or purpose she could not guess. But she was accustomed to keep her worries to herself, and Denys, as an opponent, was surely easy enough to ignore; and therefore, patching up her quarrel with Ian later, she did not mention the matter when he asked her how she had got on with Denys.

'He's a nice kid,' said Ian during the course of the conversation, by no means exclusively a verbal one. 'Rather orthodox, though. What did you talk about?'

'Oh, nothing much.' She smiled. 'I bitched him a bit, as a matter of fact. I thought it might make things smoother.'

'You needn't bother to make them too smooth, you know.'

She smiled again. 'It's all right, darling. You're not likely to find yourself out of a job yet awhile.'

Mrs Carrington walked back from the *concours* with Frau Franck. The two of them made an odd combination, perhaps, but then the whole family was curiously disjointed that afternoon: Mr Carrington was romping with the Jacksons, Helen had disappeared by herself, and Denys had temporarily supplanted Ian on Jill's horizon. And after all, what was more natural than for these two to walk back together, at a tranquil old-ladyish pace, after watching with rather fearful eyes the dangerous antics of the ski-jumpers? They were contemporaries, they had known each other a long time: and though other women in the hotel might hold themselves a cut above the proprietor's wife, that did not, in Mrs Carrington's eyes, render her any the less eligible for companionship.

This camaraderie, indeed, this readiness to make friends with what Helen called 'odd' people, was a trait with which the latter continually found fault: it seemed to her that she was always having to rescue her mother from straying away into company totally unsuitable for her. At parties she was invariably to be found, sooner or later, commiserating with one of the waiters on his long hours and insufficient wages: lose sight of her for a moment in the street, and ten to one she was talking to a commissionaire or a street singer. 'But they're human beings, after all,' she would say unrepentantly, on being dragged away. 'Why can't I talk to whom I choose?' Not that Helen ever bothered to find an answer: the thing was so obvious, if you looked at it from the proper angle.

In the present case Mrs Carrington knew well that Helen would have had no patience with her at all: she would have hustled her towards the hotel, murmuring angrily that they were late, very late for tea, and that the others would be anxious; and thus the opportunity for a nice chat with a woman she liked would have been lost for all time.

Although it was not in fact a *very* nice chat, both of them being rather too worried about exactly the same thing. . . . Naturally Mrs Carrington had no idea of referring to this thing directly – at least, not to start with: but by asides and oblique references she had contrived to find out what was in the other's mind, and the knowledge was not of the sort to increase her contentment.

Frau Franck however did not want the occasion to pass without exploring the matter further and letting her own point of view be known; and she worked hard to bring the conversation to the required point without seeming inquisitive or over-eager. Presently, by a roundabout path, she achieved the subject of child-welfare, which Mrs Carrington was unaware existed in Switzerland – everyone looked so healthy and happy that child-bearing and rearing was surely almost a gooseberry-bush affair, a handful of coloured pictures to be flipped over at an even pace. . . . When the problem had been satisfactorily dealt with:

'And how is young Mrs Carrington?' asked Frau Franck, with a great air of nonchalance. 'The little one has not yet arrived, of course?'

'Not yet, no. But only a few more days, I think.' She spoke as if it were something she was looking forward to, though that was very far from being the true state of her feelings: indeed, the whole idea, by reason of its new aspects and associations, had steadily become more distasteful to her. 'Then we'll be getting news from England.'

'It will be good to have the anxiety over,' went on her companion. 'But to think of you as a grandmother is strange.'

Mrs Carrington, though quite unable to think of herself as a grandmother, her cares as plain mother being sufficiently overwhelming, took the gambit dutifully.

'Time passes very quickly, doesn't it? Ten years go like a summer evening. It seems only yesterday that Helen and Ian were children: and now . . .'

Her voice died away, and Frau Franck sympathized with her implied disillusionment. And now, she thought, completing the sentence for her companion, they were children no longer: the daughter was apparently well mixed up with young Mr Wilder, and the son was behaving like – well, Frau Franck had never seen such behaviour, nor considered it possible. She had remarked to her husband the previous night: 'I tell you, in place of a heart he must have a stone ...' and it was for her a trenchant stricture. Kind hearts might not be, commercially, worth more than coronets, but they had their own ethical Debrett to which she was a constant subscriber.

Now she turned to Mrs Carrington, her voice warm with friendliness, determined not to communicate her own forebodings.

'You have many anxieties, I know. But I'm sure everything will be all right: these things pass, and are forgotten, and there is happiness again.'

'I sometimes wonder whether we oughtn't all to go home.' The lacuna in their conversation was safely bridged by the understanding between them. 'It would be easier in many ways.'

'No, you mustn't do that,' answered Frau Franck firmly. The words and the tone had a professional ring, but to do her justice, she was not thinking even remotely of her own position or of the loss of custom to the hotel; she only wanted to help the worried, rather pathetic figure by her side. 'You all need your full holiday, especially Mr Carrington who works so hard. He must not suffer just because ...' She spread her hands expressively, to indicate once more that topic which must never be directly alluded to. 'My husband is very angry with the girl, but you will understand that he can do nothing – her room is booked for another week, arranged through a travel bureau, and all in order.'

At her words Mrs Carrington began to look rather alarmed, seeing herself precipitating a crisis while really intending nothing beyond a minor indignation meeting. It was one thing to protest, in confidence, about a right of way, but quite another to confront and threaten the Lord of the Manor. ... 'Oh no, I don't want you to worry about it,' she said quickly. 'You've always been so good to us, so considerate, and it isn't right that you should have trouble over a thing like this.'

'Trouble!' Frau Franck repeated the word indignantly. 'Trouble enough, indeed, when girls of such a type come to us through a respectable agency. Must we then employ the police to examine each applicant for rooms?'

It was clear that she had made up her mind with regard to Jill's status, and that for her the current differentiation between professional and amateur carried little significance and no weight. The cash-basis was an affair not of morality but of competence. 'We know what young men are, to be sure – they are wild sometimes, they go through a certain phase – but there is no great harm in it, unless there is a temptation of this sort close at hand. Then it is different.'

Mrs Carrington glanced across at her companion, pondering her words and above all the tone in which they had been delivered. *Was* it different here? And if so, why? Frau Franck seemed so very downright about the matter that she was beginning to wonder whether there was some definite information to be imparted.

She herself did not think that Ian had slept with Jill (or, as she phrased it, gone as far as THAT), but she suspected that it was a possibility and would have been shocked but not greatly astonished to receive proof of it. She had kept up with the world a great deal more than Helen, for instance, imagined: she was aware that sex-experience outside marriage had lost its death-rather-than-dishonour significance, and that for Jill it might even have attained the status of an innocuous pastime, rated above stamp-collecting but below draw-poker. She was sorry about this, but she accepted it as a modern phenomenon. It was only when it touched the larger loyalties that she jibbed. Adultery was still adultery, though you christened it 'a refresher' and conducted it, to all intents and purposes, beneath the public gaze; fashions might change and customs fall into disuse, but not these deeply-rooted, these eternal verities.

Thus, to bring it nearer home, Ian might flirt a little bit, perhaps, on his only holiday in the year, but it mustn't come to THAT, or indeed come anywhere near it. He was married:

marriage was a selective barrier which must never be passed. She knew in her heart where the limit was set, though she would have been profoundly embarrassed to have had to define it aloud.

'It's very strange of Ian to behave like this,' she said, pursuing her own train of thought rather than the course of their conversation. 'I was surprised that he came out here in the first place: as if he took no interest in the child and wasn't really glad that it was coming. It doesn't seem natural somehow. ... And I thought they were so happy together, he and Cynthia. They've only been married four years, and they have such a nice little home.'

'It will pass.' Frau Franck spoke with assurance, having a deep comfortable philosophy of the eternal rightness of things; her own life had been so ordered in its progress, so successful within its chosen limits, that she could only think of misfortune as the outcome of real villainy, and thus as something which could never touch the Carrington family.

'We must have patience,' she went on, drawing from the same miraculously uncloyed fountain-head. 'The baby will arrive, and your Ian will change, as all young men change. You will see how he settles down, and what a real young father he will become.'

That seemed fair enough. ... But Mrs Carrington, with her suspicion that Ian's leaning towards real young fatherhood was already out of hand, would not be comforted.

'I hope you are right,' she answered mechanically. 'If only he didn't seem so preoccupied with the girl. It's not as if she was really pretty, either. I cannot,' she went on, true to tradition, 'imagine what he sees in her.'

'We know what tricks there are,' said Frau Franck, darkly and untruthfully. 'But I tell you, the little baby will change everything, and you must stop worrying and enjoy the rest of your holiday. And now here we are, and there is Mr Carrington all ready to have tea with you.'

She smiled brightly and competently, exchanging professional for human contact, turning aside towards her own sitting room. 'Good-bye, and thank you for our little walk. It was most pleasant.' And Mrs Carrington, with the feeling that she was being 'managed' out of a justifiable anxiety, was left alone once more.

In the hall Mr Carrington came forward to meet his wife, stamping his feet loudly and heartily to rid them of the snow. Behind him the head porter, surveying the result apathetically, reached for his brush and dustpan with a certain feudal lassitude: the phrase 'the eternal snows' had for him only an indoor significance.

'Well, my dear,' said Mr Carrington, at the top of his not inconsiderable voice, 'had a good time at the jumps? Or did you hide your eyes as they came over? – I've seen lots of women do it, so there's no use denying – I can't understand what they go there for. Show off their clothes, I suppose, as usual.'

'Yes, I enjoyed it very much, thank you.' They walked through to the lounge, where tea was laid for them. Mrs Carrington looked round her inquiringly. 'Why, where are the others? I thought I'd be the last – we walked home so slowly.'

'You must have raced them after all. Did you see any of them at the jumping?'

'Ian and Denys were there. Not Helen, though: perhaps she's upstairs.' She began to pour out tea slowly, as if she were tired of the whole business of living. 'What did you do? Did you go luging?'

'Yes. Had a great time, too. You should have seen Jackson and me on one luge, coming down the Gilbach pathway.' Mr Carrington gestured widely, menacing the whole tea-table which was of wickerwork and unreliable. 'Went like the wind, absolutely like the wind. 'Course, we came a bit of a cropper at the end – some fool of a woman walking up, not looking where she was going, and we had to cram into the hedge. Still, it's a great sport.'

He drank some tea, and then sighed, repeating 'A great sport' as if he were now less sure of it. He had a stiff shoulder and a sizeable bruise on his elbow, and was wondering if he weren't getting a bit too old for that sort of thing. Every year he had exactly the same adventures and seemed to hurt himself just a little more each time.

'You ought to be more careful,' said his wife, echoing his

mood as long domestic practice had taught her to do. 'They sometimes have nasty accidents. Do you remember that man, Colonel somebody, who ran into the horse just outside the post-office?'

'I remember what the horse looked like after he'd done it.' Mr Carrington laughed titanically at his own answer, which, as the horse had had to be destroyed, was not a particularly kindly one. 'Oh, there's no danger in luging as soon as you've had a bit of practice.' He paused, looking round the room with an air of furtive caution rather overdone, like a conspirator in a weekend charade indicating 'D' for 'danger'. Then: 'Did you say Denys and Ian were together at the jumping?'

'Part of the time, yes. ... That – that girl was with him, too.'

Since this was what he had wanted to find out, and it had been thus gratuitously handed to him, Mr Carrington first looked pleased and then, recalling the majestic importance of the subject, preternaturally solemn.

'Oh yes?' he answered interestedly. 'Queer girl, that: can't make her out sometimes – behaves as if there was no one else in the hotel, no one to watch her at all. Not much shyness about these young things nowadays. They don't seem to mind who's looking on. Still, she's Ian's choice, not mine.'

Mrs Carrington shot up in her chair as though treacherously assailed in some schoolboy fashion. '*Ian's choice?* Whatever are you talking about, Henry? There's no question of choice at all. She's just someone he's met out here.'

'Sure, sure – as long as you're satisfied,' said Mr Carrington ambiguously. 'All I said was that she's a bit queer, and there's nothing criminal in that. A lot of us would be in jail,' he enlarged, with fine detachment and absolute truthfulness, 'if there was. But I thought you were worried about it. You said the other night—'

'Of course I'm worried about it.' So rarely did his wife interrupt him that he was caught quite off his guard and wasted a good deal of tea in his saucer. 'He's behaving exactly the same as before, although you had a talk with him, didn't you?'

Mr Carrington nodded without conviction, aware that the talk had been quite ineffectual. He had embarked on the subject bravely, with a fine manful heartiness, but Ian had stalled him at every point, so that he had never been able to frame a vital question.

'We had a talk, yes,' he allowed, 'and he said there was nothing in it and we weren't to worry about it any more.'

She shook her head. 'That may be so, but it *looks* so bad. You know what the Jacksons were saying last night, hinting all sorts of horrible things. And Frau Franck, just now, was saying how sorry she was that the Collier girl couldn't be sent away from the hotel.'

'Was she, by Jove? That sounds pretty definite, doesn't it? Do you mean,' he leant forward and lowered his voice, so that all the room must have known that their conversation was intimate and probably scandalous, 'do you mean she's found out something?'

'Of course not – there's nothing to find out,' answered his wife, with only moderate conviction. 'But naturally she's sorry that they're attracting so much attention, and so wants to help us all she can.'

'Can't do with a scandal, you know. Look pretty queer if this girl disappeared suddenly. ... Besides, she might object – kick up a fuss and land us all in the soup. By the look of her she's an independent sort of girl.' His mind ran vaguely on blackmail. 'If she turned nasty we'd be in a pretty queer position.'

'Well, she's not going to disappear – for which I'm very sorry. But I do think you ought to speak to Ian again: he really mustn't go on being so thoughtless. It's upsetting our whole holiday.'

This was clearly not to Mr Carrington's taste. 'But what can I say to him?' he asked almost plaintively. 'I've no facts to go on – he gave me his word last time that everything was all right, and he'll say the same this time. It seems hardly fair to keep on badgering him like that. ...'

He brightened suddenly, took a mouthful of éclair, disposed of it within two richly-filled seconds. Then he went on creamily: 'Why not have a word with him yourself – quite independent of me, as if we hadn't been talking about it – say you've been worrying over the gossip in the hotel, and about the girl's reputation too. He might see sense if you put it like that. And it's true, in a way, too: it *is* very bad for her, however little she cares about it.'

Mrs Carrington pondered the idea, as she emptied out the last of her tea-leaves preparatory to that third cumulatively refreshing cup. 'I'll think about it,' she said at length. 'I might see what Helen has to say about it first.' Unused to moving alone, she wanted to gather all the possible allies.

'That's the way – no sense in rushing it and upsetting us all.... I know – what about New Year's Eve?'

'Whatever do you mean?'

'Well, why not wait until then, and put it that way? – New Year – turn over a new leaf, make us all happy.'

She stared at him. That sort of cowardice was quite foreign to his nature. Ian must have given him a difficult time. 'But the holiday will be nearly over by the New Year.'

'So much the better,' he rejoined, with entirely bogus brilliance. 'That'll solve the whole thing, won't it? ... Yes, I like the New Year idea. And he's a good boy: he'll see it like that, I'm sure.'

'I hope so.' Her hand poised over the tea-pot, she frowned. 'Oh dear, I don't know why all this is happening to us. The other years have been so different. All this unrest. ... Why can't people be normal like they used to?'

'Just growing pains, I suppose.' He patted her knee. 'Or perhaps it's you and me, eh? – getting old, getting out of touch.'

Privately she wondered whether Henry had ever been *in* touch with such ideas, and if so whether it was worth worrying about.

'Perhaps,' she said rather fearfully, 'we ought to give up these family holidays. It's not as if the children were young any more.'

'What, give up Adelboden? – after nine years?'

The nine years had really been her reason for making the suggestion, though spoken like that they seemed to render imperative yet another nine in the same mode. But it was perfectly true that taking their holidays together was not always the success it had been in the old days: there were maladjustments, there were quarrels, there was obviously much more than one collective family will. . . . It was inevitable, the most natural development of all; but it was the passing of something which she had known and loved, and she mourned it in her own secret fashion.

Then presently Denys and Jill came in together – a final abnormality, which quite spoilt her last cup of tea. 'Denys too?' she thought as she eyed them over the rim. Really, it wasn't safe to leave the girl alone with anyone. Fancy poor little Denys coming under that grown-up spell. . . . Why, he was hardly eighteen, he probably didn't know about things at all yet.

CHAPTER XII

'Poor Helen,' said Helen, and ordered, for the fourth time, her last side-car before dinner.

Poor Helen, with so much that was unsatisfactory swamping her whole existence: poor Helen, perpetually holding the dirty end of the stick. . . . It was not, she argued to herself plaintively, that Adelboden was such a bad place, even when one was alone in a hotel bar at a quarter to seven in the evening: it was really quite a good place, if its population behaved as they ought to, without malice or lust or communicative nervousness. But they seldom paid any attention to these basic rules: at the moment malice coloured the hotel's gossip, lust ruled everywhere save the ground floor, nervousness was making a fine hash of her family: hence her discontent, her limitless frustration, her tears of boredom.

This was New Year's Eve, traditionally gay, actually abysmal; and she had already been alone all day, and, except for the sensationally Gala Dinner which would shortly be upon her, it looked as if she would be alone for the rest of the evening. And that, she reflected idly, completed the round, the full circle of boredom, that disposed of the twenty-four hours – she always *was* alone all night: that was something that never did alter. . . .

Perhaps that was the whole trouble, perhaps it was that

which must first be taken in hand and dealt with – with which thought, and a sudden lowering of her cocktail such as made the girl behind the bar wince with apprehension, she came back to the core of her dissatisfaction.

It was, of course, Denys. Denys had faded out in the most alarming fashion during the last few days: it seemed as if, like a doctored cat, he just hadn't the nerve to show himself around the place. . . . The two of them had quarrelled, of course, and the quarrel had never been properly made up, phrase for phrase and excuse for excuse so that nothing of it lingered; but that alone couldn't account for the way in which all Denys' interest had evaporated, the way in which he just wasn't *there* at any time – after lunch, or during the evening, or at such moments as this, when she could have done so well with a companion.

It was such an unlooked-for change – it had always been taken entirely for granted that they spent all their spare time together: by mutual agreement they were each other's exclusive entertainment, and he had seemed to be enjoying the arrangement until this strange lapse; now she felt that he was failing in his contract, that she was entitled to some tangible consideration in lieu of notice. . . .

But (a new thought struck her) perhaps he was disappointed in her, perhaps she had misunderstood him all along and he really wanted her and had despaired of getting what he wanted – it would be just like him, she knew, to back out of the picture altogether at such a point – not sour grapes, but a sort of acquiescent pride which became him far better than would any hot pursuit. Standing out from all the cut-throat, stroke-cheek mob, he could get his effects by disclaiming all wish for them. . . . But if that were true, if that were all that stood between them, then the solution was straightforward, attractive, and far from impossible.

Far from impossible, save for the fact that he was never with her nowadays except for meal-times – and even then his appetite was indifferently small. It was impossible to attract someone whose eyes one could never meet. . . . She felt pretty sad about the whole thing and it wasn't all side-car: she had put a lot of things in pawn with old Uncle Denys, and now he himself had contrived to walk off with the ticket – apparently unconscious that he had it, which was the most damnable part of all.

How he was filling in the time, she had no idea; but obviously there was a bad leakage somewhere – perhaps drink, for if it was another girl he was keeping her mighty quiet.

Which was more, she reflected weightily, than could be said for some other people: if Denys made no show at all, that didn't mean that the public went without entertainment. For Ian was now giving a practically continuous performance as the Great Lover: he and Jill had become a self-contained (or perhaps a not very self-contained) community of two, and the spectacle was free-for-all – indeed, that morning Helen had actually met him coming downstairs from the second floor as she went along to her bath. One of the chamber-maids had given him a particularly sprightly good morning. . . . Obviously he didn't give a damn what anybody thought, in the heroic tradition – which was all very well for the heroes themselves, but a burden for those who had to stand by and clean up the mess.

She herself had greeted him with an ironic cheer which covered up her nervousness: an open parade of the tiles was all very well, but if either of the parents had seen him, that would have been the end of *that* holiday. As it was, a bulletin probably went straight down to the Francks.

Jill looked well on it, of course, exhibiting that flushed sparkle, that glow of completed exhilaration which she herself had never been able to achieve; and the fact that (as she guessed) not only Ian but anyone else would have sufficed to give it her did not alter the case or make it less disturbing. Rather aggravated it: for it meant that Ian in the near future was going to be made unhappy – he would be dropped, he would have to go back to Cynthia who, with the mocking addition of a child, would be his whole and sole future. ... And Helen, being fond of Ian, knew that she would rather anything happened to him than a freezing dying anti-climax of that sort.

She drained the last of her drink, noted the time (which was seven o'clock) and prepared to take her leave. They were not changing for dinner that night: there was a fancy dress dance after it – the event of the hotel year – and it was understood that the energies of toilette-making could be held in reserve for that.

Her own costume was to be a simple one, involving a flame-coloured silk brassière and part of a grass skirt: planned a week ago with an eye to the greatest good of the greatest number (and a powerful glance at Denys) it had by now lost all attraction for her. And so many people would make fatuous jokes about that grass skirt, jokes about hay-making and sunshine, about borrowing a mowing-machine, about Hula-girls. . . . Still, Denys would be at the dance too, probably disguised as the rough side of a tongue; and in any case she would put on her dress, aimlessly, as she had come into the bar aimlessly, because even if Denys took no notice of her it was the nearest thing at hand, the easiest thing for her to do.

No, that wasn't quite true about the bar: her hour's session there had been no idle time-wasting, but a matter of necessity. The bar had been a bolt-hole, a refuge, the only place where her mother wouldn't think of following her. For throughout that day her mother had been cornering her at odd intervals, to talk to her about Ian; it was clear that she was extremely worried about the whole thing, and clearer still that she thought Helen ought to do something to help.

What that something was, had not come to light: her mother spoke vaguely of 'using her influence', of 'bringing Ian to his senses', even of 'having a little chat with the girl' . . . That was a grossly unfair suggestion, that was one of the less tolerable parent-tricks – the way they treated you as a child, consistently ignoring your own view-point for years at a stretch, until there was some stroke of dirty work to be done, when they co-opted you quite shamelessly and expected you to jump their hoop or roll their log at the crack of the whip.

That was it, exactly – a circus with all the performers drilled to uniformity, with a sign over the door: 'All done by kindness', with not even the smallest waggiest little dog allowed to misbehave. That was their family life. Walk up and pat the Shetland ponies – their manes are curled, their hooves encased in velvet, their teeth drawn. . . . But it wasn't always workable, as she had straitly told her mother; and in this case there was nothing she could do, family or not, brother or not, Cynthia, scandal, arrant immorality or not. Lovers' knot or not, in fact and ha ha . . .

And when her mother persisted Helen had merely told her, in so many words, to do it herself: knowing that she would make a warm parental mess of it, putting forward a hesitant protest which Ian would stem, mop up, and hand back in the neatest, politest way imaginable. He had an elegant way with official opposition: and, even if his elegance deserted him and he found himself in the wrong, it was his game anyway, because he had done exactly what he wanted and the holiday was nearly finished. The boys always seemed to handle things better than the girls. Of course biology was on their side.

She stood up, and nodded to the girl behind the bar; and then, as luck would have it, Mr Jackson came in, wearing a pirate costume with such an unnatural air that he would have been shot for passive insubordination on any pirate ship afloat. (Or, if not shot, at least perpetually suspect. One could imagine the sneers in the fo'c'sle, the open hints that Jackson wasn't a pirate at all, that he had just come for the trip, that he was the Captain's favourite who got drunk on the smell of a cork and would faint at the sight of blood. Yah pansy! Yo ho ho and a bottle of bay-rum. Have his bags, boys – he doesn't need them.)

'What's this?' he cried on the instant as he caught sight of Helen. 'No fancy dress? Aren't you joining in the fun tonight?'

'Of course I am,' said Helen defensively. 'But I don't want to change until after dinner. It means such a long time sitting about doing nothing.'

'Afraid of catching cold, hey?' As usual, he underestimated the force of his grip on her arm. 'I know what you girls are when it comes to fancy dress – a few bits of rag here and there, a string of beads maybe, and you think you're ready to go anywhere.'

'Oh, I think my costume's quite adequate.'

'Then I bet you won't be wearing breeches like these,' said Mr Jackson indelicately. 'Made for one of these athletic young chaps, I should say – all leg and no – er – no room,' he concluded primly. He looked towards the bar. 'Had your drink yet? How about another?'

'No, I don't think I'll have another, thank you. As a matter of fact I was just going.'

'Oh, come on – New Year's Eve, you know – no harm in being matey, once in a while.' And then, remembering his standing joke: 'Denys isn't likely to be along yet awhile, and I'll square it if he does turn up.'

Meekly she suffered herself to be led back to a table, and confronted yet once again with a side-car: she felt herself quite unable to make her escape without being rude or unsociable, and it did not seem that she had sufficient energy even for that. Behind the bar the girl sat frowning, in doubt as to whether or not she was being loyal to her sex in continuing to serve Helen. For the latter had already been there for the best part of an hour, the brandy bottle was ebbing away like expensive bath-water, and girls should stick together, particularly when men of Herr Jackson's stamp were about. It was the usual villain's trick, to fill a girl up with hootch beforehand. Funny that books never said anything about self-filling girls who started a good half-bottle ahead....

'Well, well,' exclaimed the latter, quickly halving his whisky-and-soda, 'here we are again, a year older and a year wiser. Thought up any good resolutions yet?'

Helen smiled. 'One or two – the usual ones, you know. Less drink, more think.' She'd only just thought of that and it sounded quite funny.

'Think, eh? Strikes me you girls do a bit too much of that nowadays – doesn't give the fellows a chance.' Helen pondered, but was unable to interpret this save in terms of extreme masculine unworthiness. Or else of some calculating strategy – the Equation of Disappointment: Think before you Leap = No Leap = No Fun at All for The Fellows. Therefore don't think, girls: I'm here, and Euclid's been dead a long time. 'Think? Well, well ... And what about the rest of the family? Does Ian turn over a new leaf, too?'

Helen laughed to herself, recognizing the poke-nasal twang of the bow-at-a-venture. That was why he had joined her, that was really all he was interested in – it ranked Number One Scandal for everyone in the hotel, and he wanted to keep up to date.

'I suppose he does, like everyone else,' she answered tranquilly. 'Do you think he needs to?'

'Well, as a matter of fact,' he exchanged the hearty for the confidential with barefaced facility, 'I rather thought he was kicking over the traces a bit. Nothing serious, of course, and he's got a right to enjoy his holiday, but that's not to say that everybody thinks the same as me. Not by a long chalk. One way and another, there's been a bit of talk, as you can guess.'

'What about?' asked Helen obtusely.

'Why, this girl of course.' It was clear that Mr Jackson had discussed the subject so exhaustively with everyone with whom he had come in contact that he could not understand Helen being uninformed about it.

'Don't say you haven't noticed him and the Collier girl all over the place together?'

Helen decided to do a little exploring. 'I don't think I *have* noticed anything very special – you know I'm down at the rink all day. What's been happening?'

He looked at her suspiciously, trying to decide whether she was serious or not. 'Why, those two go everywhere together. … Another whisky and another side-car please, Fräulein. … I was talking about it to your father only yesterday. And the Van Geysels, *and* old Novak – blind as a bat he is, but he'd noticed it all right. By the way he was talking you'd think he'd been cut out by Ian and was trying to get a bit of his own back.'

'Well, well. … And what did my father have to say about it?'

'Oh, nothing much, though I know he's worried about it, like everyone else.'

Thus did he gloss over the fact that Mr Carrington, taken by surprise, had sent him away with a resounding flea in his ear, and that relations in that quarter would probably have become distinctly strained were it not for the incidence of New Year's Eve.

'She's a pretty girl, you know – bound to attract attention.

And of course it can't come to anything between them, can it, him being married and everything?'

'Of course not,' echoed Helen. 'It's out of the question.'

'Fearful places for scandal these hotels. That's why I thought I'd mention it, see? – might save a bit of trouble if you had a talk with him on the quiet.'

'What, another one?' But she did not say it aloud: she wanted to keep her pose of ignorance; there was a perverse satisfaction in getting, at second-hand, information on something which she knew back to front already. And evidently the hotel was not entirely up-to-date in its facts, though at the present rate the final revelation could not be long delayed. She sipped her drink thoughtfully, mourning the essential triviality of the subject, wishing that Denys was by her side with the clock put back about two days. All her excitement nowadays seemed to be obtainable only at second-hand: all the fun, all the colour and significance of life seemed fated to go to other people.

Mr Jackson surveyed her face anxiously, trying to interpret its lack of expression. 'Not annoyed, are you?' he asked after some moments of silence. 'Just thought it would be for the best to mention it to you.'

'Of course I'm not annoyed – I know you want to help.' This was the easiest way to bring the session to a close. 'But I must have a talk with Ian if it's as serious as you say. I don't think for a moment that there's anything in it, but he ought to be a bit more careful – naturally he can't appreciate the effect it has inside the hotel.' She stood up. 'Time I was getting ready for dinner. I'll see you afterwards, of course?'

'You bet.' He was beaming now, convinced that he had effected a stroke of the rarest diplomacy such as no one else in the hotel could have conceived. 'We'll have a bottle of champagne, shall we? Just to see the bad old year old.'

'That will be nice.' The champagne would, anyway.

Denys, who had walked up to the far end of the village to view a reported eclipse of the moon which was actually due the following week, was wandering back to the hotel at a lazy, contented pace. Lazy because he had been ski-ing strenuously at Hahnenmoos all day, and contented because of the date, because tonight, New Year's Eve was the one night which couldn't possibly go wrong – all his plans were perfected, triply insured by that lovely smile he had encountered five days before. For of course his Alsatian girl *would* escape from her father, she *would* turn up and be as sweet and as tender as she had been before – and more so because tonight would be differently managed: he would really have her to himself, and all sorts of things – unspecified, undreamt, unhoped for – would happen of their own accord.

The five days' interval since their meeting might have been specially planned to accommodate the thoughts with which he had filled it – rising thoughts, very happy thoughts, thoughts which excluded all else save her image. And for them he was profoundly grateful to her, knowing that if he had not met her things would have been wholly different: he would have moped over Helen, he would have been worried about Cynthia, he would have been shocked beyond measure by Ian and Jill. ... But nothing like that had happened at all: with the triumph of this rival distraction, so far as these problems had been in his consciousness, he had been able to treat them impersonally, like the plot of an indifferent play which was holding no one's attention: they were there all round him, but so was the darkness when night fell, and when night fell one did not sit moping in the gloom – one switched on the lights and amused oneself agreeably. ... And she had arrived in the nick of time, and the last five days had been miraculously lit, with an increasing brilliance which no human agency could quench. He knew that he owed that to her: it made her the world's, and his, darling.

At which thought, as if to point his simile, he turned out of the dusk into the main street of the village; and seeing once again that curious friendly streak of light which marked its limits he felt himself doubly heartened and doubly happy. This was the setting with which he had also fallen in love. Each inn, each bar and shop had a focal brilliance, making its final effort to attract the passer-by: this was the busiest time of the day, when the town had swept and gathered in its full roll of inhabitants – from the outlying rinks, from the hills and snow-fields: and the whole street was a long straggling group of figures, variously coloured, gleaming under the arc lamps, talking in a dozen interwoven languages.

And as Denys strolled along loitering as idly as anyone else, the lighted windows offered him their various tribute, things smooth or useful or quaintly contrived: the fascinating sports shops with their array of equipment fit for the snow gods themselves – cunning ski bindings, polished steel luges, jerkins slashed with bright colours: the travel bureau, deftly insinuating with poster and model and photograph its visions of an even lovelier world just round the corner: the curio shops, full to overflowing with carvings, souvenirs, little metal plaques to be tacked to your walking-stick – '*Stock-nägel*' to the initiate – cuckoo clocks, musical bears – the froth of the tourist trade laid out to invite and trick the eye. . . .

Everything seemed to him alive, everything seemed brightly coloured and full of promise: threading his way through the groups of people, calling greetings to casual acquaintances, glancing into smoky, clamorous bars, he drew down deep within him a solid unassailable contentment which was, he knew, but the background for the secret joy to come.

Then, face to face with one rowdy circle of young men, he stopped and joined it, being hailed with extravagant delight and bastard phraseology: they were the people he had met the other night with the Norwegian, who himself was there, holding forth in a truculent manner in what Denys judged to be his own native tongue – a bluster of vague syllables having affinity with no other language. But he broke off immediately he caught sight of Denys, to greet him as a brother and to apologize for not having been round to see him before.

'They have been bad days,' he said impressively. 'I had to celebrate the ski-jumping, you understand, and next morning I felt not so good. So I stayed in bed, and most of the next day also owing to a mistake. And then there have been some more parties, because I meet more terrible people each day, and now,' he gestured to the group round him, 'we seem to have started again, for the new year. You will join us?'

Denys smiled at the inadequacy of the account, thinking of the contrasted ways in which the two of them had spent the interval: for the Norwegian, a period of coma, for himself an equal period of lively anticipation. Was it young to prefer, to a fantastic degree, his own method?

'I'm afraid I can't,' he answered regretfully. 'It's nearly my dinner-time, and after that there is a fancy-dress dance.'

'But later – much later. Meet us somewhere, anywhere in the village. Just say where and we will meet you, with girls and full glasses.'

'Well. ...' He made a show of considering the idea, knowing what different plans were actually in his mind. 'I might be able to, with that sort of attraction promised. Where do you think you'll be, about nine o'clock?'

The Norwegian waved his arm again, more vigorously, scoring two hats and a pair of skis. After cursing the owners' clumsiness: 'Perhaps the Français, perhaps the Adler: perhaps we shall be standing here in the snow, arguing about nothing at all. You can look for us: it will be interesting for you, you can give a loud shout when you see us.'

'I shall be in fancy dress,' Denys warned them.

'Good, that will be more respectable,' said the Norwegian obscurely.

'No, not evening dress – fancy dress. You know – *en costume*.'

Unexpectedly everyone, it appeared, found this a very droll idea indeed: loud laughter echoed down the street for some moments, startling the passers-by, making them whisper or frown.

'And what costume will it be?' asked the Norwegian as the noise died away. 'A pierrot? – an Eastern slave girl? We know what these affairs are like – the old ladies dress as *cocottes*, the old men as Don Juan. And they bring their costumes all the way from England, carefully wrapped up, and then pretend to have made them in their own bedrooms from a few old rags. ... Perhaps you do the same thing tonight?'

'I don't think I'll tell you after that,' answered Denys. 'Let it come as a surprise for you.'

The Norwegian looked at him closely, or as closely as his focus would permit.

'You are not angry?' he asked. 'Really, you can dress as a

cocotte if you wish to – we will understand. We only laugh because these costumes are famous – a joke in the town. You understand?'

'I understand,' answered Denys gravely. 'You shall see me, and have a real laugh for a change.'

He took his farewell, drawn by their friendliness into making promises for the evening which he almost certainly would not keep; but from the present temper of the party it was quite clear that they would not miss him.

Actually the evening had been difficult to plan out: the programme at the Schweizer was a dance, followed by supper at midnight, both of which he ought to attend, and the only solution seemed to be to give the dance a miss and meet the Alsatian girl then, returning to the hotel in fancy dress in time for the meal – a lengthy affair topped off by singing, speeches and intensive drinking.

From what the girl had said when making the date, and from her manner of saying it, it was obvious that she could not stay out very late: probably eleven o'clock would be her limit, and after that hour she would begin to get nervous, she would think of her father, she would keep looking at the clock and the magic would be broken. . . . But if she could stay out later than that so much the better for both of them: he would a million times rather spend the evening with her than at the Carrington supper table, no matter how prodigally the champagne flowed, and he could always make some sort of excuse for not attending – a headache, anything would do.

Then, for no reason at all except that he was thinking of celebrations, his mind went back to England and Cynthia and the baby – the baby which was probably going to be born tonight, which might have been born already.

All thoughts of it had been thrust out of sight during the last few days, but he knew the realization to be lurking in the background, only attending some interval or anti-climax to return in full measure. His knowledge about Jill and Ian was another cat waiting to pounce, a latent enemy from whom the eyes could be hidden just so long as there was effective cover; but when this was destroyed the old idea of resistance and perhaps revenge would assert itself, bringing to him a lust to prove his strength against the opposition – to pit his youth against the entrenched forces of evil. He was making the best of the interval, but an interval was the most it could be called.

A baby – New Year's Eve – new life to wash away the past and start four-square with the future. He found himself then, as he plodded through the snow and the chattering throng towards his hotel, hoping with all his might that Cynthia would have an easy time, that she was not in agony at that moment, that she would be spared pain to offset Ian's cruelty to her. He thought how awful it would be if, even as he walked along – *now* – she was suffering in the hellish way he knew women did suffer: for a few paces things glimpsed and remembered, vivid words and phrases, crowded in to rack his imagination; and then suddenly he had reached the end of his journey – the tail of street lights curled away uphill and out of his sight, and there confronted him at last, as the signature of reality, the crude glitter of the hotel and the great splashed tri-lingual placards: 'Aujourd'hui – Heute – Today – GRAND BAL COSTUME,' to mark another bloody year gone by.

That brought back the present, and the personal magic of the hour. For a little space Jill and Ian, Cynthia and her child, might wait: he had his own precious vision of contentment to foster, to cherish, to drink deep.

CHAPTER XIII

I

'Just a little drop more,' coaxed Mr Jackson anxiously. He wielded the champagne bottle like an Indian club, imperilling dresses, the table-cloth, his own coat-sleeves: Alois, hovering in the background, lamented visibly this incursion of the amateur into the orbit of the professional. 'Never did anyone any harm, this stuff didn't.'

'No, I don't think I'll have any more,' said Denys, very slowly and carefully. 'I've had lots already, you know.'

'Now then, young Denys,' broke in Mr Carrington. 'No shirking now: do your share and take a turn. ... Fill it up,

Jackson: of course he wants some more. I've never heard of anyone who didn't. What does he think it's there for?'

Denys, surrendering, removed his hand from the top of his glass and sat back, watching the bubbles as they gathered and clouded and swirled.

It was thus that, like two indifferently disguised *agents-provocateurs*, his hosts had contrived, throughout dinner, to load him with a variety of drinks ranging from Dry Martini to the present copious flow of Möet and Chandon; and thus that Denys, too contented with his lot to make an adequate protest, had suffered their ministrations.

Why they should be so eager over the matter was beyond him – it was still a long way to the stroke of twelve and the universal onset of gaiety: perhaps they had noticed his earlier preoccupation and decided that nothing must baulk the grand sweep of the evening; but whatever the reason, everyone had conspired to be charming: Mrs Carrington had continually beamed towards him, Helen opposite him was striving to regain the old standard, and, to top the display, alcohol had seeped in his direction with the regularity and the purposefulness of flood-water.

With the result that he had drunk an amount far greater than he had intended, an amount which, measured in terms of the approaching meeting, was in the wrong class altogether. He was as eager as ever to keep the appointment, but he had a vague feeling that it was even money whether he would be able to recognize his intended partner or not. And so far as he could remember she was unlikely to relish so adult an uncertainty.

For the rest of the room, dinner was nearly over, but the united Jackson-Carrington table, eating slowly and vociferously, was a good lap behind, causing a certain chaos in the kitchen (where they were eager to get dinner finished with and supper started) and also laying a formidable foundation for the evening's rejoicings. Indeed, it might even be that the foundation would prove out of proportion to the completed building: to keep up this pace, it seemed, would require a more than human staying power, or some emergency adjustment quite incompatible with dignity.

Most of the diners were still in their ski-ing clothes, but here and there an early Mephistopheles or a premature Gipsy Girl sprouted, forming a self-conscious target both for the general eye and for the small pellets of bread with which Mr Carrington signalized at once his patronage and his good humour.

Denys could not understand why it should be more satisfactory to throw bread at people in fancy dress than at people in their ordinary clothes; but it was a fact that Mr Carrington concentrated exclusively on the former, to their increasing discontent.

Jill was not down to dinner, and Ian, sitting with his family, was drinking sufficient to drown his sense of frustration – a thirsty if a transient emotion; while Helen occupied a place of some honour and more embarrassment next to Mr Jackson, who was now the abundant life and exiguous soul of the party. Of course it was New Year's Eve: but if this, she thought as she wiped the champagne from her dress, was a sample of what he could do at eight o'clock in the evening, then God (an unlikely visitor) help them all at twelve.

But still, the occasion was not all rugged despair for her: the side-cars were proving themselves a pleasant form of transport, and Denys was visibly improving in spirits under much the same steam. He only wanted a little coaxing to be back to the old exciting near-ecstatic form. ... And she still had in reserve her fancy dress, which she hoped would prove its worth without exciting notice and Heaven-knew-what verbal cracker from Mr Jackson ... Not that she minded a near-the-knuckle joke, but with her parents there she would be expected to display embarrassment, and the machinery for that had long fallen into disuse. ... Her skirt as dry as she could make it, she leant across the table:

'What are you wearing afterwards, Denys? Anything out of the ordinary?'

'I shall be a sort of Mexican,' he answered with great gravity. Gravity was rather fun: pity it needed so potent a backing. 'Outfit includes top-boots, velvet plus-fours, a liberal blouse, and one of those hats that catch in doorways.'

'Sounds good. There should be a lot of competition to dance with you.'

'To dance with me. . . .' He repeated the words gently,

unsure whether or not to tell her that he was going out. She looked eager, she looked as though she might take it rather hard. He decided to keep the news to himself.

'I suppose they'll have lots of those Paul Jones things,' he temporized amiably. 'It might be better to stay away.'

'I thought you and I had solved the Paul Jones problem. Anyway, the dance may be worth attending for a change: it won't only be the hotel people. Perhaps that Norwegian friend of yours might turn up. I should like to meet him. You're always talking about him.'

'I should think you'd probably take to him,' he agreed.

But oh dear, he thought to himself, how deeply I'm getting involved and how little I care. ... That carelessness was now, unfortunately, the motif of the evening: he knew that his balance was in doubt, or would be as soon as he tried to stand up, he knew that he would probably make the most foolish mistakes, and he could do nothing about it – even moderate drunkenness was such a novelty to him that he had no idea how to minimize it, how to conduct matters so that he betrayed himself as little as possible.

Still, that did not mean that everything was already lost beyond recapture: perhaps the Alsatian girl wouldn't be used to it either, and she'd be sweet and then he'd make another date with her, just a little bit ahead, and everything would be all right. If they sat still and he just talked a little and stared at her he might get away with it tonight. But certainly he was over-equipped for the gentle and secret meeting he had planned.

'Rather dishonest, don't you think, that Paul Jones technique of ours,' he answered Helen. 'The spectators get a bit tired of it too – they like seeing different couples and gauging clinches, and whispering about them.'

'They whisper a darned sight more about us. ... Anyway, I don't dance to entertain the spectators.'

'You can't help it. ...' It was a pity that this, the first voluntary compliment he had ever paid in his life, was exclusively a product of champagne and insincerity: that it was quite the wrong thing to say under the circumstances: that he was running higher and higher a bill which he had no intention of paying. ... If he had known exactly how high it was he might well have paused even at this stage: for Helen, taking things at their face value, was now pretty pleased with everything: she jumped ahead five hours in her thoughts and chose devirgination as the very nicest New Year's present. Connoisseurs with long memories might well have agreed with her.

The sweet was served, catapulted from the kitchen with servile resentment. They were the only people left in the room, and efforts were being made to apprise them of the fact.

'Don't you touch that, Denys,' said Mr Carrington unexpectedly. 'Finish the rest of that champagne: you've got a long evening ahead of you.'

Useless to protest, to say that the long evening ahead was the strongest reason for refusing another drop: the bubbles swirled afresh, his glass was filled, and he drank it dutifully before embarking on the *crème brûlée.*

Ian had by now disappeared, and his nearest neighbour was Mrs Carrington, who moved across to talk to him. The fact made him slightly nervous – he felt she would know immediately that he wasn't quite sober; but luckily she had just come there to talk, not to listen, and his mumbled responses passed merely for the inelegance of answering with his mouth full. And *crème brûlée*, she knew well, was a hazard for the most adroit eater.

Presently it was time to move and he stood up with the others: then he sat down again quickly and leant one elbow on the table. The ceiling whirled, shuddered and fell into place again. But whatever movement he made next must be essayed with far more circumspection. Simply to stand up was out of the question.

'I think I'd like an apple,' he said cautiously, in answer to their inquiring looks. 'But don't wait for me – I'll come through in a minute.'

'All right. We'll keep your coffee for you.'

Helen stayed and the two of them sat opposite each other, solitary keepers of the long disordered table, while he peeled an apple which he did not want. But seeing that he did not even begin to eat it, but sat there rather vacantly staring at nothing, she leant towards him again.

'Are you all right, darling? You don't look too good.'

He focused his eyes on her and smiled, still mightily contented. 'I'm fine. I felt rather queer when I got up though so I thought I'd wait for a bit and then go out by degrees.'

She was perturbed. 'What do you mean, queer? Ill?'

He touched the glass by his elbow, incidentally knocking it over. 'I think I've had a little too much of this. Your father was a bit pressing at times.'

'It's a shame – why should you drink it if you don't want to?'

'Oh, I don't mind.' He laughed suddenly, amused by the idea that she should want him to feel less marvellous than he did. He felt fine: and ready to tell her any number of lies.

'P'raps I'd better not start dancing straight away, though: I don't want to fall in a heap in the middle of the room. People notice things so easily, even on an evening like this.'

She nodded. 'You'd better rest for a bit and come down later. I'll give you an aspirin.'

He got up, very slowly this time: after a chaotic moment he found that he could stand easily and even walk, although his action gave Alois, looking through the service door, the best laugh he had had for a long time. When by easy stages they arrived at the hall:

'What about my coffee?' he asked. 'Perhaps I ought to put in an appearance.'

'I'll say you don't want it,' Helen answered. 'Go on up to your room, and I'll bring you the aspirin in a minute. And don't worry about the family: I'll do all the explaining.'

When she did bring it she kissed him rather sweetly and would have stayed, if he hadn't said that he would be better alone. He was really getting very clever at managing her. But look what the prize was. . . .

2

The first thing that Denys noticed about the Bar-Français was that it suggested a film orgy rather than a trysting-place: the room was packed, the atmosphere that of a stokehold, the noise stupendous. The second thing he noticed was the Norwegian, stripped to his not inconsiderable waist, conducting some kind of round game which involved the overturning of chairs in order to trip up one's pursuer. It said a good deal for the disposition of the room that he was exciting hardly any notice and no comment at all, except possibly from whichever women were glad to see that he had a smooth skin and no hair on his chest.

The idea of introducing the Alsatian girl to such surroundings should have been a scandalous one, but somehow Denys could not convince himself that it mattered very much. For she was coming there especially to see him and she would be able to disregard the people round her and look solely at himself; or, alternatively, she would enter into the full swing of the evening, and, short of stripping to the waist, would match even the Norwegian's high spirits and make it in truth a happy New Year. ...

Indeed, it seemed very important that she *should* do this: he had been counting on the meeting so much, and if she were going to be silly about the Bar-Français, if she were shy and wanted to leave, it would be almost as bad as if she didn't come at all. Tonight, at this late hour, he had no use for shyness, no sympathy with reserve; she must echo his own mood, or else be counted a dead loss. For if her perfection was in truth such as he had convinced himself, the quality of her environment should not affect her at all.

He launched himself across the room in the direction of the Norwegian's table. Here an immediate obstacle presented itself, for the band chanced to be playing a rather immovable sort of blues, and his way was blocked by a solid wedge of dancers, themselves with little intention of moving and none of letting him through; his passage was marked by struggles, by protests, by efforts to crowd him into the orchestra, by much laughter. ...

Presently he had effected a passage of the dance-floor and was among the tables, skirmishing with waiters, apologizing without hope of being heard, trailing unawares a great swathe of paper-streamer which played havoc with the glasses: the din, the close atmosphere, the effort of co-ordinated movement all mounted to his brain, there to mingle with the fumes of wine in a companionable if devastating confusion. ... To cap it all, the Norwegian happened to catch sight of his struggles and elected, out of the most patent devilry, to lead a sortie towards him, a spear-head attack which laid waste the tables like the passing of a hurricane; so that his final arrival, in a crescendo of laughter, bad language and breaking glass, gave him a notoriety not immediately to be allayed. People marked him down, people pointed him out to waiters as the young man who had done all the damage, people considered sending him large bills for crockery or shoulder-straps. . . .

Idly he wondered what exactly he was going to do when (as might happen at any moment) the Alsatian girl appeared in the far doorway. It would be a case for something like police protection if he were to retrace his steps: there were no police, as yet, and he could not leave her to fight her way alone.

When he was installed at the table:

'But what is this?' asked the Norwegian, peering at him. 'Is this fancy dress? It is very like the clothes you ski in. Did it win first prize? Will you give me a drink?'

'I'll give you a drink,' answered Denys, 'but it isn't fancy dress. I decided not to change until supper.'

'We are having supper now. Look.' He waved on high a length of *salami*, shaking it free of paper-streamer. 'A fine supper. How big a piece will you have?'

'No piece, thank you. Mine's ordered already.'

'You must go back to the hotel, then?'

'Later, yes. But I thought I would like to see how you were getting on: the supper is not until twelve o'clock.'

The Norwegian looked at his watch. 'Half-past nine. . . . In two hours perhaps you will think differently – perhaps you need not go back.'

Denys shook his head. 'I mustn't drink very much more. There is someone I have arranged to meet.'

'A girl?'

'Yes.'

'Hurrah! I thought perhaps you were not interested in girls, I thought you must have a very serious one at home.' The Norwegian frowned. 'I myself have a very serious one at home.'

'I'm sorry,' said Denys, rather ridiculously.

'Oh, I do not find it as bad as that. . . . But you must not go. We have girls here, more than we can use at one time. Just look.' He pointed. 'Margot, Ilse, Fräulein von Altmayer, and that one I do not know how she is called. I think she is American. This young man,' he went on loudly, 'wants a girl. Also he wants to go away soon. I tell him he need not go, I say you are all in love with him.'

But as none of them really understood, the news did not make much impression. There were vague pre-occupied smiles, and the American girl called out, 'Shame – throw him out,' in a not-caring voice; she was rather pretty, but menaced on all sides by two earnest young men both trying with all their might.

A Frenchman, who was sitting next to Denys and had met him before, suggested a drink instead of a girl – 'You wake up feeling better' – and Denys felt proud enough of what was to him rather a compliment to take his advice. (He was not to know that it was quite erroneous advice, due to a wish, on the part of the Frenchman, to put him at his ease, coupled with a startling ignorance of English grammar. On such chances do lifelong habits depend.)

Examining his neighbours, he decided that, alcoholically, they were all a good way ahead of him, and he did not want to spoil the party, even though he was only there for a little while. Everyone should respect the rules: it was like a game of sardines in a rambling country-house, where one defection meant that a rot set in from which the game never recovered until the gong sounded and beaters were sent out.

Then suddenly the band struck up an acceptable tune and nearly the whole party decided to dance: there was an empty chair next to the American girl, a chair signalling to him like a lowered eyelid, and Denys picked up his glass and wandered round to it. Walking, he noticed, wasn't getting any easier: the next section of the floor was always a little nearer than anticipated, and he would have felt safer if he could have had some trustworthy person to hold his knee-joints for him. But eventually he reached the empty place and sat down in it. She turned towards him expectantly.

'I hear you're American,' he started.

'Canadian. Your tie's crooked. Shall I fix it?'

She had rather a good voice, in the drawling class, but nice and ready, like an arching cat.

'Yes, please.'

She fixed it, carefully, taking her time. She had a warm skin and large brown eyes with fleckings of green and a shapely, an unavoidable bosom: she used a scent something like Lily of the Valley, only there was something else in it. He found that his mouth was just level with her hair but he didn't dare do anything about it: he wanted to lean forward but that would look as if he were trying to see down the space between her breasts, and after all she was only Canadian, practically English. He thought with a few more drinks he might do it, though.

She finished, but did not lean back; she said:

'There you are – what do I get for that?'

Not understanding, he just looked at her glass, and asked:

'Would you like a drink?' He saw the point of the question immediately afterwards, but then she was sitting back with one elbow on the table.

He said: 'Did you mean I could kiss you?' It was a very brave question for him, and a remarkably foolish one: her eyes, which had been mocking him, suddenly went cool and horrid.

'No, of course I didn't.' She switched away quickly to the other young man, but he had given up till his turn came round again and was looking at the dancers; then she let her eyes wander back, and saw Denys sitting so forlorn and ashamed of himself that she stopped being tough and turned on something else, something nicer.

'You're pretty sweet,' she said softly. 'But never ask a lady whether she wants to be kissed: the answer will always be the same, whatever she was thinking. Can I have that drink after all?'

He ordered it, thinking: I could have kissed her if I'd said nothing about it. ... Immediately he began to watch for other chances, but the effort of concentration was too much for him, and he soon gave up. When the others came back he stuck to his place talking to her in such a humble way that she began to wish she hadn't been nasty, even for that one daggered moment. Of course, he must be pretty juvenile or he'd have kissed her hair or something while she was fixing the tie. Even Englishmen, even Canadian ice-hockey players, didn't usually miss that.

Presently he said conversationally: 'As a matter of fact I'm waiting for a girl.'

She stared. 'Well, that's nice. ... I'm not keeping you, am I?'

Then she gave up altogether, and he saw he'd been truthful and therefore rude, and went back to the Norwegian, deciding after all that men understood him better, or would do so until the Alsatian girl arrived.

'A nice girl, isn't she?' asked the Norwegian in a stage whisper. 'Did you have a nice time?'

'Fine,' said Denys briefly. 'I think I want to go to the lavatory.'

'Do you feel ill?'

'Not yet, no.'

When he came back, both his head and his legs felt more vague than ever, but it didn't seem to have affected his spirits: he really was in terrific form, he'd drunk more than he'd ever done before and it was just making him feel better and better. He thought: I must have a good head, I must be a three-bottle man even now. Chaps who pass out must be fools, if staying conscious is as easy as this.

He touched the Frenchman on the sleeve, ready to explain how good he felt: then he saw the Alsatian girl at the very far end of the room, looking round rather hopelessly, searching for him.

He so loved her image at that moment that he could only remain where he was, staring at her across the heads of the crowd and the smoky atmosphere. She was standing at the top of the steps, and he had her body in view down to the waist: it chanced that one of the lamps fell directly on her face so as to form a separate pool of light suspended in mid-air. She wore green, with a touch of white at her throat: once again he drank in the oval of her face, the outline of head and neck so childishly and proudly set.

He knew that standing there she was yet quite apart from the room, that she was fresh where it was misted and stale, that she glowed while her surroundings were merely leaden. He knew all that – and yet somehow he did not want to take her away: he was enjoying himself, he had got used to the room and the noise and his companions, he felt that there was no real need to move on, that he could not break up the evening even for her. ... He bent over the Norwegian, and then pointed.

'There she is. I must go.'

The Norwegian followed the guiding finger, peered, smiled instantly. 'But bring her here. We must all meet her. She looks pretty.'

'She *is* pretty.'

'Then bring her here.'

Denys smiled in turn, said 'Well, I might ...' and began to move across the room in her direction. Progress was easier now, in the interval between tunes: a few people stood about talking on the dance floor, a few more overflowed from the bar, but he threaded his way through them without effort. The movement of his advance caught her attention and before he was half-way across she had recognized him; she smiled, a rather wayward smile which lit her face for a moment only, and walked down the three steps on to the floor.

To come near her suddenly was like drawing close to the fire on a cold day. ... When he was by her side he made as if to take her hand, but she seemed to shrink within herself at the gesture, and all at once he remembered that he hardly knew her at all, that the approach he had made to her in his dreams and thoughts meant nothing in their small formal acquaintanceship. ... Momentarily he had a pang of pure terror, terror that this was not going to go right and that he had been building impossibly tall castles on nothing but wisps of cloud; then he nerved himself, smiled, and spoke in that indifferent French which fell so oddly on her ears.

'I'm so glad you have come. Was it difficult?'

'No – my father himself is out, at another hotel.' That should have been a relief for her, but she was very far from being at her ease: her eyes kept going past him, glancing round the room, taking in here and there details which clearly worried her. He knew how very many of these she would find, he knew that soon she would ask if they could go somewhere else, somewhere not quite so grown up. ... He smiled again, striving to reassure her, and motioned towards the bar.

'Sit down here for a moment. Would you like a drink?'

'Oh no, thank you.'

That wasn't going to help matters, that was the code-sign of a losing sequence. ... She sat down, patently out of place on top of the long bar stool: as well might one have looked for a bowl of roses on the Nelson Column. And she wouldn't stop glancing about her in that half-appealing, half-annoying way, as if she trusted neither the room nor the people in it, nor even Denys by her side; what had before seemed a sort of dewy unawakenedness had now become rather disconcerting. She must know that there were other places in the world besides drawing-rooms and convent schools and nursery slopes. ... He tried once more to start the evening.

'Please have a drink. I've had one.'

'Yes, I see that.'

He stared at her – she was really so different from the other day, so prim and estranged; clearly she did not approve of drinking and thought Denys was rather horrid to touch the stuff at all. ... Then he laughed, trying to regain his contentment: she might be shy now, but she would warm up in a little while, and nothing could spoil her loveliness, nothing render that oval face unshapely or that skin anything but flawless. He gazed at her face until she became embarrassed and turned away; but in front of her was nothing but row upon row of bottles, and the man on her other side, swarthy and gleaming, was not of the sort to reassure the *jeane fille*. For a moment she looked so forlorn that Denys thought she was going to cry; then she said:

'Can we go somewhere else? I don't like this place very much.'

'Don't you?' He looked round it as if considering the matter for the first time: he truly thought it not such a bad place at all – it was noisy, but then so was the most dowagered charity ball – it had served him pretty well that evening, and it held a good many of his friends. He didn't want to leave it, and this reluctance made him imagine that she would get over her mood without much difficulty, so he only answered:

'Oh, it's all right – rather noisy, but that's New Year's Eve. Let's stay a little longer: everywhere else will be the same tonight. Come over and sit with my friends.'

'Friends?' She looked more unhappy than ever. 'Who are they?'

'Oh, very nice people. One's a ski-jumper.' That wasn't particularly reassuring either. 'There's a Frenchman, too. Do come.'

'I thought you wanted to talk to me.'

'So I do, but it's silly to sit here when we're not drinking.' He stood back from the bar with some resolution; as she got down from her stool he couldn't help watching her legs, and she became aware of his glance and blushed vividly. (Damn it, she must know that she had pretty legs, and that there was no harm in looking at them.) Without saying anything he took her arm and began to pilot her across the room; the meeting was so far from his expectation of it that he wished he could start all over again from where she had come in. No – it had better be from much earlier – six o'clock or thereabouts: things would have been very different if he hadn't drunk so much.

The journey across the room took some time: the noise confused her, the crowd of people was something quite novel and quite terrifying, but she hesitated to cling to his arm, she preferred death even to this small dishonour. . . . He realized that he should never have brought her here, but it was too late – even if he took her outside they could only stand about, rather foolishly, in the snow, because everywhere else was just like this, and anyway, he knew that once she left the place she would want to go straight home. Oh dear, he thought, and knocked over a chair: he turned to meet her eyes and found in them something akin to horror: she was now quite sure he was drunk, and had not the smallest idea what to do about it.

Then they had reached the table, which on the instant looked blatantly raffish. The Norwegian had resumed his shirt, but that was about all that could be said for him; he rose with an old-world courtesy as the two of them approached, bowed and sat down again in one unconvincing movement; at a first glance it was obvious that he had little control over his legs and none over his expression, which ranged at lightning speed from the infuriated to the vacuous.

Nor were the other occupants of the table any happier in their impression on her: some nodded, some laughed, a few whispered and then edged closer. ... Denys felt entirely at a loss: she was not less lovely than he had hoped, but how useless that was when the times were so conspicuously out of joint. For she would do nothing to help him, she sat there, silent, expressionless, unable to make any contribution to the party; if her dismay was her own secret, her antagonism was patent to all the world.

The Frenchman alone seemed able to do his best, asking her with some display of interest (she really was a lovely girl) whether she was enjoying her holiday, whether she could ski, how many times she had been out, but all to no purpose: he smiled too much into her eyes, he was not the kind of young man she was accustomed to, and her wary monosyllables sounded the defeat of all reasonable intercourse.

Gradually his interest flagged – one might amuse oneself for a few moments by playing fives alone in a quiet court, but one could not wait indefinitely for a partner to supply the returns – he began to look about him again, his phrases grew shorter, his hands restless. Presently he glanced across at Denys, twitching one eyebrow in a faint wink as if to say: 'I give up – she's too faithful to you,' and turned away to his other partner. At that moment Denys could not find it in his heart to be anything but ashamed of his protégée – she might be young, she might be hopelessly shy, but damn it, she could at least *try*. ...

As he himself was trying:

'Sure you wouldn't like anything to drink?'

'No, thank you.'

'Do you not drink anything?'

'Sometimes.'

'Did your father object to your coming out?'

'Yes.'

'Really? What did he say?'

'He said I was not to be too late or he would come to fetch me back.'

That would be a fitting end to the evening, some square black-bearded Frenchman storming in to rescue her and threaten a duel.

'Well, we don't want that to happen. . . . Have you been ski-ing today?'

'Yes.'

'Where did you go?'

'To Gilbach.'

'Did you knock any one else over?'

'Oh no.'

'Do you remember running into me the other day? I was very surprised.'

'Yes.'

But where *was* the girl of the other day, smiling and vital and friendly as he remembered her? Would he ever catch sight of her again, in this or any other place? Or had he after all made a mistake? Should he rather have asked: 'Have you got a sister, very like you to look at? She ran into me on the nur-sery slopes. . . .' For only in her looks did she resemble that other dreamt-of heroine, and even that resemblance was be-coming obscured, misted and spoilt by her mute inacessibility. Of course she could hardly appreciate her surroundings, of course she was suspicious about the amount he had drunk, but it wasn't as if he were rolling about the room or trying to make love to her – he was doing nothing to make her afraid.

'You ski very well, for your first season.'

'Do I?'

'Yes. Do you skate at all?'

'No, I don't like it. But my father does.'

'Yes, I know. I imagine ski-ing is much more difficult.'

'Yes, I expect so.'

That was the dead level of their conversation – jerky, dis-connected, embarrassing, entirely negative. He took another drink, looking at her covertly over the rim of his glass: if only she would smile, if only she would trust him and their surroundings just for a moment, just long enough for him to make some kind of contact. One joke, one snatch of laughter would be enough.

Out of the corner of his eye he saw the Canadian girl watching them, and he knew for certain what the expression on her face would be – amused, slightly contemptuous, wondering by what precise yardstick he had measured herself as against this odd little bundle of stage-fright. . . . He set down his glass with a rattle, frowned ferociously at the Norwegian who was reaching the singing stage, and turned again to his companion. There was only one thing more to be tried, one action which might retrieve the evening. After that he'd give up.

'Would you like to dance?'

'Oh no, thank you.'

'Yes, please do. The floor is quite good, and the band also.'

'But the music is just going to stop.'

'It will go on again – they play four tunes together.'

She was unconvinced, but she got up when he did and preceded him to the dance floor. This was as crowded as ever and they could not move very energetically: taking immense care, he held her loosely and let her hand rest unclasped in his, a symbol of his desire not to frighten her. But to be so close to her, and to be forced occasionally to press his body against hers to avoid the other dancers, brought back, with increasing sharpness, all the dreams and hopes he had built on this meeting; gentleness and diffidence were all very well, but she might surely be approached with other weapons; for she could be so sweet when she wanted to, sweet in that undefined way which would lead to a real companionship, to secret glances from those soft eyes, perhaps to kisses and . . . his arm tightened quickly and he drew her to him, using unconsciously those fierce movements which Helen had taught him and had found so rapturous in the teaching.

New discoveries crowded in to intrigue and excite him further. He learnt how small her waist was, how long and slim her legs, how supple her whole length from breast to knee – the music swayed, the roar of voices fell back, the lights rocked dimly through the close air – presently she made a small movement, a shudder which he thought was a stir of ecstasy, not seeing the white aversion of her face – and then the music died to nothing, the tempest in his blood abated as he relaxed his arm, and suddenly she was gone like the wind from his side and across the floor and out into the darkness, leaving him standing there, shaken, foolish in his defeated lust, near to tears for the lost sweetness he had so blasphemed.

When he went outside to look for her the little snow-bound street was quite empty.

CHAPTER XIV

I

Drawing near to midnight, the Carrington New Year supper, in spite of its two bleak spots, was going with a bang, or rather a series of explosions, the echo of which was never quite allowed to die down. And, no mistake about it, it *was* the Carrington New Year supper, the whole roomful of it – Carrington with a heavy shading of Jackson round the edges; the two families might form but a fraction of the total muster, but their joint table had taken complete charge of the proceedings, commanding a monopoly of the service, the cellar, the public eye, swinging the party this way and that as their own personal balance dictated.

The meal was not half-way through before the singing started, launched with resounding disharmony from this copious fountainhead; they were at the moment swamped in the intricacies of 'London's Burning', aided by such English people as were present and unself-conscious, and listened to with surprising good nature by the rest of the room, to whom the rendering must have been murderously atonal as well as incomprehensible. But the noise was not the only entertainment on offer, and even for the deafest mute the sight of Mr Carrington, with a bunch of daffodils behind his ear, beating time with a plate in one hand and the business half of a trombone in the other must have had a certain spectacular value.

The bleak spots were sitting side by side, in blank despair of the evening and of themselves: Denys, fresh from his defeat, could not bring himself to take any part in the turmoil surrounding him, could not rise above the level of his own desolation, and Helen had not yet recovered from finding out that, far from being semi-prostrate with alcohol, Denys had left the hotel as soon as her back was turned and had stayed out for over two hours.

By a mischance (for him) she had met him in the hall as he was returning from his expedition, but he had brushed past her without a word and gone straight upstairs, there (as she presently discovered) to lock himself in his room and refuse to make any communication. Probably he was too ashamed of himself to speak to her – but all that was nearly an hour ago, and he ought to have broached the subject by now, he ought to have realized what a beastly, what an *unnecessary* trick he had played her, and to have produced some sort of excuse.

The thing was fantastic: it wasn't as if she hung about him all day, or even got in his way to the smallest extent: if he'd simply said he was going out she wouldn't have minded a scrap, she wouldn't have asked him anything about it, queer though it was. But to pretend to be drunk like that – for obviously he had been pretending from the very start – and then to sneak out without a word, as if she were some sort of governess to be fooled and eluded – really it was too ridiculous of him, it was too childish altogether. Of course he *was* just a child, and she had been silly to think of him in any other way, and she wasn't going to, any more, no matter how sorry he said he was and how much he pleaded. All that was quite finished with: it had been dying before, and this final display of futility had killed it, whether he realized it or no.

Unfortunately, he was showing no signs of repentance, of pleading for her forgiveness, or even of knowing that she was by his side and very angry with him.

The tide of song swept and eddied over the room, each table and each nationality giving of its best, quite often with its mouth full. A French party offered (inevitably) 'Frère Jacques' and 'Au Clair de la Lune', the other residents attending at first in respectful silence but presently joining in, in a variety of accents mercifully obscured by the uproar; then a tableful of Austrian students gave a rendering of 'O du lieber

Augustin,' rounding it off with a folk-dance which got involved with the incoming sweet course and set that part of the meal back by half an hour. But save to the incurable sybarites the food was of little consequence: dinner had been on offer only four hours earlier, and now only noise and alcohol were the essentials, with perhaps a little dry toast to soak the latter down.

Presently Ian looked at his watch, touched Jill on the elbow, whispered to her, and rose. 'We've got to go now,' he said to the table at large. 'We're detailed to bring in the New Year. See you in a few minutes – and do cheer, otherwise we'll feel the most awful fools.'

They collected a small party of other people and left the room, while the excitement rose quickly as watches were consulted and compared: the two of them looked in fine form, thought Denys as his eyes followed them sombrely; by their glances and their close movement it was quite obvious that they were lovers, even without that insolent confession of Jill's which he suddenly recalled. A good many other eyes were on them, too, assessing, speculating, trying to pierce through to the truth. Poor Cynthia – perhaps she was being tortured by Ian's child even at this moment. What fiercer example of unfairness could there be?

With the instinct of conspiracy the noise died down as midnight approached: outside the door there were suggestive scufflings, and a peal of laughter followed by a loud 'Sh. . . .' Everyone stood up, glass in hand, as the clock began to strike and was taken up by a crashing cymbal in the hall outside; then the double doors opened and a whole gang of people came in, fantastically dressed – the Old Year, the Four Seasons, Ian as Father Christmas (a notable anachronism), Jill as an hourglass (no structural difficulty there), a number of unidentifiable sprites and skirmishers, and topping the lot a small unhealthy child borne by six men on a luge, peeping out of a cardboard egg and patently wishing itself elsewhere. . . .

At the sight of this last inhuman sacrifice cheers were raised, singing broke out again, healths were drunk: the luge wavered, the child bit its lips and blinked in the light: behind them all, half-hidden and wholly embarrassed, Herr and Frau

Franck bowed their acknowledgments and began to edge into the room to drink, as bidden, with Mr Carrington.

But here a variation on the accepted theme was introduced, for as they appeared in the doorway their names were called out by those nearest, and a moment later they found themselves being acclaimed by the whole room. It was a curious, rather affecting spectacle – Humility coming at last into its own: everyone present got to their feet again, glasses were held high, cheers and counter-cheers raised; and by the doorway stood the official management, jointly and severally overwhelmed with embarrassment, the hero and heroine of the evening – small, rather drab, their insignificant clothes contrasting with the blaze of colour round them, smiling and waving their hands, on the verge of tears at the force of the demonstration....

And as if nothing should be lacking to point the scene the band, knowing its job, struck up a lilting tune, at the first notes of which certain people here and there in the room stiffened to attention: there was a moment's indecision, and then a whisper which ricocheted this way and that like reflected light: 'Swiss National Anthem,' and everyone joined in, wordless – singing 'Ah, ah, ah,' with extreme enthusiasm, swooping at the top-notes like hawks going into reverse. ... It was a pleasant tune, like an old ballad or a hunting song; at the end it was cheered to the echo, with the fervour of exuberance if not of ardent nationalism.

'Let's sing that again,' said Mr Carrington as the cheers subsided. 'It's a pretty little thing.'

After various quite laughable mis-starts they did so, followed pantingly by the band, and cheered themselves again at the finish.

'Now then – what about "God Save the King"?' asked Mr Jackson promptly.

'No, I don't think so,' answered Mr Carrington. 'Bit difficult for the other people, you know: they mightn't know what to do. We don't want any unpleasantness. What about having that Swiss thing just once more? – everyone seems to like it.'

This time the band was silent, and the Swiss residents showed signs of rebellion – once was good, twice a decided novelty, but three times probably a studied English insult. ... But by the omission of 'God Save the King' the party had been saved from endless complications – it could hardly have compromised with current international relations without the 'Marseillaise', 'Deutschland Uber Alles', 'Giovanezza', and whatever melody the Dutch and Danish contingent thought fit to introduce to the gathering.

Anything might have happened: people might have put in Semitic crotchets and non-Nordic flourishes; people might have stuck their heads in the air and walked right out of the room. ... To insult no one during a round of national anthems needed a quick ear, a straight face, mobile thighs and endless endurance: and at this late hour someone would be sure to be found wanting, someone would sooner or later look up mildly to find himself encircled by a ring of faces black and swollen with anger. It only needed two sentences – a hiss of 'Stand up' and the meekest rejoinder of 'Sorry – thought it was just the orchestra playing' – and the accustomed massacre would ensue.

The Francks, rather moist about the eyes, sat down at the Carringtons' table and were plied with champagne; Frau Franck was next to Denys, and would have found it heavy weather if she had not been too tremulously exalted to notice his prolonged silence.

The little child out of the egg-shell, fairly twitching with relief, went round being kissed and murmured over, receiving sweets, spoonfuls of ice-pudding, salted almonds, slices of buttered toast; while its mother, a small embarrassed Frenchwoman, hovered in the background, fearful of the richly flowing tide but more fearful still of giving offence by trying to stem it. Generosity turned so swiftly to spite and backhand whispering. ... Presently, however, being refused a glass of champagne by an excessively mean old gentleman, the child started to wail and was led away to a decent obscurity before vital harm was done.

The old gentleman, whose bed-time was in any case long past, also retired, under a barrage of black looks and hissing reproaches. He was a Swede. It was, of course, just like a Swede to refuse a child a little pleasure on New Year's Eve.

Denys surveyed the mob and found it agonizing: it was out of his line at the best of times, and in his present mood it was unendurable – too boisterous, too noisy, too overflowing with song and paper streamers and hats and heartiness. And in his immediate circle was to be found the nucleus and the focal point of the gathering: the Jackson family singing again ('Three Blind Mice'), Mr Carrington playing hell with bread pellets, his wife looking very odd indeed in a paper sun-bonnet, Jackson himself leaning back at a perilous angle, trouser-legs as tight as the skin of his neck, and flirting with a Danish girl in plaits at the next table. It was all in the authentic tradition of the 'Old Bull and Bush' and 'Two Lovely Black Eyes'.

And nearer home things were in an even worse state: Helen, of course, was livid with him, and Jill and Ian (he looked round, and up and down the table, with a sharpening anger), Jill and Ian just weren't there at all – they must have gone out again immediately after the New Year entrance. ... Seeing which, and realizing its hateful significance – the two of them just couldn't be bothered with the family any longer, they only wanted to be together, in a proximity which social convenience did not permit – he himself got to his feet, uncontrollably driven to make some independent move. No one noticed him: only Helen caught his eye, inviting him to explain.

'I'm going out,' he said. His voice was low, and taut as his nerves were taut. 'I don't think I'm much good here.'

'Got a date?' she asked coldly. 'I thought you disposed of it before supper. Or is this just a picking-up expedition?'

He stared at her, for a moment unable to fight or answer the challenge: then his voice came in a little spurt of sentences, summarizing jerkily his hopelessness, his sense of defeat, his reaction to the brave good humour of a few hours before.

'Why are you like that? – even in this you won't help me.... Ian and Jill have gone: you know what that means. Why shouldn't I go too? ... Cynthia's probably having her baby to-night. Doesn't that mean anything to you? Can't you realize things, can't you see which is the right side? ... Why are you all against me?' And then suddenly, careless of his surroundings, blazing with anger at the sight of her cool, unmoved face: 'I hate you – hate you all – you're cruel, stupid and cruel – I wish to God I'd never come out here. And now I'm going, whatever you say – I've had enough of this.'

He was gone before she could think of replying, walking swiftly from the room, his shoulders hunched against its insistent clamour. Her mother stared across at her, seeing the manner of his farewell but having heard none of his words. Helen smiled back reassuringly.

'He remembered he had to meet somebody,' she called out. 'He was rather late.'

Mrs Carrington looked puzzled. 'But isn't he coming back?' she asked. 'We're having such a good time, all of us.'

'I don't know. Perhaps he'll bring his friend in. Don't worry about it, darling – he'll be all right.'

Of course he'd be all right, since he was off on his blind again: but that was the last she'd see of him that night. ... If only he didn't take things so seriously, she thought, life would be a good deal easier; she had planned such a different evening, and there was now hardly a chance of its coming to anything.

Perhaps it was her fault, perhaps if she hadn't snapped at him in the first place, when he stood up, he might still be with her, or they might have gone out together: it would have been nice to dance again as they used to, and, given the chance, she would have been so sweet to him, so very sweet and accommodating. But it didn't look as if she were going to be allowed a second opportunity: everything – her good mood, the side-cars, the brand new year – was going to be wasted after all. And even to cry over the spilt milk was no sort of satisfaction: that was not the way she had wanted it adulterated. ...

Poor Helen. ... She turned back to her glass, she started to flirt with the eldest Jackson boy; he was a dead loss, a sort of calf-bound edition of his father, but she might as well keep her hand in.

2

Considering that it was his first real pub crawl, Denys was doing pretty well.

By four in the morning he and the Norwegian had covered nearly every bar in the town: they had ranged this way and that, clumping through the snow, bursting suddenly in upon new lights, new people, new warmth and drifting smoke: drinking a little, making quick friendships and mislaying them again before they palled, and then crowding out to resume, like a marauding band, their journey and their search for a fresh thrill. They collected strange people in their train, only to lose them again within the hour: Denys felt sometimes that he ought to have kept a list of the hangers-on, a sort of New Year Roll of Honour to prove that the evening had been well and truly celebrated.

Personalities stood out here and there, vivid enough to remain in the memory. There was an American girl who went along with them for some time, slim and dark, lustrous as to eye, glimmering as to intelligence: she was memorable for the fact that when addressed, no matter in what fashion or on what topic, she would clap her hands and answer 'Goody-goody!' in a quick pattering little voice: a stranger might well have thought this promising material, but it presently appeared that these were virtually the only words she knew, and, as Denys realized after a time, they were only the same word repeated twice over. ... But in any case she got lost in a sort of genteel Sabine Rape in the Grand Bar: she was carried off shoulder-high by a muscular young man in a fez, she was laughing a good deal, and it was generally acknowledged that her last recorded words were 'Goody-goody'. Students of form were of the opinion that she might well find that she had said them once too often.

There was a pathetic young man in a fancy dress purporting to represent the Emperor of Ethiopia, but he had long ago lost the more authentic parts of it and was now just a ragged little chap with a dirty face. ... He was with them for some time, drinking copiously and paying nothing: they escaped him finally by locking him in a discreet apartment labelled 'Ladies' Cloaks' in four languages, and throwing the key into a brazier. There was a nice chap with an accordion, but he made too much noise (and, owing to the size of his instrument, kept sticking in doorways): there was a drunken Austrian student who talked politics continually, truculently, inaccurately: there was a middle-aged lady, betraying all the attributes of frustrated masculinity, who ought to have been ashamed of herself. . . .

Once Denys got temporarily involved with some young Swiss lads: they were singing a jolly lilting sort of song, and he joined the circle and it was that damned National Anthem again and he still had his ridiculous Mexican hat on. . . . The Norwegian rescued him after a bloody struggle which included a good deal of kicking not quite in the stomach and yet higher than the shins. They had to have a big drink to restore themselves, and Denys, ordering the wine, had a bitter argument with the waiter about how to pronounce 'Asti Spumante', and it went on and on and suddenly for no reason at all the manager was called and it turned out that the waiter thought Denys was saying it *wasn't* Asti Spumante at all and refusing to pay for it, and of course soon everyone was screaming at everyone else and they got off with half price which was a bull-point and only showed you.

And then it chanced that they went down the main street and there came upon something which had puzzled and worried them a little earlier, only they hadn't been able to attend to it – a tap running into a sort of drinking trough: it just ran and ran, it had been running for weeks, it would always run because it had no turning-off mechanism, and as they were trying to remedy this a kind of policeman darted out of the shadows and they themselves had to run and run, only they laughed so much that it hurt more than the most vindictive fine would have done. . . .

Oh, it was a great pub-crawl, thought Denys, picking the crusted snow out of his ear: he had hardly given a thought to Ian or Jill or Helen – they were somewhere in the dark background, but he was keeping well away from them, he was constantly cheating them out of their due recognition.

Then at one dusky little place they came upon some real friends, and among them the Canadian girl doing balancing tricks with half a plate which might well have been intact when she first handled it. She had with her her two original cavaliers, who were looking positively aghast at something or other – perhaps the crockery bill: when she saw Denys she dropped the plate for good and ran over and hugged him. That was a surprise, the first unsolicited hug of the evening, but there was more to come. She said:

'Hallo! I've been hoping I'd meet you again, all evening.'

'Me?' It seemed unlikely, remembering the way they had parted. 'Do you mean me? You remember me, don't you? You put my tie straight and nothing happened. Are you sure it's me?'

She cocked her head on one side, trying to get him in focus. 'Well, if not you, someone mighty like you.' She was fairly far gone, alcoholically: her hair was all over the place and she kept swaying and blinking at what faint light filtered through the haze; there was little doubt that one of her escorts would achieve his dividend by morning unless they killed each other in a duel first.

'Where've you been? Crawling all the time? That's a nice suit you've got on. Those trousers have got body-urge. Lemme try the hat.'

'Try the trousers if you like.'

'No, hat first – so that I can get the size.'

She put it on, but it fell forward over her eyes, and it took a long time and a good many people to convince her that she hadn't had a momentary stroke of blindness and that it wasn't liable to happen again any minute. But blind or not she seemed to have taken a fancy to Denys: she stood him a drink, for which one of the young men paid, she held his hand and put her mouth to his ear and whispered: 'I think you're sweet, I think you're swell,' over and over again like a kind of erotic wave rolling on and on and never quite breaking.

He was a bit bored at first, because at the earlier meeting he hadn't been able to think of her in that way, except momentarily, and the old habit stuck; but after a little bit he began to like it, he began to have the most entrancing thoughts and to wonder if he could somehow bring them true. One had heard of such things – instant attachments, adventures in railway carriages with palpable female spies. While he sipped his drink, which was horrible, because he'd ordered it by the sound of the name – Ski-Wasser – and it turned out to be Kirsch and soda-water, he thought of how he could cash in on the supply of warm irresponsibility beside him. It looked so easy: one only wanted to know the password.

But as it happened he didn't respond quickly enough, or else he wasn't really to her taste, or perhaps it was simply the hair over her eyes, for presently she lolled back in her chair and said:

'You're sweet, sweet but slow.' She repeated the words again, so that Denys was afraid she was going to start a new and inferior wave; but she went on in a cross voice: 'I bet you're thinking of someone else. I can tell when a chap isn't concentrating. I've met chaps like that, and bigger ones than you, too. Who are you thinking of? That dumb little girl?'

He frowned. 'What dumb little girl? The evening's been full of them.'

'And I'm another in the row? Go on, say it right out if you want to. I can take it – I can take anything that's clean and handy and not too intellectual. What I don't like is hinting and nudging and biting people in the neck when they're not looking.'

'But you were looking,' he said edgily. 'All the time. You never stop looking.'

'Well, I still don't like hints and nudging and whatever I said. And don't try and stall, anyway – you know the girl I mean. The one that came in – oh, a long time ago – at the Bar-Français. She wasn't having any, though, however much you tried: she left early and fast. She was about as much use to you as a mermaid with cramp.'

Denys got angry, very quickly and fiercely: it was like a surge of blood to a newly opened cut.

'I didn't try anything with her,' he blurted out. 'She was just a kid.'

'Sure, you made a good pair. . . . It didn't stop you, anyway. I watched you dancing.' She clasped her arms round the nearest young man, who in no way resented it. 'Like this, you were, only I can't act so rough because this chap'll go off the trigger. It was like this – all neck, and nothing to pay. I saw you: it was the only treat I've had tonight.'

Her words reminded him so vividly of the Alsatian girl

that he could answer nothing more: it was a long time since he had thought of his loss, but the hurt was fresh, the nerves waiting to leap at him.

'Pity she didn't come to hand,' his companion went on, her voice flicking him, like a spur on flesh already laid bare. 'You're technique wasn't bad, for a two-year-old.' She pointed out to the dance-floor. 'Something like Romeo over there, except that *his* girl's lapping it up and yours gave you the air.' Then she frowned suddenly. 'Say, now I come to think of it, I'm getting just about sick of that pair: everywhere I look, there they are necking like sin. It isn't polite. They ought to close it up.'

Denys, following her arm, found that she was pointing at Ian and Jill.

He gave a kind of gasp, as if taken unawares by a mortal blow. There was something in the way she had pointed the two out – as if they were the show piece, the Pride of the Garden of Love – which caught him cruelly on the raw, seeming to strip away the pretence of the whole evening and the armour of laughter with which he had warded off reality. He could carry the banner so far, but this was too much. ... As he relaxed his grip he felt come over him, wave after wave, the realization that he had been successively duped by everyone who had any concern with his holiday: Ian had gone his own careless way, Helen had lined up on the same side, the Alsatian girl had led him far into a spacious dream-land and there abandoned him. Nothing – no exhilaration, no determined pursuit of pleasure – could be proof against the bludgeon of this endless treachery; he was confronted now with the necessity of dealing with the situation realistically, of facing the concrete fact of his defeat, and of trying to amend it in whatever way he could.

He lay back, his eyes closed, oblivious at last of his surroundings. Surely there was something he could do, some blow he could strike to redress the balance, so that he would not always be the loser.

There was suddenly borne in on him, crystal clear, like an exact vision of right and wrong, the picture of what was being done against him and his code of honour, and what he had to avenge. A way must be found, for now, at long last, there must be help for Cynthia and himself; and there must be action of some kind also against Jill and Ian, against Helen, against the whole dead-weight of malice and stupidity that stood to their debit. ... For why should it be he who bore all this, who seemed to be taking the blame, in his own person, for every stroke of evil effected by the other side? He was young, young enough to be ignored or slighted at will; and thus they thought they could make him the scapegoat, the whipping boy of their own perverse desires. That was the established practice, and even when he made a break for freedom, when he tried to snatch some happiness for himself, it came to nothing, it was defeated out of hand; even the Alsatian girl, his own dear ally, had failed him when he stood most in need of her.

Then he paused, struck by a train of thought so dazzling, a glimpse of a revenge so unique, that he could not grasp the whole of it at once. He would think it out fully on the way back....

She had failed him but she had given him an idea, the best idea of the whole holiday; he could put paid to the bill with miraculous ease, he could teach Helen and all of them that he was not to be ignored any longer. ... Incontrovertible, true, direct, his thoughts came round suddenly to their logical conclusion: sweating, falsely calm, he stood up and looked round the table.

'I must go,' he said, quite simply. 'I've got a job to do.'

3

Helen, sick of her thoughts and her loneliness, had already given up trying to go to sleep when the knock on her door sounded. It was nearly five o'clock: through her shutters the light was beginning to strike down, cold and rather unfriendly, but gaining ground, outlining by stages the chairs, the ugly chest-of-drawers, the pile of clothes and the derelict stockings.

She had lain in the same position, first in darkness and then gradually aware of her surroundings, for a long time: sleep had refused to come, had retreated mockingly as she pursued it, and she had had only her discontent and her strange imaginings to take its place. And from these one tangible act emerged, taking shape before her eyes like a lowering thundercloud: the knowledge that there was really nothing to be said either for the past evening or for the whole holiday – they were both part of the same dead loss, the fact that, over Denys, she had entertained an idea incredible for her, she had played her hand wrong, and she had failed.

The knock roused but did not startle her: her recurrent sleeplessness was known to the rest of the family, and probably it was Ian returning at last and wanting to see if she were awake. She called 'Come in', and switched on the shaded bedside lamp, ready to talk or to listen to his account of the evening's amusement. Lucky Ian, to have so assured a source of contentment. ... But it was not Ian, but Denys who came in, who glanced at her without greeting, who shut the door softly and advanced to her bedside.

There was something odd in his manner, she recognized at once: he looked bottled up and slightly mad. She patted the bed and he sat down close to her: then taking one of his hands in hers she pressed it gently. She knew why he had come, and she rejoiced in it: he was sorry for the way he had behaved that night, he was ashamed of himself and wanted to apologize. But she didn't want him to apologize, she only wanted him to be sweet to her again, to kiss and make up, to rub his cheek against hers and say he loved the feel of her skin. . . . That was the full sum of any surrender she would ask him to make.

Stirred by her thoughts, she raised herself on one elbow; the bedclothes fell away at the movement so that he could see the thin stuff of her nightdress and the warm rounded body underneath. Still he did not speak, but sat as if meditating his next step; he could not know that she had made up her mind what this was to be.

In the pool of light her posed figure glowed and glowed, and inside his brain his thoughts glowed also, driving him on to fulfil his resolve. Subconsciously he noted that the amount he had drunk sufficed to overcome the hesitation he would otherwise have felt: his whole trend of action was shameful and alien to him, but alcohol had transported him to the room, and once inside his burning resentment would enable his plan to be carried through. ...

She had lovely shoulders; he stretched out his arm and touched one gently, to prove its loveliness, its divinity of texture. But for him there was neither lust in the movement nor pleasure in the contact: he had come there with the single thought of doing her harm, of completing a ritual revengeful seduction which would show her in what manner he could strike back when he wished; it was not possible to think of her as desirable when he hated her so.

He drew back his hand, and as he did so, and aided by the compliant play of her muscles, the shoulder-strap of her nightgown fell and her breast was revealed – the first woman's breast his eyes had ever rested on without hindrance and without concealment. He flushed quickly, moved in spite of himself: she looked down at her uncovered body, and then straight up at him: she smiled, telling him, as clearly as if she had spoken, that she was glad he could see her thus. And then she spoke for the first time, in the voice she had sometimes used when they were dancing or gently love-making; she said:

'You didn't really want to quarrel, did you, Denys? We're happier like this, aren't we?'

He nodded – the easiest form of falsehood at his command. And he wanted to avoid speaking to her if he could: he was no loving companion, but simply the instrument of punishment. ... His eyes left the bed and went round the room, glancing over the shutters, the light creeping in, the untidy clothes: at another moment he might have loved the intimacy of it, the unencountered secret novelty of its appeal, but now he was unaffected. He need take no account of atmosphere, and he needed no outside help, either; the driving force was from within. ... Her voice recalled him, breaking in on his detachment, reminding him that his task had a sensual element with which he must cope.

'Why did you come in?' she was asking. 'Couldn't you sleep?'

'No, I couldn't sleep.' And as he said the words he woke up to his present circumstance, feeling himself ready for battle. 'I thought I'd like to talk to you. Do you mind?'

'Of course not. I couldn't sleep either.' She knew that his eyes were on her breast again: she was conscious of a quick surge of heat within her body, a readiness to take fire from his own as he willed. 'Why not lie down here, and rest?'

'And rest?' Momentarily his heart misgave him as he observed her mood; but he knew that nothing could alter the fact that he would seduce her, that she was a virgin whom he would despoil. She might display a certain measure of welcome, but soon he would overtake it, and pass it by, and leave it shattered. 'And rest?' he repeated.

She smiled softly, secretly. 'Presently, yes ... Kiss me, Denys.'

He leant over, his hands on the pillow on either side of her head. She was very warm, very ready for him: there was perfume about her hair, and a pulse in her temple which beat and flickered against his cheek as if seeking release.

'This was what you came for, wasn't it?'

'Yes.'

But it was not. Why was she like this, why did she come to the slaughter as if she had willed it herself? It was agony to think that he might be cheated even of this revenge, it was agony that he was already committed, that he could no longer shape his plans to his own advantage.

Now she was leading him, stirring him towards her.

'I've got a lovely figure, haven't I? You do want me, don't you?'

'I do, I do.'

He was startled by the vividness of her body. Her breasts rose to him like flowers opening to warmth: she smiled mistily, as if knowing herself on the verge of great happiness; and suddenly his desire to do her harm was drowned in the other stronger flood of his hunger for her body. Now the liquor, which before had aided him, was playing him false, melting his will to a river of flowing eagerness. He was lost in its torrent: no matter if it was her triumph, no matter what its true significance was, there would be nothing like this for him, ever again.

He was clumsy and unsure, but Helen guided and helped him, seeming always to know so much more than he did. She removed his foolish Mexican outfit with gentle hands, stroked his smooth body, and brought him to eager passion; soon she had pulled him down to her, and was urging him on towards an earth-shaking moment of release.

Naturally he hurt her a good deal: but she did not mind, and later he was to be glad, savagely and secretly glad, that he had been able to do so.

CHAPTER XV

I

A peerless dawn, a fragile blue and pink sky, greeted his miserable self-disgust: closer to heaven than he deserved to be, he regarded it with humility, as if at any moment the sight might be denied him and his presence be dismissed as belonging only to darkness.

He had gone straight back to his room, he had dressed and left the hotel; and now he was walking swiftly, up the sloping track out of the town, away from human sight and human contact. A great silence hung over the whole valley, and the air round him was so magically fresh and clean that he felt himself to be a blemish on the morning, an evil element in the midst of a natural purity. No one with such a clinging burden of sin should walk in a dawn of such perfection. . . . And stronger than his self-reproach was a feeling of the most violent frustration; for he knew, beyond a shadow of doubt, that his plan had gone amiss and had been turned to his own discomfort.

Helen's eagerness should have been a strong enough warning; but the knowledge had come too late for him to act upon it. For how could he have guessed her true quality, how could he have known that even her own chastity was of no account to her: that the standard of Ian and Jill, which she had at first deprecated, was in fact her own? He had come into her room to effect what was to be the most cruel revenge he could think of, something which he hated but which would balance all that he had suffered since he left England; and she had twisted the whole thing round so that it had been his surrender and her triumph, his seduction and her achievement of it.

He had beaten down nothing – for that was to be the motif,

a conquering of opposition – he had not imposed his will in the smallest degree: even their actual love-making had been in the same mould – a pathetic awkwardness on his part, a loving accommodation on hers. And that was so far from his intention that the affair was now not even neutral, but another burden on the debit side, yet another occasion for taking a further revenge. To have his attack received and managed and turned into a childish wantonness brought the scales down against him till he must find relief or perish of shame.

He found himself wondering what he could have done to merit such punishment. For it *had* been punishment, the whole holiday, punishment prolonged and increasing: Ian and Jill had brought him a perpetual agony of mind. Helen had been a progressive disappointment, the Alsatian girl the torture of hope long deferred and finally overthrown.

There was nothing to set against it, no history of deceit or ingratitude: it had come upon him out of the blue, at the very moment when he had a tangible expectation of happiness. Nor was he at the end of it: for Cynthia's baby might precipitate immense complications, and Helen, it seemed, would be a reproach to him for the rest of his days.

Helen. ... His thoughts came back to her, as he neared the head of the valley and walked within the shadow of the great hills above. He had not the remotest understanding of her action, nor could he accept it as experience, as a *fait accompli*, and turn to other things. He had never considered it possible that decent girls could be like that: to his mind marriage was the *sine qua non*, the sole password to a sexual future.

There were girls like Jill, of course, but they weren't recognizable as a body of opinion – they were the strays by whom the orthodoxy of the rest of the flock was measured. ... It was the fault, or the justification, of his upbringing, that he knew nothing of any other code: the idea that young men and young women might have desires which it was legitimate to satisfy, without relating them to honour or 'cleanness' or a technical and incontrovertible chastity, was not yet within his grasp. He only knew that there were things that one could do at any time, and other things that one had to wait for; and if it had been remarked that the distinction was imposed for reasons largely tribal and now invalid, he would have thought it an unworthy quibble.

The irrelevance of tradition had never occurred to him: he sided by instinct with the close corporation, the strongest confederation of all – the Trade Union of Married Women – and their motto, 'Inside, or God help you', was for him as sound and as inviolable as a natural law.

He tried to puzzle it out. Was Helen, then, to be classed with Jill? Was it this that she had been waiting for, the whole holiday? Had she thought him a fool because he had hung back? There were so many questions, and he had so little to guide him and (it seemed) so short a time to act. For there were only three more days of the holiday left; and that desperation, that eagerness to hurt, which had driven him into Helen's room a few hours before, still burned for release – he must make another attempt, before the party was dispersed and his chance with it.

Helen must be counted out as a possible instrument: though by ignoring her and refusing to fall in with her wishes he might do something to off-set his failure. There had been no shrinking modesty, nothing of the deflowered virgin, about *her*: she had wanted him to stay till breakfast-time, she had told him how much nicer it would be next time ('I'm a pretty quick study,' she had said – whatever that might mean), her last words had been: 'Till tonight, then' ... He hadn't been able to protest, to say how much he loathed the idea of continuing the affair; she had taken his silence for shyness, and loved him the more because of it ... But there must be something else he could do; if Helen was no good, there was still Ian or Jill or the parents – a wide field for a plan, if only he could think of one.

At that he came to a standstill and looked about him rather vacantly, deep in his own thoughts. Though the sun would not be up for another two hours he could already make out the exact point, beyond the mountains, where it would appear: there was a lightening of the sky there, and the few small clouds were like dull gold where the approaching rays caught them. He was standing, he found, on a little promontory of rock at the roadside: above him the track wound upwards, below was the valley and the gleaming trees and a glimpse of swiftly running water.

From a chalet, almost hidden by the woods, a spiral of smoke ascended, mounting in a slow column till it was lost against the sky: there was the sound of an axe, too, breaking the silence, waiting for its own echo, continuing again as if fearful of losing time. The world was waking up; soon he himself must go to meet it, taking on its burdens again, playing his part in whatever fashion the circumstances dictated. And somehow or other he must find a way of dictating to circumstances himself.

He felt very tired, and afraid of the future: there was too much against him, and not enough help on his side. There should be some way, some simple stroke, by which he could square the account. If only ... He turned back and began to retrace his steps down the path to the village, pondering the rat-trap of his position; Care sat on his shoulders, Hatred walked by his side.

2

'But what I can't understand,' said Ian, striding resolutely about the room as if he were breaking in a pair of shoes, 'is why you chose him. Denys, of all people. ... Good God, he's only a kid.'

'He's nearly nineteen,' said Helen defensively. She was sitting up in bed, trying to butter a roll with one hand; a cup of coffee was steaming by her elbow. 'Getting on, you know. What were you doing at his age?

'Running after shop girls. ... If you can see any parallel, you're welcome to it.'

She smiled. 'Dear Ian – always ready with a kindly word. I wouldn't have told you if I'd have thought you were going to be difficult about it.'

'I'm not being difficult – I'm being surprised. God knows you must have been bored enough with being a virgin, but why pick on someone like that? You might have aimed a bit higher, if only for the look of the thing.'

'I thought I'd like to keep it in the family. If Cynthia is your heart's delight, there's no reason why her brother shouldn't be mine, is there?'

He frowned. 'It's important, you know, even if you don't take it seriously.'

'I do take it seriously. I'm waiting for you to say that I'm old enough to be his mother. Then I'll lose my temper. What the devil has it got to do with you, who seduces me? And why is it important?'

'Because presumably he'll want to go on with it, and it's going to be a bit more difficult in London.'

'Why more than with any other man?'

'Because the family will pay more attention to him, if it's obvious that he's hanging round you. It'll be more noticeable.'

'I should say it would be less – a sort of natural camouflage.' She stretched. 'Oh well, it's done now. And he's rather sweet, Ian. But whether he'll want to go on with it in London, I'm not so sure.'

Ian stopped in his tracks, and stared at her. 'You can't be as bad as that, surely. . . . Why ever shouldn't he?'

'I don't know. I've been wondering about him.' She frowned in thought. 'Sometimes I think he's gone a little mad, lately – really mad, I mean. He's changed so much. You see, he didn't want to sleep with me at first: I don't believe he gave it a single thought the whole of the first week. And then suddenly he walked into my room as if – as if he'd set himself to do something he didn't care much about. He was sort of impersonal, and rather frightening.'

'Just shy, I should think.'

'No, more than that.' Once more she frowned, wrinkling her brow, tapping the eiderdown restlessly: her coffee stood unheeded. 'Has it ever occurred to you that he might have a grudge against us – against both you and me? He was terribly worried about Jill, and he thought I was backing you up. At times he must have really hated both of us. It's just possible that he thought he was – well, punishing me for what I'd done, that it was his way of getting back at me.'

'Rather far-fetched, don't you think?'

'Perhaps. But it's a possibility, and it would explain a lot of things.'

'But he'd choose some more obvious way. He must have known that you didn't mind. It's not as if he'd raped you – at least, that wasn't your version of the affair.'

'He's old-fashioned in lots of ways: he may still believe in seduction as a fate worse than death.'

'Then I'd better counter with a riding-whip. ... And when do you suppose I'm to be punished?'

She smiled. 'Who knows? Perhaps today? You'd better pad your trousers, or whatever you do before a beating.'

Ian laughed suddenly. 'Well, as long as he doesn't choose the same punishment as he gave you. ...'

'That'll do from you. ... I must get up, I think. What are you doing today?'

'Going round with Jill, I suppose. I must practise for that race some time.'

She looked at him curiously. 'How's Jill going? Still interested?'

'Oh, moderately. ... She's a grand girl, Helen, and this holiday's been absolute bliss.'

'And after this holiday? Are you going to carry on with it?'

'I hope so.'

'Divorce?'

'Perhaps.'

'Of course, there's the baby, you know. You ought to hear pretty soon.'

'Yes, I'm expecting news any time now.'

She frowned, stirred by some instinct to a mild protest.

'Just how much conscience have you got?'

'Being married wears it out.'

3

Jill, reviewing her programme for the day and weighing it against other possible or imagined programmes, found that the result was a sense of discontent. Ian was all right in his way but it was a limited way and she had no patience with limitations: already it did not seem possible that their affair would outlast their stay in Adelboden. For in spite of his attraction, and the fact that he had been ready enough for adultery, she had found him at heart a conventional being –

he could still protest, he could still be shocked, at sayings and actions of hers which she herself considered wholly normal. When they were talking, she continually had the feeling that he was letting her down – in their companionship, in their community of ideas: she would indulge her imagination and he would pull her back to the mundane, she would speak of fearless unthinking loves and he would talk divorce and children – pathos caught at its nadir, its foolish details in sharp relief, its pants down....

That was not the sort of companion she wanted: she needed spark for spark, and a flame ready, without fail, to answer her own: she had no use for a wet-handled fire-extinguisher whose mechanism she did not really understand. Thus she had come to the conclusion that Ian would last out the holiday, and then be abandoned; but that was a routine decision, in the sense that it wasn't worth giving it any deep thought – he was only another slice of experience to add to the gathering store, just another male in her coffin.

In a way she wanted explaining, this girl – not to herself, certainly, but to the normal world, matching and hatching (never *vice versa*) and living by rule of a thumb which, where the conventions were concerned, never by any chance strayed within snooking distance of its nose.

Jill lived in a curious section of society, and she was at once the product of it, and its virtual leader. Her friends, drawn with few exceptions from Pimlico, her own quarter of London, had banded themselves together into a coterie on much the same lines as those of Bloomsbury or Chelsea; they called themselves The Pimlicans, they concentrated on their own circle, they had evolved a common design for living which they agreed was the highest one attainable by human nature. Much of it was the customary cant – 'free' love, an atheism traceable to sheer laziness, an instinctive dislike of authority, an attack on every existing institution, no matter what its merit: all coupled with a quite sincere belief that only in themselves rested the fountain-head of culture, of intelligence, and of progress. In fact the whole thing might have passed for a sort of juvenile New Republic, with no harm done, if they had not taken it and themselves with such deadly seriousness.

For then it became a bore, as seriousness does when applied even to the most elaborate charade. They were bogus. Even the fact of their living in Pimlico was bogus: it was a slum, but they chose to live in it because the local landlords turned an agreeably blind eye on their tenants, and they could do quaint and original things, such as dropping bottles out of upper windows or going shopping in their dressing-gowns, without being stared at by anyone except the lower classes, who of course didn't count.

The men were either fat, shiny, and far gone in liquor, or bearded, unkempt, and curiously dressed in green: they were usually to be seen at eleven o'clock at night at the lower end of their favourite bar, standing drinks to someone else's wife and expecting her to pay for them. The women were often beautiful, always untidy, and always having abortions: in social contacts they would ape what they took to be their betters, rushing vehemently at each other and crying: 'Darling ...' but the effect was that of foals at play rather than the hallmark of well-bred affection.

All of them were selfish, inept, and preferred talking to anything else except copulation, which they conducted with marathonic vitality. True, they had a few positive achievements: the men occasionally produced novels about their schooldays, the women painted pictures or appeared at the Arts Theatre on a dirty Sunday night or got three days' crowd work at Shepherd's Bush. But there really wasn't time for that sort of thing, what with the latest scandal, and the latest man or woman, and the latest abortion; the world went by, but what must be settled, discussed *ad nauseam*, and settled once more, was the basic, the eternal problem, of who sleeps with whom. ... For that was reality: all else was worthless, the mere froth of existence, and interesting only to very stupid or very wrong-headed people.

And finally, in this matter of free love, the corner-stone of their small world, they missed the point so profoundly that they wrought destruction wherever they touched upon it. They wanted sexual freedom purely for its own sake: they never realized the essential rule – that one may dispense with the legal tie of marriage as being a social imposition, an elaborate and sustained piece of cheek to which one should not submit, but what one cannot jettison is the loyalty which that tie is meant to ensure and which should be intrinsic in any personal contract, whether the Church has its big malignant eye on you or no. But this they could not stomach, however well-garnished the plate on which it was handed to them.

As a result they lived with each other jerkily, chopping and changing according to their moods, pursuing odd by-ways as passion or pique directed them: they did not see that there was even more need for concentration and faithfulness in 'illicit' love than in marriage. They had no use for continuity, and they never missed being able to count on their partners because they were themselves wholly untrustworthy. They were free – that was all that mattered; and for them, freedom meant an unconditional licence.

Occasionally one of the men would get married, for a variety of reasons – he wanted a child, he wanted a housekeeper, he wanted a girl he couldn't get otherwise; but the old habits, the old lack of self-discipline, never retreated very far, and within a year or so he would be back in the gang and at the service of such young women as had need of him.

The women in their turn had a habit of marrying their first lovers and then returning to their second or third: it was no doubt a colourful and satisfactory arrangement, but it made it very difficult for the outsider to keep his records up to date. If one missed one evening at Jill's or one single penetrating discussion in the pub, one was liable to be left holding only yesterday's news – the most bastard, deformed, and futureless child imaginable.

Into these surroundings Jill fitted perfectly: she was the prototype, the prize pupil of the system. Equipped by nature with a generous sort of body, she gave it full play: she was the most popular, the busiest, the most talkative, the most entirely useless of all the Pimlicans. She played her own hand every minute of the day and night; she would live with people at top pitch for about a month and then leave them very quickly, so that for some little time they were persuaded that she had done them a favour. Of course, there were recriminations and jealous scenes, but they were part and parcel of her way of life; and somehow retribution never quite caught up with her – she would smile, she would argue, she would plead an incurable frailty, she would square things somehow and make off like a flash. . . .

Once she had had three men living with her at the same time, in the same house, and had managed to keep them there for six weeks without scrapping. She had been widely applauded for the effort, since this, her friends said, was proof that their code was workable to the most extreme degree, this signalized their plan's perfection. . . . All that it did signalize was the fact, never in doubt, that people who want a thing badly enough, as the young men wanted her, are prepared to deny their own instincts, their own fastidiousness, their own sense of decency in order to get it: but if it were put like that, if she were told that she was brutalizing something rather fine and rather precious, she was liable to laugh a good deal and remark that her accuser would grow up one of these days.

The men had divided up the week between them, without rancour and apparently without further ambition; and since they had not the wit to liken themselves to three little dogs hanging about a street-corner bitch, they were contented enough. But Jill, lighting on the affair in her thoughts as she was dressing that morning, knew that if Ian were confronted with the story he would be horror-struck, quite apart from any question of jealousy; since sex used in that way, as a series of contrasted refreshments, did not enter into his scheme of things – his mind would never encompass it without complete mental distortion.

And that being so, there was little point in keeping him by her: he brought nothing special to the partnership, he was just a new body to which she had now become used. And there were plenty of those in London, plenty and to spare; in fact she wouldn't have wasted her time on this rather alien creature if she hadn't wanted her holiday to be a complete change for her in every respect. But there were, anyway, only three more days of it left. . . . Ian would rave a bit, no doubt: people always did – in fact it would be a distinct poke in the ego if they didn't; but he'd get over it as (once again) people always did if they had to.

Perhaps, she thought, it might be as well if she brought the matter up before they left Adelboden: she didn't want him hanging round and pestering her in London, she wanted the cut to be clean, as their departure from Switzerland would be clean.

He must know already that she wasn't in love with him: she had given him nothing more than smiles by day and some very disturbed nights' rest. ... He'd settle down again; he had his wife, after all, and probably a baby, too, by this time. No man was really entitled to much more than that. It was the common human share on earth, it was what those sort of people wanted: it would suffice for him.

Ian *did* rave a good deal when she told him: in fact he behaved as if she'd been beastly to him the whole holiday, instead of marvellous, which was the truth. Blow, blow, thou winter wind. ... And why was he such a fool? The Aware Man was he who brushed himself aside before the Great Road-Sweeper did it for him. (She could play God as easily as Jill Collier: in fact the parts were interchangeable.)

Of course she picked rather a bad time, just after breakfast, and she wasn't very careful about choosing her words – something like 'making the most of our last three days', a quick question and answer, and then a really shattering argument, furious on his part, impatient on hers.

She dealt with it as she usually did: that was another part that she knew inside out. Surely he must have known ... why on earth should he imagine that she was in love with him? ... that wasn't how people behaved nowadays, nobody thought sleeping together meant anything at all ... if he were a bit less conceited ... why did he take things so *seriously* ... and so on, further and further apart, rending impossible, by that one scene, any more tenderness of any sort between them.

Ian knew he had a genuine grievance, for though they hadn't actually talked of the future she had behaved as though they belonged to each other, she had been exclusively his; and that sort of faith-breaking was, to his mind, the only true treachery.

But he was really moved: he would have let the grievance go by if he had only been given a chance of winning her favour again.

'Why not at least try it?' he said finally, when he really knew her to be in earnest. 'Things may not be so different in London: you may want to go on.'

She smiled at him ironically, wondering to find him so stupid. 'Things won't be any different in London. That's just why I want a break. There's no point in aiming at the same thing all one's life, you know.'

He was genuinely perplexed by this. 'What nonsense that is. If you're enjoying something, you don't change it just for the sake of changing: you carry on, and make the most of it.'

'Do you?'

'Of course you do.'

'I must be different. A thing may be good, but that's not to say it's the best yet. I like to keep moving, peering round corners, taking a chance on the next throw.'

'I think it's a perfectly damnable idea.'

She laughed again. 'All sorts to make a world. ... That's understood, then, is it? Three more days, and then finish. But we'll make the most of them, of course.'

He gave an angry exclamation. 'How can we make the most of them? How do you suppose I can go on—'

'Sleeping with me?'

'Yes – sleeping with you, if I know that it's going to end in three days? It must mean more than that: it isn't just a way of filling in the time.'

She shrugged. 'Isn't it? What else do you want it to be? A sort of haze? – shut your eyes and live in dreamland? You can't conduct affairs like that: you have to be alive all the time, knowing exactly what's going on – physically, mentally, everything. You must *handle* things, not let them slide.'

'That isn't the way I look at it,' he answered slowly. He took her hand. 'Jill darling, do think it over. Do let me see you in London, just at first. I won't be a nuisance.'

'Sorry. ...' It was that attitude which she could not stand, the sort of faithful-dog, I'm-here-when-you-want-me idea so very popular on the stage and so burdensome in real life. The Adoring Suitor in the Background might be a suitable theme for heroics, but in her view his position as one of Nature's lap-dogs was unchallenged.

'It really wouldn't work, Ian: I know – I've tried it before ...' She looked at her watch. 'Eleven o'clock. What shall we do? Are you having lunch in?'

'No, I'm not.'

He was suddenly furious again, realizing how completely she was in command, how she had in fact always been so – pulling the strings, making her toy figures dance.

'I think you're the bloodiest young woman I've ever met, and you can get someone else for your last three days – I wouldn't touch them with a barge-pole.'

Maddeningly, she clapped her hands and smiled. 'That's the way to do it – make up your mind, take a line and stick to it. You're learning already, you see.'

'I've learnt something else, too: not to trust anyone like you ever again.'

'Then I haven't really wasted my time.' She gave him a last brilliant smile, and was gone.

Thus it came about that when the telegram arrived for Ian that afternoon, he was by himself up at Gilbach, practising for a Visitors' Race due on the morrow. The fact cost him his life.

CHAPTER XVI

I

Both Denys and Helen were in to lunch, as well as the two parents; and the telegram, which was opened in case it should be important, brought an immediate sense of crisis to them all.

Mr Carrington left the room to put through a call to London, while the others, after a half-hearted attempt to finish their meal, went up to Mrs Carrington's bedroom to wait for further news. There they disposed themselves according to their several tastes: Helen sat on the bed, thinking of nothing in particular, Denys stood by the window and wondered, while he stared at the mountains opposite, whether Cynthia was really going to die, and Mrs Carrington did her best to cheer things up without admitting that there was any cause for anxiety.

'We mustn't worry until we hear more definitely,' she began in a brisk fashion. 'You know how doctors are always fussing about nothing at all. I expect Dr Armstrong thinks it would be good for Cynthia to see Ian. It will cheer her up.'

Nobody said anything. The clock on the bedside table ticked away the seconds; whatever happened round it, whatever pain or distress the four walls of the room enclosed, time passed evenly and was lost for ever.

'And a baby, too,' she went on. 'Won't that be lovely, Denys? Why, you're actually an uncle. ... I wonder whether it's a boy or a girl. Dr Armstrong might have remembered to tell us.'

Helen roused herself. 'I don't suppose he thought it was very important,' she said rather sharply. 'It's just a child to him. And it's Cynthia he's chiefly concerned with now.'

'It would have been nice to know, all the same. Wouldn't it, Denys?'

He turned. 'I beg your pardon – I wasn't listening.'

'We were wondering whether it was a boy or a girl.'

'Oh yes. ... Which does Ian want?'

There was a silence at that. 'A boy, I think,' answered Mrs Carrington after a moment. 'People usually want a boy first, don't they?' She considered the point. 'Yes, I think he said a boy, when I asked him once.'

But that must have been a long time ago, thought Denys: long ago, two or even three years back; for now Ian doesn't want a child at all – a child will be in the way: he would like Cynthia to die, so that he can marry Jill. And Cynthia *will* die, and he will have his wish.

'I wonder where Ian is?' said Helen. 'Do you know, Denys? Is he up at Hahnenmoos?'

Why were they all bothering him now. ...

'I don't know,' he answered. 'I don't think he went out till quite late, so perhaps he's only gone to Boden or Gilbach.'

'Someone will have to fetch him,' put in Mrs Carrington. 'He must be ready to leave tonight.'

There was another silence. The idea of fetching Ian home seemed somehow to increase the chance of tragedy, as well as to bring the realization of it tangibly nearer; it was the first link of the chain and the chain ended at Cynthia's death. If only they could be persuaded (or if Mr Carrington learnt on the telephone) that Ian needn't start for home, then the chain would have no beginning and Cynthia would be safe.

Denys said, half to himself:

'Perhaps he won't want to go home: perhaps he won't think there's any need.'

'Denys!' Mrs Carrington was genuinely shocked, the more so as her own thoughts had been of much the same sort. 'Whatever makes you say that? Of course he'll want to go: he'll catch the train tonight.'

She wanted to add much more to this, but she did not like to dwell on the subject at such a time: she would have liked to explain, quietly and convincingly, that just because Ian had been running after that silly little girl it didn't mean that he didn't love Cynthia any longer – that he was a good boy really, her only son – that he wasn't bad, but just forgetful at times. . . .

She was lost in her own thoughts, wishing with all her heart that the holiday had gone differently or that Ian had stayed behind in London in the first place. Then nothing would have gone wrong, because Cynthia wouldn't have been anxious: it was worry, of course, which did so much harm at times like that. . . .

Then her husband came in, and she knew that he had grave news because he shut the door quite softly behind him and hesitated before speaking. It was to Denys that he spoke first.

'Can you find Ian, do you think? He must go back, and he'll want a little time to get ready.'

The words were ominous: they left so much unsaid, they had about them that quality of furtiveness so much harder to endure than a direct avowal. Denys wanted to ask straight out: 'What's happened? What have you heard?' but even at this moment he hesitated – illness was the concern of the grown-ups, Death was an adult preserve. . . .

Mrs Carrington put the question for them all.

'Did you get through? What did they say?'

'Well,' he glanced at Denys, and then away again, 'I'm afraid it's serious. She's had a difficult time, and Armstrong is very anxious – he's called in a specialist. The kid's fine, I'm glad to say: it's a boy. But Ian must go home tonight. He can get to Frutigen on the bus after dinner, and catch the ordinary train.' He paused, and turned to Denys again. 'Will you look about for him, old boy? I suppose he must be out ski-ing.'

Helen spoke suddenly. 'He may be anywhere. How can Denys find him? It's two o'clock now: he'll be in by four, anyway. Why bother to fetch him?'

There was sense in this, of course, since Ian need not start from the hotel till nine that evening at the earliest; but the idea of leaving him in the dark until he chanced to come home was not an appealing one. His was the chief part in the drama, and he deserved all the help they could give him.

'Oh, I think he ought to know as soon as possible,' said Mrs Carrington. 'It'll be such a shock for him, poor boy.'

'Well, I don't think there's any need,' answered Helen obstinately. 'It's just wasting Denys' time.'

'Suppose I don't mind my time being wasted?' Denys' voice cracked out suddenly, startling them all, surprising even himself by its sheer virulence. 'Do you think Ian isn't interested in the subject? Or are you afraid he's somewhere with Jill, and mustn't be disturbed? Perhaps they might excuse an interruption, under the circumstances. And I wouldn't tip-toe up to them – I'd let them know I was coming.'

He looked down at Helen with hatred, knowing her to be an enemy, and she thought suddenly: 'God, he's going to tell them here and now that he slept with me last night. . . .' She strove to placate him with a smile, willing him to remember the night before with pride instead of with anger, so that it might remain a secret between them. Then Mr Carrington spoke, making for the first time an open acknowledgment of the situation.

'You mustn't think too much about that, Denys,' he said, with something like humility. 'We've all been worried over it, but it's got nothing to do with things as they stand now. Ian may have made a bit of a fool of himself out here, but it can't affect this – he'll want to go home all right.'

'Then you'll admit, sir, that he – that he hasn't—' Denys paused. He did not know how to phrase it, but he wanted the affair to be brought at last right into the open, he wanted them all to acknowledge the case against Ian, where before they had ignored it.

'We know he's been running after this girl,' Mr Carrington agreed. 'There may have been something in it, and there may not, but as far as I'm concerned ...'

'There was something in it.' Denys swept round at Helen. 'And you know it too, don't you?'

She nodded simply 'Yes', afraid of provoking him in any way.

'Well, it's finished with now,' said her father. 'He'll go home – we'll all go home – and forget about it.'

His tone was challenging, seeming to imply that Denys was straying out of his rightful, his eighteen-year-old province, but the latter insisted, tasting the small savour of power for the first time.

'How do we know it's finished with now?' he countered brutally, trying to hurt them and hurting himself at the same time. 'Ian's still going about with her, isn't he? And what if Cynthia dies? That'll just suit him, won't it? He'll have a free hand then, just as he's been wanting all this time.'

Mrs Carrington gasped. 'You mustn't say such things – it's absolutely wicked. I'm sure such a thought has never entered his head. Why—'

Her husband soothed her. 'It's all right, my dear. We mustn't get excited over this; it won't help at all.' He turned to Denys, authority in his movement. 'Now look here. Whatever the rights and wrongs of this, there's no need to make it worse by suggestions of that sort. Let's patch it up as best we can: let's not argue about it any longer.'

He was ready to say more, but Denys had relaxed, content with the ground he had made. For they had faced it, they had admitted that Ian had behaved badly, there had been tacit agreement with his own point of view; even Helen, confronted with the essentials, had not spoken to the contrary. He looked once more out of the window, and up at the declining sun: it would be behind the hills in two hours, and dusk would follow swiftly. ... He turned away, and nodded to Mr Carrington.

'All right,' he said softly, tranquilly, 'I'll go and fetch him.'

2

Ian was neither on the nursery slopes, nor at Boden: Gilbach was the other possibility, and this lay two miles down the road. Denys, trudging along with his skis shouldered, found himself scanning the faces of the people as they passed, fearing that Ian would be among them: for with the day's decline everyone was making for the town in a slow procession, and he wanted to meet Ian out on the snow fields, alone and uninterrupted.

He had no plan in his mind, only a glowing resentment and a vague determination to 'have it out' with Ian; the latter had had so much in his favour, and had gone scot-free so long, that Denys knew that he could not let him get away to England without putting some sort of spoke in his wheel. Even if he only called him a swine, it was better than letting the occasion go unmarked....

People continued to pass him, in groups and twos and threes: they walked with care, still and contented in their weariness, looking forward to the lights of the town and the warm evening ahead. Their voices would ring out of the dusk, their footsteps crunched in the snow, their forms were vaguely seen and then were suddenly within focus: they stepped aside to let him pass, they called greetings or murmured good night, they were gone as the daylight was gone, vanished out of sight, leaving only blurred tracks in the snow and perhaps the tang of a cigarette.

Denys plodded on, and they passed him like a continuous frieze: presently he became confused at their number, he forgot to answer their greetings, he withdrew within himself and thought only of his meeting with Ian. Among the trees on either side there were lights flickering, and occasionally he would glance at these, as at some will-of-the-wisp which he would have followed but could not: mostly they were rough peasants' chalets, the outcrop of the town which he had now left behind: it was borne in upon him that they were the only traces of friendliness in a world suddenly hateful and hating.

For as surely as he knew that the dying light would soon

have vanished, so he had become convinced that Cynthia was already dead. The telegram had told nothing: it had read simply 'Child well but anxiety about wife Suggest you return home': it was the most that Armstrong could have said at that stage. But there had been something in Mr Carrington's manner when he came back from the telephone – not so much that he had heard definite news as that no hope had been held out to him; and if that had been the case at two o'clock, by now she was no longer alive. So she, his own companion, to whom he had drawn closer as his father receded to the background, had now vanished for ever. And with that established, he thought as he left the valley and began to climb once more, a wholly different situation had arisen which he must meet, not with a mere gesture but with action.

And here his steps began to falter, so that for some moments he walked as if blindfold: the skis on his shoulder weighed him down cruelly, and the snow slope ahead made his eyes burn as he stared at it. Soon he became breathless, knowing that he was thinking of impossible things which he desired with his whole being and would shortly bring to pass: like a tight iron cage, there pressed on his brain the whole futile story of the past two weeks, the successive insults, the successive defeats, and he found himself saying aloud: 'It is too much – too much: it is something I cannot endure.' The wind in the trees sighed the same words, and presently others were mingled with them – Jill, Helen, the little Alsatian girl. . . .

He started as a bird rustled through the leaves at his side: he staggered and nearly fell, he sobbed, not knowing that a man and a girl who were passing stopped and stared and would have helped him: a little further on, within sight of the inn at Gilbach, all control passed from his mind as if reins had been slashed through and severed, and he was, for a space, not less than mad. The only thoughts left in his mind were mad thoughts, and he pressed forward eagerly, breaking into a limping run, to make them come true as soon as he could.

CHAPTER XVII

Ian lay in agony where he had fallen, by the wooden fence: there was blood, and a great weal, on his forehead, and his leg, broken below the knee, brought him an unbelievable torture even in its half frozen state.

He had tried to do a remarkably silly thing – to go at speed through a gateway between two fields: the space had not been more than three feet across and, travelling too fast, he had attempted a stem at the last moment and run full-tilt into the gate itself as it swung at right angles to the fence. It had been late in the afternoon when it happened, and he was too high up for anyone to be ski-ing near him: he had been unconscious for nearly an hour, and when he recovered, half dead with cold, it was almost dark.

Not far off, and within his view, was a small shelter, rough built of logs and with a black hole marking its window, but though he had shouted there had been no answer, only the stamping of cattle and the jangle of a cow-bell; he lay now, listening to that jangle, calling weakly at intervals, while the cold mercifully froze his leg and crept upwards to his stomach. There was blood all over his clothes and on the surrounding snow, blood on his skis, blood on the splintered gateway; from the scored wound on his forehead a trickle of it ebbed away, dripping on to the snow and there melting for itself a little rust-coloured cavern, deeper, darker, soaking perhaps into the grass which lay hidden beneath. He knew that within an hour night would have succeeded the dusk, and that he would die where he lay.

He was afraid of dying, but not stricken with panic, as he had thought he would be: at first the pain of his leg had been so intolerable that he would have welcomed oblivion, and later the cold and the increasing dusk together combined to induce a feeling of drowsiness, a gradual ebbing of vitality comparable to the ebbing of some slow tide in a forgotten backwater. The phrase 'sinking to rest' occurred to him, and he found it a satisfying and comforting one: if it meant anything at all, it meant that he had only to lie there, letting the cold do its work, and within a little while the natural elements of his body would resign their function and life would leave him at peace.

But then he fell to thinking of how young he was, and of the wastage – of power, of ambition, of potential success – involved in his death; and once more he was roused, once more he called out and feebly waved one of his ski-sticks in the hope that someone's eyes might chance to be turned in his direction. Death might be welcome when it came, but the future still held chances and promises for him, guiding torches on which his gaze could still be fixed and his individual secret hopes take fire.

The effort with the ski-stick, short-lived and ineffective, was a severe one, and after it he sank into drowsiness again; when he revived, and opened his eyes, Denys was standing over him, looking into his face intently.

He managed to smile, and whisper: 'Thank God you've come.' Then he waited for comfort and help to be brought to him.

Nothing happened. Denys stood there in silence, leaning on his skis, staring down at Ian: his face, luminous in the dusk, had an astonishing lack of expression – there was in it no anxiety, no concern, no surprise even that Ian should be lying there in such a case. After a long scrutiny Denys shifted his gaze and looked about him: Ian watched his eyes, drawn by the cowbell, light first on the nearby hut, then on the blood-strewn snow, the road far below them and almost out of sight, and lastly the heavy sky already pricked with stars.

There was something terrifying in his immobility, as if he were only a watcher, or a judge without power to help or wish to acquit; Ian knew that there was, unaccountably, something wrong, some vital flaw in the train of events, but he was too spent to consider what it was. He said weakly: 'Help me to sit up and get comfortable. Then you'd better fetch some more people. They'll have a stretcher at the inn.'

There was still no answer: Denys, seeming not to have heard him, stood as before, leaning on his skis. But his lips were moving, and presently a succession of sounds came out, a murmur of which Ian could not catch the drift.

'What did you say?'

Then the words fell clearly:

'You have a son.'

Ian managed a weak laugh. 'That's fine. ... But give me a hand now, old boy: we'll see about the celebration later.'

Then, as he saw his companion still immobile, his voice sharpened, like a violin string plucked and tightened: 'For Christ's sake wake up. Can't you see the state I'm in?'

His words battered violently against the darkness, and were lost: he knew as they vanished traceless that there was no help at hand, but that this was rather an enemy who would destroy him. He waited, wondering what devil had taken hold of Denys, and how far its madness would drive him. Again there was a murmur, and again a single dulled sentence falling like the shadow of death across his body.

'But Cynthia is dead.'

Ian caught his breath, forgetting his pain and his frozen limbs and seeing only the white face hanging above him. So that was it: Cynthia had died in childbirth, and Denys had got hold of some crazy idea. ... He gathered himself to speak, and to try to pierce through to Denys's true intelligence, but before he could say anything, or indeed light upon an adequate form of words, Denys forestalled him.

It was as if the bonds of the other's spirit had suddenly fallen away, leaving some monstrous animal shape free to range as it willed. The result was a bestial incoherence – wild words tumbled out of his mouth like the flow of saliva, mad irrelevances horribly tangled: he spoke with tongues, and they were the aimless tongues of a mind distorted and wrenched out of human control. People and places and snatches of once-vital speech were jumbled up together – 'Jill – the Grand Bar – Helen – Cynthia dead – this was what you came for, wasn't it? – anxiety about wife – her name is Miss Collier – cheating, lying all the time—' and then the words 'Swine ... swine ... swine. . .' repeated on a rising note till they became a shriek of fury, flung out as if they had the taste and the savour of the grave itself.

Ian was appalled at what he heard, and appalled too at his own helplessness: it was clear that Denys was out of his mind and would never help him, and it was by now too dark for them to be seen by anyone else. ... He raised his hand, and wiped the blood from his eyes: at the movement an excruciating pain travelled the whole length of his body from leg to shoulder, so that he was forced to cry out. Then he clenched his free hand round his ski stick, and summoning his last remaining strength gasped out:

'Denys ... listen to me ... for God's sake pull yourself together. ... I can't help what I've done, and it's over now, isn't it? – you can't change any of it. ... But I didn't kill Cynthia, she would have died anyway, she wasn't strong enough to have a child. ... Listen, go down to the inn and see if you can get help. Don't you see that I can't stand the cold much longer? ... I'll be dead in another hour. ... Please go.'

Then he fell silent, not through weakness – though he was nearly spent – but in horror at what he had said. He had betrayed himself, for at the words 'I'll be dead in another hour' the expression on Denys' face had changed and he had nodded to himself as though suddenly lighting on a solution of a secret problem; it was immediately clear that he desired Ian's death and now understood how to bring it about, without further effort to himself. And as if to offer him the proof of this, Denys inclined his head again and said, quite simply and gently:

'I needn't kill you after all. I needn't do anything else. You will be dead soon. The snow will do it for me.'

Then he bent down and began to strap on his skis.

Inside the hut the cattle stamped, and the bell clanged like an echo of the death-knell. From Ian's throat a cry of anguish was wrung. 'Denys, for God's sake. ... What are you going to do? Are you joking? Don't play with me – I can't stand any more. Are you going to get help?'

There was no reply, only a steady and purposeful breathing by his side. One ski was securely buckled and the other had been slipped into place, and the toe-grip clamped home.

'Think what you're doing. You can't leave me here. It's murder, don't you see? – murder.'

It was as though he had not spoken. Denys stood up, gathered his sticks, prepared to begin his run.

'Answer. Say something.' The words were sobbed out: it was as though he could already feel the clutch of death.

Denys said, in his normal voice: 'Good-bye, Ian,' and set off down the hill.

A great cry followed him, reaching his ears just as he misjudged his first turn, and fell. Lying in the snow, he looked back and upwards: twenty yards away in the darkness he could just see Ian's form prostrate between the gateposts, and one ski stick propped at an angle like a signal of distress. Denys knew that Ian was physically helpless, but the strength of the cry worried him: it was louder than he had expected, it might yet bring help. . . .

The evil and blood-thirsty man shall not live out half his days, he thought, as he got to his feet and began to climb the slope again, step by step, digging the edges of his skis firmly into the snow to gain a foothold, as the Norwegian had taught him. When he reached Ian he found him crying, sobbing out his thanks for Denys' change of mind. 'I knew you wouldn't leave me here, I knew you wouldn't,' he said over and over again, until Denys had slipped through the gate, past the blood-stained snow, and was still continuing his climb. Then he stammered and stopped speaking, and waited in terror.

Denys plodded upwards – ten yards, twenty yards – looking back occasionally to judge his distance: if it didn't work the first time he could try again until he attained an entire success. . . . His skis made a neat herring-bone pattern as he swung into the alternating rhythm – left stick, right ski, right stick, left ski – which carried him upwards at a slow labouring pace. Finally, thirty yards above the fence, he turned in his tracks and stood still, waiting to recover his breath.

Ian cursed the blood which filled his eyes. He could only just see Denys – a black shape against the snow, an avenging form poised for the leap. He called out 'What are you doing?' in a voice thin and reedy with fear. But he knew already.

He tried to turn his head away as the swift downward rush began, but the sound of the skis, increasing like a furious escape of steam, hypnotized him so that for the last few moments he was compelled to face them. He tried to wrench his body out of the way and could not move it at all: he tried to raise his head, but in spite of all his efforts it lolled sideways, a listless and foolish target, and he could only watch with frantic eyes the black figure approaching.

He had a last glimpse of Denys' face, coming at him like a mask swinging down from the sky, and then the fury was upon him. His head dropped finally on to the snow, on to the mush of his own blood: the tip of the foremost ski entered his eye at an angle, splintered and crushed the surrounding bone, and drove on upwards. He gave a cry of extreme agony, twitched and lay still.

Part Two

'AND A HAPPY ISSUE...'

CHAPTER I

From the very beginning it was never assumed by the authorities that Ian's death was anything but a lamentable ski-ing accident of a kind fortunately rare in Switzerland: and the wild words and explanations, which the young man who found the body let fall when he burst in upon the inn at Gilbach, were put down (in so far as they were understood at all) to natural agitation at so horrible an experience. Apparently he had stumbled right on to the corpse, which was that of a close relation – enough to give any young man a shock which might affect his mind for some little time.

It was not even thought necessary to wait until Denys, who was in bed with a nervous breakdown, recovered sufficiently to answer questions, before concluding the affair: clearly he was not a material witness, clearly there were no material witnesses to an event in which luck and ill-judgment had so obviously played the critical parts. He could tell them nothing that they did not know already; and, after such an experience, it would be kinder to leave him in peace. The rules must be observed, naturally, but humanity set a limit to their rigidness.

Two other factors contributed largely to the acceptability of the official version. The first was that Ian's body was brought down in pitch darkness, and none of the three bearers could remember the exact position, in relation to the fence, in which it had been lying – they had taken it for granted, they said, that he had simply run at full speed into the gate and then collapsed; nor had they noticed whether any jagged piece of wood was especially near the body or had dropped away from it as it was moved. The second was that snow fell heavily the same night and obliterated all tracks. But next morning they found, two feet deep, the splintered gate, and on it traces of blood: and it was natural to assume that one of the cross-bars had inflicted the horrifying wound by which Ian met his death.

Thus they reconstructed it, after a cursory medical examination: a crash at high speed, a broken leg, penetration of the eye by one of the many pieces of wood now lying about, followed by death from exposure and loss of blood. ... A post-mortem would have told them a great many surprising things, among them the fact that though the subject had bled a great deal, death was in fact due to laceration of the brain and must have been instantaneous. But there was no post-mortem: it was a simple case, they said, and fearing adverse publicity they speedily dismissed it as such.

It was a pity, of course, that such a thing should happen particularly at the height of the season in a district having such a good accident record: but what could be done about it? Young men, especially young Englishmen, had always skied fast and would always do so, no matter what warnings were given them: and indeed it was a safe enough proceeding until some combination of chances, such as (in this case) failing light and a narrow gateway, contrived to bring disaster.

One could not legislate for that sort of thing: one saw in it the hand of God. ... It was, however, recommended that sharper watch be kept at dusk on single skiers who were still on the snowfields; and the principal hotels were asked to exhibit notices warning everyone, no matter how expert, against going through gaps at more than normal speed. There, officially and otherwise, the matter rested.

Ian was buried in the little village churchyard: Helen and her mother went home to be with Cynthia, who was out of danger but still weak: and Mr Carrington stayed on for another fortnight to complete the interminable formalities and to look after Denys, who at first was very ill indeed. It was agreed by everyone that he must have suffered a tremendous shock: imagine, they said, going out to look for one's brother-in-law and finding him lying dead like that. ... The local paper indeed produced a telling word picture of the scene, characterized by a high degree of detail and conspicuous lack of taste: it enjoyed wide publicity and an avalanche of protest from the British visitors.

But clearly the event was enough to unhinge any young man: only time and complete rest could efface the memory of it and restore him to health. For the present it was thought best for him to stay in Adelboden, gaining strength for the painful journey home.

In the Schweizer hotel itself there was, naturally enough, a certain amount of gossip about the situation between the two young men prior to the accident: there were some even who hinted that Denys would have suffered no great shock if Ian had simply been brought home dead – it was only the fact of finding him which had had such a serious effect. But the whispers could never gather real volume or malignancy, for the very good reason that the whisperers did not stay long enough for this to happen: the hotel's population continually renewed itself, and a week after the accident there were very few people left who had been *au fait* with the previous state of affairs.

Herr Franck had to answer a multitude of questions, and did so admirably: but whenever this aspect of the case was touched upon he straightway became stern and denounced such an idea as the wildest kind of scandal-mongering. What he himself really thought was less clear; but he did occasionally find himself admitting that Ian's death was the neatest possible solution to a number of very real problems. Even considering that it was the tail-end of the season, things seemed a good deal more rosy now than in the days when Ian was padding about the second floor, not always in his stockinged feet, and when Denys was having to compete with no one at all for Helen's favours.

He could thank God also that Jill Collier, retreating before the wave of unpopularity that Ian's death brought her, had left for England on the following day. There was no doubt that many people in the hotel found her presence there unwelcome, and it would not have been easy to curb the general unrest if she had stayed on.

Denys himself was in bed for ten days, during which time he returned perhaps half-way towards his normal state of mind.

The first few days – until Ian was buried, in fact – had been full of nothing but the sheer terror of discovery: it seemed impossible that one morning the door would not open, to admit a detective who had nosed out the whole story, and finally caught up with him. . . . There were nights, too, when he was visited by dreams so horrible – dreams of pursuit across wastes of snow, of a trial, of waiting for death in some mean and secret cell – that he would wake screaming in terror: Mr Carrington would come from the next room, and the night porter, and a rather kind Frenchwoman who had the room above and sometimes sat with him during the day-time; and they would strive to comfort him, saying that it was all over, that he was with friends, that he need not think of it any more.

Worried, they would stand about the room, talking to reassure him or watching him sip a warm drink; and he would lie back and look at them one after another, and wonder how much longer he could keep his secret. Almost, it seemed, the waking nightmare was more terrible than the sleeping.

It was hardest of all, of course, to bear Mr Carrington's presence near him. Try as he would, he could only see in him a man whose son he had murdered, a man who was showing him every kindness in the midst of a great personal grief, and who, knowing the truth, would have been ready, and entitled, to sign his death sentence. To accept any favour from him was more than treachery.

So he was silent when Mr Carrington talked or tried to entertain him, almost surly in his rejection of all advances: he would lie very still, willing the other to go, revolting with all his soul against the despicable part which he must still play. Murder in hot blood, or goaded by an insane rage, was one thing; but this continuous betrayal stretched his nerves to a fresh breaking-point at each encounter.

On the fifth day came a measure of relief. It was a dull afternoon, and the Frenchwoman – faded, grey-haired, soft in manner – was sitting by his bedside, trying to interest him in a game of chess. But presently, seeing him preoccupied, she set the board on one side: then she took his hand and pressed it gently.

'You cannot think completely of the game?' She had a

welcome voice, low-pitched and slow: in her youth it must have delighted many men, now it was a sexless pleasure for any hearer. 'Then it is better not to try. What would you like? A cigarette? Or to go to sleep? Last night was a bad one, wasn't it?'

Denys nodded his head. 'Yes, it was bad. But if I sleep now I won't be able to tonight.' His eyes wandered round the room, and then to the window: within his view there was nothing but a far-away fringe of trees and a patch of grey sky which would soon be darkened. The sky had been darkened when he had found Ian. 'Tell me what's happening outside? Is there jumping today?'

'No. But there is ice-hockey, I think – Adelboden against the Wengen team. Do you like the game?'

He nodded. 'Very much. It's so fast, and they're usually so very clever on their feet. But it's a pity they lose their tempers so much.'

'That is only human,' she smiled. 'They care so much to win: naturally they are angry.'

'Naturally they are angry,' he repeated. Naturally he had been angry in defeat, naturally he had lost all control. ... 'Tell me something else. Tell me – what happened about Ian.'

She hesitated. The subject had never been raised between them or directly referred to: the doctor himself had warned her against it.

'What do you want to know about him?' she asked at length.

'Everything. None of you tell me anything: I have just to lie here and guess. ... Has he – has he been buried?'

'You must not think of such things.'

'No, please tell me. Otherwise,' he smiled desperately, 'I'll start worrying again, and have a bad night and scream like a baby.'

'But why should you worry?' she asked in her low soothing voice. 'For you it is all over – you know that.'

'But it still concerns me. He married my sister, after all. Or is there something wrong? Hasn't he been buried after all?'

Seeing him agitated, she took the easiest course. 'Naturally he has been buried,' she assured him. 'A quiet affair, though there were many people, and lovely flowers too. There was a wreath from the hotel, and another from the Ski Club. Of course it was a great shock for everyone, to have a thing like that happen in the holiday season.'

'But what did they say about it? The papers, for instance?'

He had an idea that she was hiding something, something which they were keeping until he was better able to bear it: his sick terror began to return, and the dreadful feeling of being unable to share his secret with anyone. If there were someone in whom he could confide he would not feel so helpless and unprotected.

'What did they say?' he repeated. 'Did they write anything about it?'

'Oh, there was a list of those who attended, and a photograph taken outside the church. It is the same in England, is it not? One cuts it out, and keeps it for a little while, and then perhaps it is lost.'

Now he knew that she was hiding something from him, talking away from the subject so as to lose it as soon as possible. ... Better, far better, to know the truth than lie here trembling in the most miserable panic he had ever suffered.

'No, I don't mean the funeral,' he began, his voice elaborately calm. 'I mean the accident itself. Wasn't there an inquiry of some sort? How did they think it happened?'

She saw that, underneath the quietness of his voice, he was pitiably agitated: she thought that in his disjointed state of mind he connected the finding of the body with the accident itself, so that he felt in some queer fashion as if he were responsible for it.

At the inn, she remembered, they said that the same thing had happened when he stumbled in that night – he had told of a body out on the hill-side, and how he had run into it in the darkness – that it was a mistake, that he had not meant to do so dreadful a thing. ... She knew nothing of psychology nor of the effects of shock upon thought processes, but her instinct told her that this association and confusion of ideas was a possibility.

'There was an inquiry,' she told him gently. 'It is the usual formality when there is an accident. But it was soon over: it was clear to all what had happened, and one cannot prevent such misfortune – one knows that ski-ing is sometimes dangerous, and that occasionally there comes a tragedy of this sort.'

'But what about me?' he began, and stopped, suddenly afraid of betraying himself. She seemed, however, to be prepared for the question, for she replied immediately:

'Please try to understand that it does not concern you at all. It was not your fault that you found your poor brother-in-law, and everyone is sorry that such a thing should happen to you.'

'Then they won't want to question me? – they won't ask me about it at all?'

His tone of voice told her that this fear of official examination was probably at the root of his present condition, and she laid special emphasis on her answer.

'No, they will not question you. The whole matter is finished, and no one connects you with it in any way. Your name was in the newspaper, of course, as the finder of Ian's body, but that is all.'

Once more she pressed his hand, trying to reassure him finally and completely. 'You must forget about it, as everyone else is trying to do.'

And at her words, and the comforting pressure of her hand, there came flooding back to him a heavenly sense of security, of the beginning of a returning peace of mind. If what she said was true, and she was not saying it simply to aid his convalescence, then he could well rejoice at his escape; he could come out of the shadows, he need not always be looking back over his shoulder in guilt-stricken expectant misery....

Elated with relief, he longed to confide in her the whole story, and held it back with difficulty. But he sat up in bed, and smiled at her so sweetly and so thankfully that she felt the tears suddenly near her eyes.

'You're sure of that?' he asked, in a voice more brisk and controlled than she had yet heard him use. 'You're not just trying to keep me from worrying?'

She smiled in answer, pleased at the welcome change in his manner. 'I am trying to keep you from worrying, yes. Because there is no need to worry, no need at all. Your part in the affair is forgotten. And now I will ring for tea, and you shall eat lots of cherry jam, to show that you are sensible again. But first there is a surprise, and I must prepare everything for it.'

She pressed the bell over his head, and then rose to set the coverlet straight and tidy his bedside table. He watched her idly for a moment, enjoying her grace of movement. Then he asked:

'A surprise? What is it?'

She turned, her laughing face challenging his in gentle mockery.

'Something that all young men like – a visitor.'

He was on edge immediately: the old terror returned, the old sick inability scarcely to breathe for fear of walking further into a trap. Could it be that she was still only reassuring him, keeping him quiet until something – someone – arrived?

He heard the tramp of feet in the corridor: they missed their mark and passed, but there might be more to come. He couldn't lie here and wait for them. ... He feared to speak again, but somehow words struggled to the surface, somehow he put on a normal expression – helped by the curtained twilight, muffled by the pillow, he said:

'A visitor? Who is it? A – a man?'

She smiled again, seeing in the question only a young desire not to commit himself, a romantic shyness in keeping with what she knew of boys in love.

'Ah, who can tell? A man or a woman – that is the secret, that is part of the surprise.'

She continued to tidy the room and set his bed-clothes in order, while he watched her in agony, convinced now that he was only being humoured, that she was playing for time, while below, only one flight below, the iron forces of the law gathered their strength to grip and encircle him. But he would not submit, he would fight and ...

There was a knock at the door, a knock which startled him pitiably. He half sat up in bed as she crossed to the doorway, trying to speak, trying to attract her attention: but the words would not come. At the door she turned and smiled once again.

'Now I will leave you. Tea will be here soon. Mind you enjoy it.'

Then she was in the passage outside, and he was alone without aid. He heard a murmur of voices, a light laugh. He hid his face, finding the pause unendurable. Someone came into the room and stood waiting. Presently he looked up.

It was the little Alsatian girl, her face bright with happiness, aglow with adventure.

His relief was so immediate and so devastating that he could have cried out. He stared and stared at her, drinking in her darling loveliness, until she became embarrassed and looked away. She had her ski clothes on, the clothes he remembered so well at their first meeting: she looked fantastically slim and boyish, the skin of her face as smooth and creamy and warm as he had ever dreamt it: the little corded forage cap dangled from one hand, like a hesitant shy-nymph offering or a flag of truce to be used if the necessity arose.

Presently she walked over to the bed and, after a tiny moment of hesitation, bent and kissed him on the lips. He answered it with a little caressing movement of his own, acknowledging her sweetness, her brave generosity.

But the touch of her mouth made him infinitely sad. He could see that she had dramatized their meeting – the lovely young girl comforts the stricken invalid – and was simply playing a part which she had rehearsed and hugged to herself perhaps for many days: but it was not this childlike insincerity which was the core of his unhappiness. What struck him immediately, even as she sat down on the edge of his bed and smiled expectantly at him, was that she had come too late.

Once he would have died for such a moment as this, once she had been his natural partner, and if he had clung to her world all would have been well. But he had not done so, he had tried to leave it behind and enter another – worse still, he had tried to emancipate her at the same time and lead her into a room full, for her, of nameless terrors which she could never conquer....

Now too many things intervened – and above all Helen stood between them, Helen whom, in a way, he had taken as second-best instead of the girl sitting by his side. With such a history behind him he could never reach again the plane of their first meeting.

But he was still amazed: he said wonderingly:

'Now how on earth did you get here?'

Tea came and they talked, while unnecessarily she prepared little sandwiches of bread and jam and put them into his mouth as if he were quite helpless. Dramatization again. . . . She explained how she had seen his photograph in the papers, had heard he was ill and wanted to visit him, had arranged it all with her father. ... It was brave of her, he recognized, and clearly she was proud of this bravery and shyly eager that he should admire it.

But he could not warm to her, he could only listen and answer gently and lament her late arrival. If only their New Year's Eve meeting had held such promise as this....

'Are you feeling better now?'

'Yes, thank you. Don't I look better?'

'You look rather pale. Do you want some books? Shall I get you a book in the village?'

'It's very nice of you, but I have plenty. Mr Carrington sends them up.'

'I like him. He was kind to me. He said—'

'Yes?'

'He said I would be the best medicine for you, better than all sorts of pills and mixtures.'

'Oh, he was quite right.'

'Will you be able to ski again before you leave?'

'I don't think so. We go back to England as soon as I get up.'

'What a pity. You loved ski-ing, didn't you?'

'Very much, yes.'

It was like their conversation in the Bar-Français that other night, save that now the roles were reversed, she trying her utmost to interest and amuse him, and he failing to respond. He knew exactly how she felt about it. ... No, her visit was a failure, as a romantic episode: it could hardly be otherwise, though he would have given anything to have been able to rise to the occasion, to joke with her, to make the most of her coming and rekindle the animation of that warm oval face.

But when finally she left him, with a sad, rather puzzled little smile which betrayed her own disappointment (she did not kiss him again), he realized that he had not lost by the encounter.

He lay back and stared at the ceiling, feeling soothed and comforted in his spirit, recalling the little scene before she came in, when the Frenchwoman had been trying to reassure him about Ian. It seemed that she had done so. ... Yes, he could begin to be sensible again now, as she had urged him: he could gradually lose his sense of danger, he could begin to see that night and that encounter with Ian simply as a stroke of madness, as a successful attempt at vindication which time would bury but not destroy.

For he had won: helped by an entire loss of control, by an interlude wherein he must have retained no shred of human feeling at all, he had demonstrated that he could fight for his ideals, that purity was not bloodless nor evil all-triumphant, that youth must and could be served when the circumstances were sufficiently compelling.

From that day, from that moment, he left illness and nervous exhaustion behind, and began to repair his spirit. The knowledge of what he had done was still a frightful burden, returning to him at any hour of the day or night; but it was a burden which he had under control, which would grow lighter as his journey away from the past progressed.

CHAPTER II

On his last morning in Adelboden Denys walked again down the little friendly street, carrying his skis across his shoulder, his head bared to the mounting sun. He had been at the travel bureau, changing the last of his Swiss money back into sterling – usually the final sad rite of any holiday, but in this case bringing a curious sense of satisfaction to him. The transaction seemed to mark the close of the account, in more senses than one: it signified the end of Switzerland altogether, the completion of a lengthy and distressful episode.

He wanted to carry nothing away with him save memories –

perishable stuff which did not travel well and would in turn be lost: there was to be no link with the past, no kind of echo, no looking back at all. For, despite the sunlight and the brilliant sky Adelboden was for him a place of shadows; and it was time he came out into the true day again, the day of freedom, the day of peace and self-control. The act of changing his money seemed to be a small step in this direction, a pointer towards the road he wished to take.

The next step, of the same quality, was to return his hired skis, and it was on this errand that he was now making his way through the trodden, rutted snow and the aimless crowds of holiday-makers.

On a journey of another kind he had reached something like normality. He had lost the sense of immediate and urgent guilt, he had lost much of that first terror which had threatened to affect his reason; and already he could move about, in the hotel, in the street, without feeling that every single passer-by was staring at him or that every whisper or comment concerned him and his story.

The feeling of isolation returned intermittently, in spasms of unrest which drove him to his bedroom and the shelter of its locked doors: but even this was losing its force, subdued by his returning self-confidence and the knowledge that he was now beyond reach of the law or of the consequences of his action. All that was buried with the dead, and its ghost would never walk on this side of Judgment Day.

In his own mind he had dealt with Ian's death in a curious way. Searching for a true perspective, the idea had come to him that at the critical moment another person must have taken command of the whole course of events, a tougher, more independent Denys who did not surrender to circumstance as he himself did, who would be neither slighted nor denied. Murder was so out of character for his normal self, he must have been 'possessed' by forces of a different quality and fibre altogether.

Thus the blame, and the burden of conscience, could be laid elsewhere, upon a *doppel-ganger* grown to super-human proportions and usurping all controlling functions.

And being in this manner excused responsibility, he could

even weigh the accomplished fact in the balance and decide that he was satisfied with it. Even the fact that Cynthia and the child were both well did not alter the essentials of the matter: for if Ian had not done his best to bring about her death he had at any rate so conducted himself that her death would have fitted in with his plans – the guilty mind, if not the guilt itself, was there. And with that established, what need was there for regret?

So his thoughts covered and recovered the old ground, as he picked his way down the street on his last errand. The future would be difficult, he knew well: Mr Carrington's presence was continually an unhappy reminder of his secret, and in England the rest of the family, and especially Cynthia, would have the same distressing function for a long time to come. About Cynthia he was most worried of all: the loyalty and comradeship between them demanded different treatment for her, and he could not for ever face her with a whole part of his mind barred up and hidden away. Probably, he decided, he would tell her the story, at some later time when she was reconciled to Ian's death and the full knowledge would hurt her less.

He could even forecast her reactions: horror, perhaps, at the beginning, and then a striving to understand his motives and the undeniable force which had moved him. And she *would* be able to understand it – she had that kind of piercing intuitive sympathy which could appreciate and reconcile all his actions, no matter how strange they might appear at first. And then it would be their shared secret, and the true alignment (which had always been present in embryo) of Wilder against Carrington would be operative in actual fact. For the two sides didn't mix; and Cynthia's marriage to Ian had been no more than a small excursion to prove this fact, and Ian's death the signature and seal and deliverance of the proof.

Denys smiled at this point, for contentment with his glance into the future, for the prickings of the returning joy of life. He need only wait, keeping his counsel and drawing close to Cynthia again, and his forecast would be fulfilled. If the matter could be arranged, he would go to live with her and the little boy – his godson, as had been long promised: they would be happy together, they would keep the world at bay ... He lowered his skis from his shoulder, not without the sense of completing a task and throwing off a much greater burden, and turned into the little sports shop from which he had hired them at the beginning of the holiday.

There were many people in the shop already, and while he was waiting his turn he looked through the jumble of the shop window and out into the street. People drifted past as he watched them idly: sometimes they were on skis, moving through the trodden slush with that curious skating motion so very difficult to acquire: now and then a tailing party went by, with the line of luges keeping distance and direction as if they were a string of beads drawn slowly across a table.

The stream of people and the moving colours pleased him: it symbolized the non-stop variety of Switzerland, the free by-product of something essentially commercialized and exploited. It was like the Lord Mayor's Show in London – a spectacle tossed to the crowd by a company and a tradition concerned with something wholly different – the chance largesse of an avaricious city....

And then he became aware that everyone within his view was not a passer-by: and that his glance had been caught and held by another pair of eyes, piercing eyes which did not waver but glared and glared at him through the plate-glass window.

There was something horrible in those anonymous hateful eyes watching him so steadily, and something more horrible still in the aspect of the watcher. The lower half of his body was hidden by the mass of things in the shop window, but clearly he was a dwarf, a dwarf with a big head and a shock of clipped black hair. He seemed to have no relation to his surroundings: he was dressed, not in ski-ing clothes, but in a loosely-cut suit of black cloth such as a clerk might wear: he was not part of the snow scene, but a strange importation standing out like a smudge of soot on a gay party frock. But there was something more than strangeness in the poor body and the big face with its clefts from nose to jaw: there was menace, and a kind of upstart insolence backed by power. ...

Presently the man's eyes flickered and fell, as though, intent on his own scrutiny, he had suddenly realized that Denys in his turn was watching: but he did not move away from his position, remaining with his eyes shifting from side to side over the array of goods before him. To Denys it was obvious that presently he would glance up again to resume his vigilance.

Denys could not remember having seen the man before, though there had been recognition in the glowing eyes. Nor had he been mistaken about the danger in them, and naturally he connected it, on the instant, with the only danger he was aware of – the true story of Ian's death. 'Policeman' flashed to his mind, only to be dismissed as impossible and to have 'detective' substituted for it: the latter might be nearer the mark, and certainly the furtive little figure fulfilled all Denys' ideas of what a spy or an informer should look like.

At that, as if answering the challenge, the dwarf glanced up again, this time meeting Denys' eyes voluntarily and boldly: he even nodded slightly, the movement seeming to accuse rather than recognize. ... Momentarily scared, Denys backed trapped, since the place had only one exit, and the dwarf stood away into the body of the shop: it appeared that he was within a few feet of it. Then a voice spoke at his elbow:

'What may I do for you?'

He took control of his nerves, persuading himself that he had been needlessly frightened: it was only the dwarf's strange appearance which had started a guilty train of thought, and he had not nodded, he had simply settled his neck in his collar. ... Denys handed over his skis, and the proprietor, a brisk little man with a gay smile, reached for his ledger.

'What name is it, please?'

'Wilder. I hired them about three weeks ago.'

The man paused, and looked across at him swiftly. 'Ah, yes. Mr Denys Wilder, is it not?'

'Yes.'

The gay smile had vanished altogether, to be succeeded by a blank and rather hostile stare. For a moment Denys thought that he had walked into some trap; and then he followed the other man's glance and understood. He was looking now at the skis propped against the wall: obviously he was thinking

'With these very skis – my skis, hired in good faith – you tripped over the dead body of that poor young man. You are Mr Wilder, who was in all the newspapers. . . .'

It was a moment which Denys hated: it combined with the presence of the dwarf behind him to form a little flash of pure unhappiness, a shaft of pain which took him unawares. But it was a moment only: the proprietor relaxed, and smiled again, the skis were forgotten, the comfortable order of the universe fell into place.

'That is one extra week,' said the little man. 'Let us say ten francs.'

Denys paid, and the proprietor, suddenly at a loss, prepared to bow him out. He was at a loss because his invariable formula for departing English visitors was: 'You have rejoiced yourself? Come again next year and do better,' and in the present case the young man had lost a near relative and would probably think twice about coming within fifty miles of Adelboden again. He compromised by murmuring vague German platitudes and finishing strongly with: 'I hope you have the finest journey home.' He was very pleased with this, and told a lot of people about it during the course of the evening.

Still vaguely disquieted, Denys emerged into the sunlight and stood pondering his next move. There was still an hour till lunch-time: he could go for a short walk, or he could finish his packing – taking care not to encounter Mr Carrington in the process. Through his thoughts he was aware, sharply, that the dwarf was still outside the shop, and looking in his direction: he wanted to loiter for a moment, to test his nerve and prove that he had been frightened about nothing, and then move off at an unhurried pace. And that was what he would have done had not the dwarf looked round swiftly and then taken a step towards him. Denys turned, feeling rather sick.

'What do you want?' he asked.

'Mr Wilder – Mr Denys Wilder, is it not?' The words were the same as the shop-keeper's, but it was a statement rather than a question: the man's voice was low, as if he were tremendously angry about something and was trying to hide it. Denys stared at him, too nervous to take in much of what he saw – received no more than the impression of darkness, of a mean body full of hatred. After a moment he answered: 'Yes.' And repeated: 'What do you want?'

'You are on holiday here. Your brother-in-law was killed in an accident. An accident, yes.' He spoke English with the thick grumbling Swiss accent: his eyes were slate-grey, and their glance never wavered. 'That is true, yes?'

'Of course it's true.' It seemed to Denys as if he had no spirit left at all, as if no matter what he said, his words would betray him. 'What do you want to know? And who are you? Are you – the police?'

A flicker crossed the dwarf's face, a fleeting change of expression which might have been laughter. 'No, I am not the police, I am one of the Swiss inhabitants – the people you do not notice.' Again he glanced round swiftly. 'Perhaps you will come to drink with me. There is a place near.'

'I don't think I want a drink.'

'There is something we must discuss.' The menace was back in the man's voice and eyes: he was looking at Denys as he had first looked, through the shop window. 'We must discuss the winter sports.'

Denys waited, knowing within his heart that he was lost.

'You have been taking back your skis, your hired skis,' the dwarf went on. His voice became a malignant sing-song, foreshadowing death itself. 'Much money is made in that way, if one is clever: and the people of Switzerland, the makers of Switzerland, are forgotten. ... How much did you pay for your skis?'

'Ten francs.'

'For how long?'

'A week.'

'Ten francs a week – money easily made. They were good skis, yes?'

'Yes.'

The great heavy face lit suddenly, as if a fire burnt up within. 'Yes, they were nice skis, fine skis. . . ' And then, in a voice full of venom: 'Fine skis, Mr Wilder. Skis of murder.'

CHAPTER III

Ten minutes later it was out – set down in black and white, to form a very evil pattern indeed. It was blackmail, without a weak spot anywhere: it was the age-old force of wickedness fighting for its own. It was inescapable.

The dwarf sat back against the rough-cast wall, fingering his glass, eyeing Denys with the same insolent contempt as he had displayed before. His head was still no higher than Denys' shoulder, but he held the whip – the whip of complete knowledge.

'You see I am reasonable, Mr Wilder,' he said almost gently. 'I do not denounce you, as I should: I ask nothing impossible, but just the promise, the written promise, of this small sum – every week or month, as you will. Indeed, it is lucky that I am the man who saw you – I could name others who would not help you like this.'

Denys did not look up, but kept his eyes on the table.

'I have no money,' he answered. 'I can give you nothing.'

'You can borrow.' The other's voice hardened. 'You have rich friends. I saw the coffin and the funeral – there was nothing poor there, nothing mean or sparing. You will find people who will help you.'

'I can't.'

'But you will do so. Otherwise I have information of great interest to the authorities, and I will do my duty. It is for you to choose.'

It was for him to choose. ... Denys raised his eyes at last and looked round him, like a dog in a strange unfriendly room. It was a place he had never been in before, a small bar frequented only by peasants and the poorer guides: the smoke-filled, dirty room, with benches round the walls and stained trestle tables, was half-full of a gruff, talkative crowd. He had been stared at when he came in, and the serving man had eyed them both with little favour; but interest had soon waned, until finally they were left to themselves in a corner, unwatched and unheeded. And they were indeed alone, isolated with a secret which no one else must ever share.

When the dwarf had first began to talk Denys had wanted to cry out, to appeal to those near by for help against this new unspeakable menace; but that moment had passed swiftly, to be succeeded by terror lest anyone should learn the truth, a sweat of fear lest they should be overheard by someone who could speak English.

The dwarf had observed this, of course, as he observed everything in his sly hard manner: he talked a little louder, to press his advantage, so that Denys was forced to edge close to him and beg for quietness. The proximity made him feel physically sick, but he was driven by a panic which transcended everything else. He could endure all things – the mean body, the black, peering eyes, the scent of stale sweat and alcohol which overhung his companion – if only he would speak low, if only he would consent to whisper his dreadful threats so that no one else should hear.

Denys' glance left his surroundings and dropped to the table again. There was one gleam of hope, one tiny pin-prick of light, and on it he fastened.

'What about your own position?' he began, as briskly as he could. 'If you were in the hut all evening, why did you not help him? You must have seen him when he fell. How will you explain that to the – the police?'

The dwarf sipped his tankard, eyeing Denys over its rim. Then he set it down. 'The police will have quite enough work to do without questioning me about my own movements.'

'But you let him lie there – helpless – probably dying.'

'I let him lie there. . . .' His voice rose suddenly to a brutal climax. 'I wish the whole number of swine who come here to play were lying in the same position so that I could let them rot or freeze. I could cut my own throat rather than help them.'

'You will tell that to the police?'

'They know it already.'

Denys turned towards him. 'Who are you? How is it you speak English so well?'

He despised himself for what he was doing, for trying to

appease his companion, but he knew that he would do anything and stoop to any horror of filthiness if it could help him to escape.

The dwarf smiled, without mirth. 'Who am I? You flatter me, Mr Wilder.'

'Why do you hate us so?'

'You cannot understand it?' He nodded to himself. 'That is the worst side of you – of you Englishmen especially: you do not know how the people hate you.' He leant forward. 'They hate you, do you understand? You come here, with your laughter and your money and your silly proud faces, and we have to smile and bow and make you welcome.' He spat, as if he were spitting out the whole alien race. 'We have to welcome you, when we would rather cut out your hearts.'

'But the hotels,' Denys stammered. 'They do well, they make money. Surely they want visitors?'

'The hotels. …' There was such anger and contempt in the dwarf's voice that Denys shrank away. 'What are the hotels? They are not Switzerland: they are something forced on us, something that we hate. The proprietors are not the Swiss – they are traitors, pimps, international brothel-keepers.'

He jerked his hand round the mean room. 'Look – look and learn. These are the Swiss: the country rests on these people: they starve and sweat and scratch a living out of the earth so that others may live soft and grow fat. They are treated like dirt, these peasants: they die so poor that they are buried like dogs, in a hole in the ground, with no stone to mark it. If you meet one of them, what do you do? You say "Grüss Gott,"' he mimicked savagely, '"Grüss Gott," because it is something you have learnt, something rather clever, and you expect the same answer back again – as if you were speaking to a doll, or listening to your own silly echo. And then you pass on, to your drinks and your play and your soft women, and they go back to their filthy holes and try to understand what is crushing them. They are beasts, I tell you – they are the Swiss – and it is you and people like you who have made them so.'

His voice died away, trembling with anger: drops of sweat stood out on his forehead, and his hands jerked and drummed on the table as if he was about to have a seizure. Denys watched him, appalled at his malignancy, and knew that he could expect no pity. Round them the hum of talk went on, and now it had a sort of menace about it: even the peasants it seemed had only hatred for him, and wished to destroy him and his people.

He looked again at his companion, and saw that he was staring straight ahead of him, his face pale but composed. Denys had understood very little of what he had said, and did not know whether it was just or not – it was something to which he had never given the smallest thought, save that he had sometimes noticed the poverty of a passing labourer and pitied him for it. But he was ready to believe anything, and sympathize with it, if it would save his own skin.

'Who are you?' He tried to make his voice as gentle and sympathetic as he could. 'You're not – not a peasant, are you?'

Slowly his companion's eyes came round, and in them the old contempt and the old hatred. 'What is it to you?'

'I want to understand.'

'You want to understand. And when I have told you, and you have said, "How sad," you hope that I will be friends with you and forget what I have seen. Is that it?'

'No.'

'You lie. . . . But I will tell you – and after that we will go back to the other thing.' He leant back in his old position again. 'My parents were peasants – among the poorest in the valley – and I was to be the same – or so it seemed. But I hated it: I saw that there was no future for me, only the same toil and the same miserable death. I wanted to escape it.' His voice had softened somewhat. 'I did escape it – for a time. I got a position in a hotel here – a kitchen-boy: I worked hard, I became a *commis* – a junior waiter. I was very small, but at first that did not matter – customers laughed at me and made me a favourite. Then I exchanged, and went to England for five years: I worked hard, I learnt to speak correctly, my future would have been assured. But soon it was clear that I could not succeed, because I was too small.' He turned to Denys, his eyes hard and accusing. 'I am a dwarf – people still laughed at me, but now it was bad, bad for trade, bad for a hotel's reputation. You understand that?'

'Yes. But it is not your fault.'

'It is *your* fault. ... You kept my parents and my grandparents poor: they lived on nothing – filthy milk, diseased meat – what hope is there for a child of such stock?' He paused, his eyes smouldering, staring into the past. 'I lost my work – I wandered without money – I turned to other things. ... I have been in your prisons. Then I was deported. I was dangerous – an agitator, a Communist, a thief. And other things, too. But one must live, even on women, even on one's own body.'

Denys was looking at him in horror, but he noticed nothing, he was far away in the fog of the past. 'I came back here – to the land. I starved, as we all starved: I watched my mother die, and my brothers, while all round us there was wealth and laughter and easy living. ... My father died that night, in the hut: he was not old, only fifty, but he was worn out, like a horse that is worked till it drops dead. I looked out of the window, I saw the young man fall. Why should I help him? He was one of the murderers, he and his class together. I left him there, I heard his agony and rejoiced in it. Then you came.'

Once again he paused, as if he had forgotten the rest of the story. But there was something in his face, some reflection of suffering, which made Denys begin to hope again: he might be an evil character, but he could understand how one could be driven to desperation, he would appreciate and sympathize. ... Denys signalled to the barman and fresh drinks were brought: then he turned again to his companion.

'Yes?' he prompted.

'Then you came,' the dwarf repeated. He laughed softly to himself. 'I was afraid that you would save him, but you did not. It seemed that you hated him as much as I did. Why so?'

'He was married to my sister, but he was unfaithful, while she was having a child.'

The dwarf raised his eyebrows. 'A moralist? I did not know that the English were so strict.'

'There were other things, too.'

'Well, it is no matter.' Suddenly he seemed to come to life again, and Denys could read his thoughts – they were wasting time, they were getting away from the subject in hand. Desperately he sought for some means of further distracting his attention, but he knew it was hopeless: and even as he cast about for an opening phrase the dwarf spoke.

'It is no matter, because what you did is over and cannot be changed.' His voice warmed to its former pitch, he remembered his reins of power and drew them to hand again. 'So we may get to business. You understand what I want? Money regularly paid, so that I may buy peace again, and live higher than my father and my father's animals. You will arrange this?'

The old sick terror returned, increased by the short respite. 'I tell you I can't,' Denys said desperately. 'It is more money than I have to live on myself.'

'That is your answer?'

'Yes. ... No, no, it isn't. Listen, I'll send you what I can; I'll send you a pound every week.'

'I have told you my figure.'

'But I can't do it. Five pounds a week – there's nowhere I can get it from. Don't you see that?'

The other's eyes flashed suddenly. 'I can only see that you come out here to enjoy yourself, that you can throw your money about, while I and my people fight for every franc, for every centime that we earn. Throw some of your money to me, Mr Wilder: I can put it to better uses.' He fumbled in his breast pocket and drew out a paper. 'I have here a small document – quite simple, quite easy to understand. You will please sign it.'

'No!' Denys looked about him desperately, in terror of reading what was on the typewritten sheet. 'Give me time. Can't you see that I'll do what I can? But if it isn't possible for me to ...'

'You will make it possible. You have a pen?'

'No, no. ...' In agony, he turned and seized his companion's arm. 'Give me till this evening – let me meet you again here. Perhaps I could get some money in the meantime.'

The dwarf eyed him narrowly. 'Very well,' he said at last. 'But you will not leave Adelboden before you sign this. What day do you go?'

'Tonight.'

'So. . . . You will meet me here at six, with this paper signed, and with five pounds in Swiss money. If you do not come I shall be at the bus stop with the police. You understand?'

'But if you tell them you will get nothing.'

The dwarf's eyes went dead suddenly. 'I shall get two lives for my father's, instead of one.'

Denys shivered. 'All right,' he said slowly. 'I'll do my best for you.'

'That is good.' He folded the paper and held it out. 'Take this now. Sign it when you get back to your hotel. I shall wait for you here for half a hour – no more. If you do not come I shall know what to do.' He stood up, looked at his empty glass, and smiled suddenly, hideously. 'And as a first instalment, Mr Wilder, you may pay for our drinks. *Auf wiedersehen.*'

CHAPTER IV

I

He dared not go into the restaurant for lunch, he dared not meet anyone or talk to anyone, so sure was he that he carried the mark of his guilt plainly upon him for any passer-by to see: he lay on his bed, with the silence of the upper floors of the hotel all round him, clutching the soiled typewritten sheet in one hand, and gave way to terror.

But now it was terror of a new sort, terror perfectly defined and dreadfully menacing: before, it had been only a general fear of discovery; now he could put his finger on the exact point and say: 'This is the danger, this is death, and I cannot escape it. . . .' He knew himself to be delivered over to the enemy, bound in a servitude from which there was no release; and the proof of it was the paper in his hand, the paper which set forth in two crisp, harsh sentences a confession of murder and a surrender to blackmail:

> 'I acknowledge fully that I killed my relation Ian Carrington by means of running into him while on skis.
>
> I promise to pay to Hermann Gottlieb the sum of Five

English Pounds every week for as long as he does not betray this acknowledgment to anyone.'

Underneath was the space where he was to sign his name. The date was already filled in.

Re-reading it, Denys began to tremble suddenly, as if taken with a deadly sickness. What he had gone through since Ian's death was proving too much for his endurance – there had been panic at first, then the birth of hope, then a growing security, and now as a climax this dreadful rebuff.

It was something he couldn't cope with at all: even if he had had a plan he could not have put it into execution, so finally had his courage and strength been taken from him. There was not even a choice of ways, for even if he signed the paper he could not pay what the dwarf asked: whether he signed, or ran away, or just lay there in quickening, sweating terror, he was lost, and his life was forfeit. (Perhaps it wasn't forfeit – perhaps this was one of the cantons where there was no death penalty – perhaps they didn't hang foreigners, anyway; but the effect would be the same – publicity, shame, hatred, long imprisonment....)

He nodded to himself in sick and hopeless understanding. Yes, he was filling the post of whipping boy mighty well, right up to the last moment: no one could say he wasn't taking his full share of punishment, just as had been ordained, just as he had done all through the holiday.

There was a step in the passage outside his door, and then a knock. He sat up, his face set in a mask of anguish: they were coming for him already, the dwarf had decided to forgo the money and take his life as revenge. ... The knock was repeated: he tried to say 'Who's there?' but his throat was dry, dry as sand, as if he were being strangled, and the hoarse murmur could not be heard outside the room. Then came a voice:

'Hallo there! Denys?'

It was Mr Carrington. Denys slipped to the floor, and his instinct, the instinct of the hunted animal, took him across the room to the window: it was the only escape left open. As he moved stealthily over the wooden boards he thought: what's the old devil doing up here at this hour? Had he been sent on ahead by the authorities to smooth things out and get him away without a scandal? At the window he pulled himself together: outside was a twenty-foot drop, and he could be seen both from the rink and from the ground-floor windows. He called:

'Yes? What do you want?'

'It's half-way through lunch,' came the answer. 'Aren't you coming down?'

'I'm not feeling very well. I thought I'd give lunch a miss. But don't bother about me.'

'What's this? Not well?' Mr Carrington was stirred to his customary noisy solicitude. The door-handle rattled. 'Let's have a look at you. Let me in.'

'I'm lying down. I just want to keep quiet.' It was suddenly essential to Denys that he should keep the room to himself, that Mr Carrington should not come in. 'It's all right, really. Only a bit of a headache.'

'What about an aspirin?'

'I've just taken one.'

There was a mumble of dissatisfaction – the discontent of a born organizer forestalled. 'But what about your lunch? Shall I get Alois to send something up to you? You ought to eat something, you know. There's a nice bit of fish. Or you could have a sandwich. What about it?'

'No, honestly I don't want anything.'

'Well. ...' The door-handle clicked again, persuasively, as if Mr Carrington thought his soft words might have affected the lock. 'As long as you're sure. ... I'll be up again later, to see how you are.'

'Thank you very much. I'll be all right.' Breathless, Denys listened as the footsteps died away down the corridor. For some reason it had seemed a desperate moment: he had felt as if Mr Carrington's presence in the room would bring a complete breakdown, would shatter the tenuous margin of self-control which was still his: to keep him out was to make a start in the new and vital struggle for escape and liberty. But looking round him now he knew that he was in no better case: solitude might preserve a surface calm, but it could not alter the menace and the imminence of the facts.

His eyes went again to the window, and he knew that if it

had been the police he would have chanced the drop without giving it a second thought – nor would it have mattered much if he had broken his neck. And as that thought came to him he began to realize that he had found the solution, the only sure release from all his troubles.

Death – freely chosen and freely embraced – was the true path for him: anything else was but to delay the end, to scuttle hither and thither like a coursed hare which will never win sanctuary. For there was no sanctuary – every retreat was blocked. And surely to choose death would be to round the whole thing off aptly, and give the holiday a measure of the dignity to which it had never hitherto come near attaining: Fortune had called the tune and made him dance for a long and weary time, but this would strike a balance, this would square the account at one stroke.

He could even suppose that the dwarf's name, Gottlieb, had been put forward as some kind of final pointer – that the instrument of coercion was in truth Beloved of God and therefore not to be withstood or challenged. ... And thus standing there, in the sunlit room, hardly seeing the noble mountain slope within his view across the valley, he resolved to escape his pursuers by taking his own life.

But not from the hotel window – for he might only cripple himself, and then he would be patched up and delivered over to judgment again as soon as human skill could mend his body. It must be outside somewhere, among the snows which had been the only friendly companion of this holiday. Hidden in those hills there were heights, there were steep places, there were easy falls to oblivion.

He was swift to act, swift as the thought which had clipped upon his brain. On the dressing-table he made a neat pile of his passport and odd letters, his money and his keys. On top he placed the typewritten confession, as an explanation to the world and as an earnest of his own behaviour, a reminder to himself that he could not come back. Then he wound his boot-ties and buckled on his ski-jacket, glad to have put an end to inaction, and to be moving according to his own set purpose.

2

As Denys passed along the road up the valley he found it deserted – the lazy stay-at-homes were still at their lunch, the strenuous as yet far afield. He recalled the last time he had passed that way, when he had set out to kill Ian, and the constant stream of people who had passed him and so confused his mind: but then of course he had been a little mad, and now he was sane – quite sane and resigned and content. For he was leaving the essentially evil town behind him, and taking refuge among the enfolding silence of the hills: at his back was pain, danger, distress, and in front an easy journey and the promise of peace.

Faced with such a choice, who would choose otherwise or hesitate in the choosing? – only the over-eager and the grabbing, only such as Ian, who had clung so hard to life and made such an agony of dying. Faced with the thought and image of that agony he shivered uncontrollably, and then summoned all his strength to throw off the feeling of revulsion: his last hour was to have no icy shadow of that sort, but was to be filled with light, imbued with the sweet knowledge of release. For it *was* release: and if the winning of it called for courage and resolution, how else was he to meet his life's end except with all the spirit that life had left him?

Time passed: his journey unfolded like a curling strand of ribbon: presently he left the road and began to strike up the hillside, after putting on his skis, the skis which he had chosen at random from the rack outside the Schweizer Hotel. The snow was firm, and he made good progress, careful to present always a crisp ski-edge to the slope, surmounting the steeper places herring-bone fashion, resting sometimes on his sticks as the climb took toll of his breath.

His field of vision enlarged as he gained each successive vantage-point: the valley behind him assumed far-away proportions, the pigmy village three miles away came into view and then vanished again behind a shoulder of rock: he drew himself upwards instinctively, seeking the heights rather than governing his direction, and it was some little time before he realized that he was making for the ski-jumping ground. . . .

Startled, he stopped to consider the idea, and found that it held promise for him: having gathered speed on the slope, it would be easy to launch oneself into the air, like a bird trying its wings, and easy too to fail in one's balance, to fall as even the most skilful jumpers sometimes fell – like the same bird shot through the heart, like a derelict kite. . . .

One need only mount the run-way, and keep direction, and sail into space, and then renounce control. And he would be brave enough to do it, both because he was primed by despair and because he couldn't turn back in any case – already it was too late, already Mr Carrington would have gone up to his room, and found the paper, and learnt the whole truth at last. That paper, forlorn upon his dressing-table, was his safeguard, the sure passport for his last voyage.

And now as he climbed, and rested, and climbed again, he fell to thinking of the holiday that was already past, and of the successive strokes of ill-fortune which had come his way; although he could only picture them in little snatches, quick pin-pricks of remembrance and sorrow and resentment, yet even at this late hour they banded together to impress and subdue him.

He remembered especially the scene at Victoria, and saw in it the starting-point of his downfall: if he had not been so eager to touch Helen's arm and win her interest, if he had held on to those vaguely formed principles of his, then he might have been spared all the later anguish. For normally he would not have been so close to Helen during the holiday, nor so concerned with Ian's behaviour and the family reaction to it: normally he would have been outside it all, enjoying himself simply and fully, and hardly noticing the individuals around him save where they made a direct contact: normally he would not have drunk so much, and by it lost the little Alsatian girl, he would not have been stirred to the bloody-minded vigour which had culminated in that filthy seduction of Helen and the final blinding insanity of Ian's murder.

But even this normality was speculation, and perhaps everything would have taken the same course, whatever reserves he had clung to: perhaps he had been chosen both as the instrument of punishment and the scapegoat for all evil, and the doubled part had to be played no matter how reluctant he might have been.

But in other circumstances, he thought regretfully, how happy he might have been in Adelboden: he had quickly learned to love all the thrills of ski-ing, all the woven perfection which sun and snow and high hills offered to the eye, and with the Norwegian's good-comradeship and the sweet promise of the Alsatian girl's smile to aid him, he could have had a most secure heaven for himself in this enchanting corner of the earth. Given time over again, the tools would be his to shape and carve an image of delight.

But there was no time over again: time had run on, and was burnt up in the fires of his improvidence. ... Resting on his ski-sticks within sight of his goal, he presently became aware of sound and action in the valley below him; and as if seeking some last evidence of the earth's immutable loveliness, his eyes swept down across the waste of snow, across his own deep-bitten tracks, and lighted at last upon a moving figure. It was only a girl ski-joring – towing behind a horse along the valley road; but there was something about her swift and flowing movement, instinct with the very triumph of life, which went straight to his heart.

It was at once the perfect snow-scene, and the loveliest sight his eyes had ever found: the white valley crowned with its pinnacles of rock, the sunlight glancing on the trees, the unchanging peace which was the jewel of this setting – and then, fleeing across it like a storm-cloud, the great black horse, at full gallop with mane and tail streaming in the wind, its two guide-ropes joined by a flaming red banner, and the girl tailing far behind, laughing and calling out, her trim green suit catching the sun, her golden hair plucked by the wind as she sped on. ...

He watched them, as they passed beneath him, his heart turning over at the beauty of it; and thereafter, when they were out of sight and he retained in his memory only the tossing red of the banner, and the girl's crown of hair, he turned and set his face towards his final target. That beauty, that swift and varied streamer of coloured movement, was his *envoi* from the living world.

It was the girl herself, wretched with fear, and with all her breathless happiness stolen from her, who later saw him fall and was the first to come upon the wrecked body – the face torn by a chance ridge of ice, the head cruelly wrenched, the brown hands dug some way into the snow they had so much loved.

Nicholas Monsarrat

'One of those novelists – they are growing fewer – who have not forgotten that the primary aim of the novel is to tell a story, to tell it interestingly and to tell it convincingly.'

RICHER THAN ALL HIS TRIBE 35p

Monsarrat returns to the African island of Pharamaul for his gripping successor to *THE* TRIBE THAT LOST ITS HEAD.

'Not so much a novel, more a slab of dynamite'
– SUNDAY MIRROR

Other Nicholas Monsarrat titles available in Pan.

SMITH AND JONES	12½p
THE PILLOW FIGHT	35p
THE TRIBE THAT LOST ITS HEAD	40p
THE WHITE RAJAH	35p
SOMETHING TO HIDE	25p
THE SHIP THAT DIED OF SHAME	25p

These and other PAN Books are obtainable from all booksellers and newsagents. If you have any difficulty please send purchase price plus 7p postage to P.O. Box 11, Falmouth, Cornwall.
While every effort is made to keep prices low, it is sometimes necessary to increase prices at short notice. PAN Books reserve the right to show new retail prices on covers which may differ from those previously advertised in the text or elsewhere.